"I have a deal to propose."

Cara's suspicions flared. "What kind of deal?"

"I need help with my kids. I was thinking of you."

"No." She jerked back so quickly she bumped into the door.

"Hear me out first. You show me the ropes, and I'll help you with the sanctuary."

Did he not realize how hard this would be for her?

She looked at Nathan, smashing the last bite of hot dog into his plate rather than eating it. Kimberly had just started stirring and would whimper any second. Cara wanted to run and not stop until she was a thousand miles away. She also wanted to hold Kimberly. The two longings waged a war inside her. Eventually, one prevailed.

Going over to the carrier, she undid the straps and lifted the baby into her arms. "All right," she murmured, and gently rocked the baby. "We have a deal."

Dear Reader,

When the idea for *Come Home, Cowboy* first came to me, I was hesitant to explore it. In fact, I put the piece of notepaper on which I'd scrawled the basic premise into a file folder where it resided for several years. I convinced myself that a woman who tragically lost her child was too dark of a story line for a romance novel. As a mother myself, I couldn't imagine how anyone went on, much less fell in love, in the wake of something so horrific.

Eventually, while brainstorming my new Mustang Valley series, I remembered my idea and instantly knew this was the perfect time. Maybe I finally felt ready to tackle such an emotionally layered story and such a deeply wounded character as Cara Alverez. Maybe I felt Josh Dempsey was exactly the kind of man a woman like her needed. Maybe the pieces just simply came together as they sometimes do.

Rather than being sad and depressing, Cara and Josh's story was, for me, uplifting and inspiring and wonderfully satisfying. Their journey is anything but easy. In the end, however, their struggles prove worthwhile when they finally find their happy ending.

As always, warmest wishes,

Cathy McDavid

Facebook.com/pages/Cathy-Mcdavid-Books

Twitter.com/CathyMcDavid

COME HOME, COWBOY

CATHY McDAVID

HARLEQUIN® AMERICAN ROMANCE®

ISBN-13: 978-0-373-75605-6

Come Home, Cowboy

Copyright © 2016 by Cathy McDavid

The publisher acknowledges the copyright holder of the additional work:

My Funny Valentine
Copyright © 1991 by Debbie Macomber

Recycling programs
for this product may
not exist in your area.

Printed in U.S.A.

CONTENTS

For the past eighteen years *New York Times* bestselling author **Cathy McDavid** has been juggling a family, a job and writing, and doing pretty well at it, except for the housecleaning part. "Mostly" retired from the corporate business world, she writes full-time from her home in Scottsdale, Arizona, near the breathtaking McDowell Mountains. Her twins have "mostly" left home, returning every now and then to raid her refrigerator. On weekends, she heads to her cabin in the mountains, always taking her laptop with her. You can visit her website at cathymcdavid.com.

Books by Cathy McDavid

Harlequin American Romance

Mustang Valley

Last Chance Cowboy
Her Cowboy's Christmas Wish
Baby's First Homecoming
Cowboy for Keeps
Her Holiday Rancher

Sweetheart, Nevada

The Rancher's Homecoming
His Christmas Sweetheart
Most Eligible Sheriff

Reckless, Arizona

More Than a Cowboy
Her Rodeo Man
The Bull Rider's Son

Visit the Author Profile page
at Harlequin.com for more titles.

COME HOME, COWBOY

Cathy McDavid

To Caitlin, who continues to fill my life with joy and make me the proudest mom in the world. I miss you, honey, but I know you are having the time of your life.

Chapter One

Twice every year, Cara Alverez fell apart. First, on the day of her sweet little boy's birthday. Second, on the anniversary of his death. Today happened to be the latter.

Crying constantly since early morning and not fit company for anyone, she had kept to herself, shunning well-meaning, but ineffectual platitudes. After seven hours of hard work on one task or another, her chores were done. One problem remained. Her watch read 2:17 p.m. Far too much time left in the day to fill…and survive.

Dabbing at her damp eyes with a wadded-up tissue, Cara wandered to the horse stable. Yesterday, in preparation for this moment, she'd moved Hurry Up from the mustang sanctuary to a stall for the night.

The small gelding, with his mousy brown coat, Roman nose and stubby legs, was perhaps the homeliest horse Cara had ever seen. He was also the slowest, hence the name. But all that mattered little because Hurry Up had the disposition of a kitten and an eagerness to please. Of the over two hundred head of abandoned and rescued mustangs residing at the sanctuary, Hurry Up displayed the most potential for an excellent child's mount.

Had Cara's son, Javier, lived, he'd have been four, almost five. The perfect age for his first horse.

Fresh tears threatened to flow, but Cara kept them at bay. Barely. Removing a halter from the row hanging outside the tack room, she walked to the stall where Hurry Up waited. Patiently, of course, as was his nature.

"*Hola, chiquito.* Ready for a workout?"

The gelding nuzzled her affectionately while she buckled the halter.

"Wait, wait," she said, pretending to scold him. "We'll get there."

"There," in this case, was a small corral adjacent to the round pen where Cara planned to exercise Hurry Up and maybe reinforce a lesson or two.

Dos Estrellas was a cattle ranch currently running over two thousand cows, calves and young steer. The mustang sanctuary occupied sections six and seven of the ranch, about five hundred acres. The late owner, August Dempsey, had bequeathed the land to Cara for her exclusive use.

August had been under no obligation to name Cara in his will, though he'd loved her like a daughter and she him like a father. But he had named her. The sanctuary, with its neglected and sometimes abused mustangs, was what gave Cara a reason to rise every morning and step outside her room when she'd rather remain buried beneath the covers.

Saddled and bridled, Hurry Up looked a little less ugly. He waited stoically at the gate for her to open it, then stood while she mounted. After several laps at a leisurely walk, she nudged the horse into a trot and circled the corral. Eventually, they practiced reining. Hurry Up executed perfect figure eights and zigzags.

"Come on, *chiquito*." Cara attempted to coax the horse into a lope, to no avail. Hurry Up had exactly three speeds: slow, slower and slowest.

On the plus side, there was never any danger of him running away or bucking. The only way a rider could fall off this plug was to misjudge the distance while dismounting.

Her son, Javier, had been fearless and wouldn't have thought twice about leaping from a horse's back. Had he been a tiny bit more timid, he might not have…have climbed up the shelving unit and—

Cara promptly burst into tears. This time, there was no stopping them.

A cold January breeze, originating in the nearby Mc-Dowell Mountains, chased through Mustang Valley and across Dos Estrellas, drying Cara's cheeks almost the moment they were wet. Hurry Up stumbled—probably because he was getting mixed signals from his rider—then quit moving altogether.

Vaguely aware that someone might see her, she climbed off the horse. That was as far as she got. Holding on to him for support, she buried her face in the side of his smooth neck and allowed grief to consume her.

Cara mourned more than the death of her beautiful little boy. She also mourned the demise of her marriage to Javier's father and the loss of a life she'd never know again.

It wasn't fair. It was also her fault. Everything.

Cara's crying jag was nearing an end when a soft, concerned and decidedly male voice interrupted her. It came from the other side of Hurry Up, just outside of the corral.

"Are you all right?"

She winced, then quickly gathered herself, using the sleeve of her denim jacket to wipe her face. Apparently, she'd lost her wadded-up tissue.

"I'm fine," she said, sounding stronger than she felt.

"You sure?"

She dared a peek over the top of Hurry Up's mane, only to quickly duck down.

Josh Dempsey, August's oldest son, stood watching her. She recognized his brown Resistol cowboy hat and tan canvas duster through the sucker rod railing. Of all the people to find her, why him?

Heat raced up her neck and engulfed her face. Not from embarrassment, but anger. It wasn't that she didn't like Josh. Okay, to be honest, she didn't like him. He'd made it clear from the moment he'd arrived at Dos Estrellas a few months ago that he wanted the land belonging to the mustang sanctuary.

She understood. To a degree. The cattle operation was the sole source of income for the ranch, and the sanctuary—operating mostly on donations—occupied a significant amount of valuable pastureland. In addition, Cara didn't technically own the land. She'd simply been granted use of the two sections and the right to reside in the ranch house for as long as she wanted or for as long as the ranch remained in the family.

Sympathy for the struggling cattle operation didn't change her feelings. She needed the sanctuary. She and the two-hundred-plus horses that would otherwise be homeless. For those reasons, she refused to concede, causing friction in the family.

Additional friction. Gabe Dempsey and his half brothers, Josh and Cole, were frequently at odds over the ranch, the terms of their late father's will and the mustang sanctuary.

"You need some help?" Josh asked from the other side of the corral.

"No."

"Okay."

But he didn't leave.

A minute passed, then two. What was the matter with him? Was he truly dense or simply being obtuse? She'd told him she was fine.

"Is there something you want?" she called, then grimaced at hearing the sound of the gate squeaking. He wasn't coming in, was he? She gasped softly. He *was* coming in.

"Your cinch is loose."

Certain her face looked a mess, she refused to step out from behind Hurry Up. "Thanks. I'll get it."

"Let me."

He was right there. On the other side of the horse. A few feet away. She averted her face, but that didn't prevent him from completely invading every one of her senses. She supposed men like him couldn't help it.

Without having to glance up, she felt his height and the breadth of his wide shoulders. The saddle shifted, which meant he'd unfastened the cinch buckle with his strong, capable hands and was taking in the slack. He finished, at last, and she was certain he stared at the back of her head with those piercing blue eyes of his.

She'd seen his eyes flash with anger—at his brother Gabe and at her for having the audacity to stand up to him. She'd also seen them soften when he talked about his two children.

"I'm sorry," he said with a tenderness in his voice

that she'd never heard before. "Violet told me earlier. About your son."

Dos Estrellas's livestock foreman was a friend of Cara's and also, obviously, a blabbermouth. Cara wanted to be angry, but to what end and at whom? People talked about her. It was the inevitable consequence of losing your child under tragic circumstances.

"Thank you." Cara's standard response. She found it better to acknowledge the condolence. If not, the person would just keep going on and on. She couldn't handle that. Not today and not from him.

"I can't imagine how terrible it must have been for you."

Something inside Cara snapped. Perhaps because she was hanging on to her emotions by the thinnest of threads. Or perhaps because this was the man who, given a chance, would take away the one thing left in the entire world that mattered to her. Whatever the reason, she lost control, and the words spilled from her mouth.

"No, you can't imagine. Not unless it happens to you, which I pray to God it doesn't." Spinning, she stood on her tiptoes, her hands gripping Hurry Up's mane like a lifeline, and stared Josh in the face. "Now, if you please, leave me alone. I don't need your help and I sure as heck don't crave your company."

He stepped back, she thought more to give her space than because she'd intimidated him. Someone like Josh Dempsey didn't scare easily. If that were the case, he and his brother Cole would have left after the first week when Gabe had made it clear they weren't welcome.

August Dempsey's three sons didn't get along. No surprise. August had many fine qualities and had been a remarkable human being. But he'd also made a lot of mistakes in his life before succumbing to colon cancer at an early age. His greatest one had been driving a wedge between his two legitimate sons and the one he had out of wedlock. His last act before dying had been an attempt to reconcile them. So far, it hadn't worked.

The brothers might be living and working together, and though they sometimes got along, they weren't close.

"I'm sorry I upset you," Josh said.

Cara turned her back to him, leaned against Hurry Up, who had yet to move, and squeezed her eyes shut. This day couldn't get any worse. "I'm going to ask you one more time to leave me alone."

"I will, but you need to come with me first." He spoke softly, yet insistently.

"You don't say." The idea was ludicrous. "And why's that?"

"Some of your mustangs are loose. They broke through the fence and are in section eight."

"I see." Horses mingling with cattle in and of itself wasn't so bad. Horses eating grass reserved for the cattle was cause for action.

Weathercasters across the state were calling the current conditions—rain only once in the past four months—a drought. As a result, grazing land across Arizona was at a premium, especially at Dos Estrellas, where the naturally craggy and rocky hills resisted vegetation. Lack of available grass was also the motivation behind Josh and Cole wanting the land their father had bequeathed Cara. They were already short on money, and supplemental feed in the midst of a drought was expensive.

"I'm willing to round up the horses and return them

to the sanctuary," Josh offered. "Cole's already on his way."

As if she'd allow that to happen. Josh probably thought he knew everything about rounding up horses simply because he was a former rodeo champion.

"Not on your life." She didn't wait. Grabbing the reins, she raced toward the gate, pulling the small horse behind her. For once, he kept up.

At the stable, she tethered Hurry Up to the hitching post, where he would wait quietly for her return. Then, fishing in her jacket pocket, she retrieved her keys and rushed to where she'd parked her Jeep.

No sooner did she climb in than the Jeep rocked beneath her. Another person had thrown himself into the passenger seat.

Josh Dempsey. He was harder to get rid of than a case of poison ivy. And just as irritating.

"What are you doing?" she demanded.

He buckled his seat belt. "Going with you."

It was then she noticed the coiled rope he balanced on his lap.

"Why bring that along?" She nodded at the rope while turning the ignition key. The Jeep roared to life.

"Figured it may come in handy."

Short of physically ejecting him from the vehicle, which was a near impossibility considering he had a good seven inches on her, she was stuck with him.

Silently fuming, she backed up the Jeep, shifted and hit the gas. They skidded on the hard ground as she accelerated, then bounced roughly along the uneven dirt road leading from the ranch and into the hills. Every few minutes, Cara glanced at Josh. He stared stoically ahead, one hand holding his hat in place, the other hanging on to the grab bar.

Only when they reached the outskirts of section eight did Cara realize it had been a full fifteen minutes since she'd thought about Javier.

AT THE TOP of a rocky rise, Cara downshifted and brought the Jeep to a stop. Josh spotted Violet, Dos Estrellas' livestock manager, and Joey, a young hand with a goofy smile and an aw-shucks personality, attempting to temporarily repair the break in the fence with wire, wooden planks and a pair of pliers.

Josh, however, was far more interested in Cara. She was an enigma. One minute, usually when she was with his half brother Gabe or Gabe's mother, Raquel, Cara was sweet natured and friendly, though quiet. Around Josh or Cole, she became a different person. Cool to the point of being rude.

Josh tolerated her treatment of him, though he didn't like it. She was fiercely loyal to Gabe and Raquel, as well as to Josh's late father, something Josh admired. She no doubt saw him and Cole as a threat. Possibly even the enemy.

None of that stopped him from studying her at every opportunity, however. He thought about her at random moments during the day and wondered how he might breach her defenses.

But to what end? With his two kids arriving at the end of next week and single fatherhood in his immediate future, he was hardly in a position to consider dating anyone, especially an emotionally wounded woman like Cara. Josh liked a challenge as much as the next guy, but he wasn't about to tackle the impossible.

That aside, she intrigued him, and not just because of her exotic beauty and knockout figure. He wished he had known her before her son had died. Seen the attractive spark in her dark eyes and hear the laughter he suspected was once there in her sultry voice.

Cara turned in her seat to face him. "Well?"

He decided he could take her question one of two ways. She might be asking his opinion on what to do next. The horses, fifty or more, were stretched out over a quarter mile in the ravine below, eating grass or standing and staring at the human intruders, their manes and tails blowing in the cold January wind. She could also be expecting him to vacate the Jeep, having delivered him to their destination.

He leaned toward the latter. She was wearing that scowl, after all, the one she constantly affected in his presence. For fun, he decided to go with the former, if simply to get a rise out of her.

"Drive closer," he said and lifted his rope.

"What exactly are you planning?"

"Getting those horses back onto sanctuary land."

She didn't move. "How?"

He retrieved his leather gloves from his duster pocket and put them on. Slowly.

Her scowl deepened, though it didn't detract from her loveliness.

"Well?" she demanded again.

"I'm going to rope the black."

She crossed her arms over her middle. "Do tell."

"Then we'll lead him back to the sanctuary. The other horses will follow."

"I'd like to see that." She didn't bother hiding her sarcasm.

"Good." He adjusted the coiled rope, sliding it between his gloved fingers, liking the familiar feel. "Because you're going to drive the Jeep up beside him so I can throw this rope around his neck."

"You're joking."

"I'm open to a better suggestion." When she didn't respond, he continued. "We can get my brothers and a few more hands on horseback. Or round up the mustangs with the quads, though that might cause a stampede."

He could see by her creased brow she disliked that idea. Probably too reminiscent of how the mustangs were captured in the first place. Josh had learned from Violet while having a beer at the Poco Dinero Bar that the horses came from all over Arizona, driven in from the remote regions by a fleet of four-wheel vehicles or sometimes helicopters.

"Give me thirty minutes." He allowed himself a small grin, certain his confidence would annoy her. "I'll have the mustangs safe and secure."

"He'll run," Cara said, referring to the black.

"Undoubtedly. All I need is for you to get me close enough."

The black was fast. Josh had observed him more than once in the sanctuary, tearing hell-bent for election across the grazing land. He was also fiery, smart and a natural leader, qualities Josh sought in a horse. The black had been the reigning king of his harem of mares before being captured four months ago. He wasn't ready to abdicate his position anytime soon.

Cara chewed her lower lip thoughtfully, distracting Josh. Or was she enticing him? She had a great mouth. Full and lush and wide. He found it hard to look away.

"What if you don't?" she asked. "Rope him."

"I'll help you get the mustangs back to the sanctuary any way you choose."

Her gaze narrowed. "You swear?"

What way was she thinking? On foot? They'd never catch the black. Maybe Josh should reconsider.

He didn't. "You have my word."

She pushed down on the clutch and shifted gears. "Let's go."

The next instant, they were flying down the rise. Had he been with anyone else, Josh would have let loose with a whoop and a holler. Cara was a competent driver. Make that a great driver, he amended as they reached the bottom and turned on a dime with just the right amount of daring.

The open Jeep, with its roll bar overhead, allowed him the room he needed to maneuver. Ground flew by at increasing speed. At times, the late-afternoon sun blinded him as they drove into it. The wind grabbed at his cowboy hat. Frustrated, Josh whisked it off and dropped it on the floorboard.

Nearing the mustangs, he unbuckled his seat belt and half stood, bracing his right knee on his seat and his right shoulder on the roll bar.

"Be careful," Cara said over the noise of the engine. "I wouldn't want you falling out."

Was she being sarcastic again? Josh couldn't be sure. He kind of hoped so, liking to think she hid a sense of humor somewhere beneath all those layers of pain.

The mustangs nervously eyed the approaching Jeep. A young colt ran in a circle around his mother, kicking up his back feet.

"Cut to the left," Josh ordered, pointing at the black. "He'll bolt that way."

"How can you be sure?"

"He won't take the herd up the ravine. Too many cholla cactus."

Cara nodded, then swung the Jeep hard to the left. As if someone had flipped a switch, the entire herd collected itself, then broke into a full gallop. The black stayed in front. It was a position that enabled him to both act as lookout and defend against possible danger.

Josh raised the rope above his head, the force of the wind nearly ripping it from his hand. "Move in first chance you get. Don't worry if the other horses scatter."

Once again, Cara proved her exceptional driving abilities. She maneuvered the Jeep so they were driving parallel to the black, about fifty feet away from him.

Only a half mile of flat ground remained before the next hill. Josh needed to make his move quickly or kiss opportunity goodbye.

"Get closer." He didn't add, *Now or never.*

Cara seemed to figure it out. Glancing over her shoulder, she eased the Jeep nearer and nearer, narrowly avoiding ruts, holes, boulders and brush. The fifty feet separating them from the black shrunk to twenty. Josh raised the rope…and hesitated.

Powerful, athletic, with a coat the color of charcoal and sleek as satin, the horse moved with breathtaking beauty. Head and tail raised high, he charged ahead, the image of the outlaw horse he was.

What would it be like to ride that magnificent animal? Josh wanted to know. More than that, he wanted to own the black. Train him. Gain his trust. Command him. He would, too, he was suddenly certain.

Lifting his arm, he studied his target. Josh had a drawer filled with gold and silver buckles, testament to his abilities at calf roping, bronc busting and bull riding. Once a rodeo man, always a rodeo man. He had no doubt he'd place the rope precisely where it needed to go—over the black's head and around his neck.

Moving his arm in a counterclockwise direction, he let out enough rope for a perfect loop and twirled it over his head. Holding the excess loosely in his other hand, he took aim, sensing Cara's stare on him.

Good. Josh performed best under pressure.

She seemed to read his mind and eased the Jeep into position. Eighteen feet. Fifteen feet. Twelve feet. Josh could now see the whites of the stallion's eyes.

Still, he waited, fighting the wind for control of the rope. The galloping horses made a thunderous noise, one Josh could feel echoing inside his chest. Adrenaline coursed through him. His nerves tingled as if on fire, and every muscle in him tensed in preparation.

The black pushed for even greater speed. Josh swore the horse knew what was about to happen and was intentionally defying him.

"Steady, boy," he said, more to himself than the horse. "Easy does it."

An instant later, the perfect moment arrived. Josh let the rope fly, his entire system on automatic. He grinned with satisfaction. Damned if the rope didn't sail true despite the blasted wind.

As soon as the rope made contact, the black shook his head angrily, but didn't break pace. When the rope settled around his neck and Josh reeled in the slack, the horse kicked out his powerful back legs. The other horses faltered, as if unsure about continuing. The ones farther back were already slowing to a trot.

"Take it down," Josh hollered to Cara. "A few miles at a time."

She responded quickly. Josh felt the rope grow slack and was careful not to let go. He'd hate to lose the horse now, not after all their hard work capturing him, but he would if the black was in danger of being hurt.

The black fought the rope, swinging his head wildly, bucking and stopping long enough to rear up and paw the air before breaking into a fresh run.

Josh kept his end of the rope wrapped tightly, his hand cemented to the side of his leg. Each of the black's movements transmitted through the rope like a telegraph signal traveling a line.

"That's right," he coaxed when Cara had slowed the Jeep enough that the black trotted alongside them. "No need to fight."

Except the black did just that. Refusing to surrender, he snorted lustily and pranced, showing off the spirit that made him a rebel and the sharp action of his gait. Josh fell a little bit more in love with the horse. He wouldn't be satisfied until the black was his.

By now, Cara was driving no more than five miles an hour. They were mere feet away from the hill. Had the capture taken a minute longer, they wouldn't have made it.

"Should I stop?" she asked.

Josh dropped down into the passenger seat, the rope gripped in his hand. "Let's turn around and head back."

With little choice, the black went along. Every few steps, he shook his head, snorted and attempted to change direction. Josh held firm. In this contest of wills, he was determined to emerge the victor.

As he'd hoped, the remaining horses followed their leader. Violet and Joey hopped on their quads and brought up the rear, careful to stay a safe distance behind. Their job was to make sure there were no stragglers.

Thirty minutes later, they had pushed the mustangs through the gate into section seven of the sanctuary. With some reluctance, Josh cut the black loose. After that, the horse did his job, circling his herd and making sure they were once again safely under his command.

Cara had parked the Jeep and stood by the gate, watching the mustangs pass through like a mother monitoring her many children. Josh strode over to her.

She glanced up at his approach but didn't say anything. He hadn't expected her to thank him. Well, maybe he had expected it.

"I'd like to talk to you," he said, admiring the rosy glow of her cheeks and the way her long black hair whipped around her face. Winter suited her. Then again, he could picture her in shorts and a tank top, her tanned legs and slender arms—

"About what?"

His thoughts splintered at her sharp tone. "The black," he said. "And that horse you were working with earlier."

Suspicion flared in her eyes.

Josh didn't give her a chance to rebuke him. "I'd like to buy them from you."

"They're not for sale."

"I thought all your mustangs were for sale. Isn't that

the purpose of the sanctuary? To rehabilitate the horses and find them a permanent home?"

"There's a detailed adoption process. Prospective owners have to meet certain qualifications. You don't."

With that, she walked through the gate and into the sanctuary.

"Fine," Josh mumbled to himself, watching some of the friendlier mustangs surround her and beg for attention. "But you can't avoid me forever."

And she couldn't. Thanks to the terms of his late father's will and the agreement he'd reached with Gabe, they were both stuck at Dos Estrellas, for the next year at least, working and living side by side.

The situation appealed to Josh far more than he'd ever admit.

Chapter Two

Josh examined the brilliant blue sky from astride Wanderer, one of the roping horses he'd brought with him from California. Wanderer had helped Josh win half of those buckles in the drawer at his grandparents' house. He was a good, reliable mount. He was also getting a bit long in the tooth. Josh hated to think about retiring his good friend, but the day would come eventually.

"You catch the news last night?" Cole asked, then answered his own question without waiting for an answer. "No rain for another two weeks, if then."

"So I hear."

Josh's younger brother sat beside him on one of Cara's rehabilitated mustangs. Cole, too, examined the sky. They did a lot of that. For cattle ranchers, weather was a thrice daily topic of discussion.

Cole's horse, like Wanderer, also stood patiently. One month of training and already the horse showed considerable promise of being a reliable cow pony.

Hmph, Josh mused silently. Cara hadn't minded when Cole expressed an interest in acquiring the young mustang. In fact, he hadn't bothered to buy the horse like Josh had offered. Cole had simply assumed care of the horse and started training him.

Then again, Cole had sold his four best roping horses just before Christmas to pay off some of the ranch's more pressing bills—leftover medical expenses from their father's cancer treatments—as well as purchase supplemental feed for the cattle. That sacrifice, apparently, earned Cole better treatment from Cara.

All Josh had done was return her escaped mustangs to the sanctuary.

Yeah, he might have once suggested she relinquish the five hundred acres left to her for the sake of Dos Estrellas. More than once, actually. But he wasn't alone. Cole had also suggested it. He'd practically insisted on it. Yet Cara gave *him* one of her precious mustangs and refused Josh.

He groaned in frustration. If he lived to be a hundred, he'd never understand the fairer sex.

"What's wrong?" Cole asked.

"This drought." He lied rather than admit a woman was getting under his skin. "I understand Arizona is supposed to be dry, but at the rate we're going, we'll have to sell off more cattle by March or go under."

They'd recently purchased four hundred young steer, bringing their total to two thousand head. It was a calculated move. The steer were purchased at a good price and could be sold later at a profit. That was, if the weather cooperated. Without grass, the steer wouldn't grow fat and sleek, a necessity for their plan to work. If not, they might all be looking for a new home.

That included Cara and her precious mustangs. Yet she continually refused to cooperate.

Cole tossed aside the stalk of dried grass he'd been chewing. "Violet says rainy season is twice a year, late summer and winter."

"Except it's rained once in the last four months and late summer is a long ways off."

"No accounting for Mother Nature." Cole clucked to the gelding.

Break time was apparently at an end. Josh followed his brother's example and set off after him.

They were inspecting fences. In light of yesterday's fiasco with the mustangs, it seemed the thing to do.

Especially since mustangs weren't the only culprits after the cattle's grass. Deer from the mountains and wild horses from the neighboring reservation made a habit of visiting Dos Estrellas. Though when it came to the nimble deer, a fence didn't provide much deterrent. Just last week, Josh had observed a small herd of mule deer sail effortlessly over a five-foot fence and onto ranch land.

"You're the one who decided we should live here," Cole said.

Their horses walked the fence line nose to tail, needing little guidance.

"You agreed."

"Like I had a choice." Cole chuckled humorously. "You'd have had my hide if I'd stayed in California."

Josh knew Cole wasn't as mad as he pretended to be. They had returned to Mustang Valley and their childhood home last November after the death of their father, and then because they were named as beneficiaries in the will.

Josh wouldn't deny it. They'd both been hoping for money or some asset they could convert into quick cash. Josh mostly because he'd drained his bank account fighting for custody of his kids, and Cole because he wanted nothing attaching him to his father. Instead, they'd each inherited one-third ownership in the ranch their great-grandfather had built and their late father had loved above all else, including them.

They'd also inherited a somewhat hostile partnership with their half brother, Gabe, who made no secret of wanting to buy out Josh's and Cole's shares, as well as a debt that would soon bury them if they didn't find another source of income. In addition to the inheritance came two housemates named Cara and Raquel.

By all accounts, Josh and Cole should dislike Raquel. Their father began an affair with her over thirty years ago while still married to their mother. The result of that union was Gabe, born in between Josh and Cole. Raquel was the reason their mother had left Mustang Valley, taking Josh and Cole with her to Northern California. It was the last time either brother had seen their father alive. Josh had been seven, Cole five.

Returning to Mustang Valley, living under the same roof with their father's second family, wasn't easy for Josh. It was harder for Cole. Good-natured Raquel, however, had extended the hand of friendship and treated them with kindness, welcoming them into a home that technically wasn't hers. It was an unusual and complex situation none of them were managing easily.

Josh, Cole and Gabe each had their reasons for working together and running the ranch. The all-important question was, would any of their reasons pay off?

"Look there," Josh said.

Seeing a potential weak spot in the fence, he reined in Wanderer. The horse immediately stopped, tugging on the bit. Josh dismounted. He'd hardly begun inspecting the splintered wire when Cole appeared beside him.

"What do you think?"

Josh tested the wire. "Worth a second look."

For about the tenth time that morning, he removed his cell phone and snapped a picture of the potential trouble spot in the fence. He then entered a few comments in the notes app, including location and description of the necessary repair.

"Some cowboys we are." Cole straightened, a wry smile on his face. "Using a cell phone to track fence breaks. What would Grandpa think?"

"He'd probably have himself a good laugh."

By Grandpa, Cole referred to their mother's father. They knew hardly anyone on their father's side of the family save Gabe, and him only since the death of their father.

How much their lives had changed in the past two months. Especially the past year, for Josh. First, he divorced his ex, followed by a lengthy and expensive custody battle over his two-year-old son and nine-month-old daughter. He was leaving soon to pick them up and bring them back to Dos Estrellas. He wasn't returning to the circuit.

He was trading one career for another, that of pro rodeo cowboy for cattle rancher. Never had he thought he'd follow in his father's footsteps or once again live at Dos Estrellas.

His gaze strayed to the ranch house and outbuildings, which appeared small from this distance. Smoke rising in a lazy curl from the chimney and a tractor driving across the open area lent the scene a charming, country feel.

Josh experienced a tug on his heartstrings. Odd. He wasn't the sentimental sort, certainly not about this place.

"Do you remember living here at all?" he asked Cole.

"Barely." Cole, too, stared at the ranch. "We shared a room. With bunk beds. I can remember being jealous because Mom let you have the top bunk."

Josh remembered, too. It was the room Cara now occupied. He and Cole were staying in a guest suite that had been added to the main house about ten years ago. Once Josh returned with the kids, he'd occupy the apartment above the horse stable. It was Raquel's idea, and Josh appreciated it. That way, Cole could keep the guest suite and the kids wouldn't wake up the entire household with their crying.

"We had a pony," Josh said.

"Thunder." Cole smiled. The memory must not have haunted him like most of the others from when they lived with their father. "You tried to rope a cow from him."

Josh also smiled. He'd been six at the time. "No trying about it. I did rope a cow."

"And, if I recall correctly, you got jerked clean out of the saddle and dragged across the pasture."

Josh chuckled. "After Dad rescued me and cleaned me up, he hollered at me for a full twenty minutes until my ears rang."

"Figures." Cole's mood changed in an instant. "Parenting wasn't his strong suit."

"Actually, I think he was scared. It was a pretty foolhardy stunt. I was lucky to wind up with no more than a few cuts and bruises." Josh didn't often defend his father. Funny that he did now. Being a father himself had given him a new perspective.

"I guess." Cole shrugged.

"It wasn't all bad when we lived here." Josh pocketed his phone and mounted Wanderer. Once in the saddle, he surveyed their surroundings. Beyond the ranch house lay the quaint community of Mustang Valley, with its equestrian trails and green belt park at its center. To the south, the striking McDowell Mountains shimmered tans, browns and gold in the midafternoon sun. "I could pick a worse spot to raise the kids."

Cole sent Josh an arch look before hauling himself up into the saddle. "Are you ready for fatherhood?"

"I've been a father for almost three years."

"Yeah, and you've spent maybe one of those years with the rug rats."

Partially Josh's fault, as a rodeo man was on the road a lot. But partially his ex-wife's fault, too. Twice she'd taken off with the children for weeks at a stretch without telling Josh where they'd gone. Twice he'd hired a private investigator and tracked them down.

Her actions had gone a long way in convincing the judge that Josh deserved full custody, as well as her acute drug addiction. She'd recently completed a third stint in rehab and was moving into a halfway house for the foreseeable future. If she remained in the program and stayed sober for three straight months, Josh had agreed to supervised visitation.

For now, the children were staying with his former in-laws, having a last visit with them and Josh's ex before he assumed custody. His former in-laws' promise to watch his children carefully was the main reason he'd agreed to the stay. That, and his respect and affection for them. They loved their grandchildren and hated the mess their daughter's addiction had made of everyone's lives as much as Josh did.

"We're done here." He turned Wanderer's head toward the ranch and pushed the horse into a jog. Thinking of his ex-wife soured his mood as much as thinking of their late father did Cole's. "Let's get back—" He almost said "home," but stopped himself at the last second.

"Why the hurry?"

"I want to talk to Cara."

"What about?"

They rode along the narrow trail. Josh had to speak over his shoulder to be heard.

"She had a small dead-broke gelding that would make a good horse for the kids." He didn't mention the black, deciding to keep that piece of news to himself.

"Look, I admit I know squat about kids, but aren't they a little young to ride?"

"Nathan's almost three." True, baby Kimberly wasn't walking yet, but she would at some point. "We were that age when Dad started us riding."

It was probably the only thing their parents hadn't argued about. Coming from a rodeo family, their mother had loved riding as much as their father and encouraged her sons from an early age. She hadn't yelled at Josh after he'd hurt himself roping the cow. Instead, she'd gone out the next day and bought him his first real lariat.

"You sure you just don't want to see Violet?" Cole flashed Josh a sly grin. "She's due back from the grain supplier about this time."

For some reason, Cole and Gabe believed Josh was interested in the livestock manager. Not that Violet wasn't pretty, and Josh did like her. As a friend. Nothing more.

Nonetheless, he didn't correct his brother. The same uncertainty that had him keeping his interest in the black mustang to himself also made him keep his fascination with Cara a secret. Cole might not appreciate Josh's plan to get to know Cara better. Then again, Cara might not appreciate it, either.

No matter. He was determined. Josh hadn't successfully competed at a championship level the past twelve years because he gave up quickly. Cara, he'd begun to suspect, was worth the effort.

USING THE POCKETKNIFE she always carried, Cara sliced through the twine binding a bale of hay. With practiced ease, she yanked the twine loose, then quickly wound it into a small ball, which she tossed into the bed of the pickup truck with all the rest.

Next she grabbed four flakes of hay and tossed them into the feeder. Dust and tiny particles swirled in the air, and she wiped her nose on her jacket sleeve, banishing the tickle. More flakes followed until the entire bale was gone and the feeder overflowing.

That done, she moved to the next one. Twenty bales for this trip. She alone had loaded them onto the flatbed trailer and driven the pickup and trailer across two miles of pastureland to the mustang sanctuary.

An old cattle barn sat at the center of the sanctuary. With the help of volunteers, Cara had converted the structure into a feeding station that, as it turned out, was seldom used. Then came the drought. With grass in short supply, Cara now made the trek three times a week, loading hay purchased with their donated money into the dozen metal feeders—a gift to the sanctuary from an elderly woman who retired last year and sold off her ranch.

Cara continued stuffing the feeders full of hay, looking at her audience every few minutes. Nearly half of the sanctuary's two hundred mustangs surrounded the cattle barn, milling impatiently. The remainder had stayed in the hills. Eventually, however, they'd come down. If not today, then tomorrow or the next day, driven by hunger and the slim pickings.

Rubbing the palm of her right hand through the leather gloves she wore, Cara rolled her head from side to side. Aches and pains were a constant.

No wonder. Feeding and caring for two hundred horses was hard work. Thank God. Most nights, she fell into an exhaustion-induced slumber in which she could escape the guilt and grief that filled her days.

On those rare nights when sleep evaded her, she sat alone in the rocking chair by her window, revisiting her worst memories and blaming herself for something no amount of counseling had convinced her wasn't her fault.

"I'm not sure why, but I think we got off on the wrong foot."

Cara rounded and bit back a retort. The last person she wanted to see stood before her. When had he arrived and how had he gotten into the feeding station without her hearing? Catching sight of his horse tethered to the railing behind him explained it. No roaring engine to alert her.

"I don't know what you're talking about." She resumed cutting open hay bales.

Josh grabbed a thick stack of flakes before she could and added them to the feeder. "Two months I've been here, and you still try to avoid me."

"You actually have to ask why?"

"I'm not the enemy, Cara."

"You're not my friend, either." She moved in front of him. "And I don't need your help."

He ignored her and lifted the remaining flakes as if they weighed nothing. "We're going to be living together for the next year, at least. It would serve us both to get along."

"We're not living together." Apparently, he didn't carry a pocketknife, for he waited for her to cut open the next bale. "You're staying in the guest suite."

"Living at the ranch, then."

"I get along with you." As best she could. He didn't make it easy.

"You tolerate me."

"August promised the ranch to Gabe." She stood back, hands on her hips. "He's the one who worked alongside August. The one August trained to take over."

Josh took advantage of her irritation and lifted half the bale into the next feeder. "So I'm told. By you and Gabe and Raquel. Repeatedly. Yet he left the ranch to all three of his sons." The remaining hay followed.

The man was persistent, and she didn't like persistent people. Too reminiscent of her ex-husband. Though in all fairness to Josh and anyone else, her ex went above and beyond. If not for him demanding she stay and continue their argument, Javier might not have—

"I'm sorry," Josh said between armfuls. "I know you don't like the situation."

"None of us do."

"You have your sanctuary."

She crossed her arms and eyed him. "Which you want."

He stopped. "The cattle operation is barely getting

by. The sanctuary pastureland is some of the best on the ranch."

"Grass wouldn't be in such sort supply if you hadn't bought four hundred steer last month."

"That wasn't my decision alone. Gabe is the one who suggested we buy the steer."

"And it's *his* fault they were sick with red nose?"

Josh's expression hardened. "I didn't say that. Don't put words in my mouth."

She had. Mostly because she understood why Gabe had pushed for the purchase of the steer. He wanted his half brothers gone more than Cara did.

With the help of their neighbor, Theo McGraw, and the money Cole had received from selling his championship horses, the steer were now healthy and thriving, recovered from the virus. They were also eating. A lot.

"Cattle are what put the roof over our heads and the food on our table," Josh said.

"I'll pay rent," Cara answered stiffly. Donations were down, but she'd find the money somehow.

"We don't want your money."

She resisted lashing out. The fact was, she did depend on Dos Estrellas for her room and board. The arrangement hadn't felt one-sided when August was alive. Cara had contributed to the household by running errands, cooking and cleaning so that Raquel could devote herself entirely to August's care.

Since his death, Cara had poured herself even more into the sanctuary, her contributions at home not needed as much. She supposed it was possible for others, like Josh, to view her as a freeloader. He didn't see her as part of the family like Raquel and Gabe did. The way August had. They'd taken in her and Javier without a single qualm or hesitation after she and her ex separated. She loved them for it.

"What do you want?" she asked testily.

"If this ranch goes under, you'll lose the sanctuary."

"Hmm. Either I lose the sanctuary by giving the land back to you and your brother, or I lose it because the ranch goes under." Her voice dripped sarcasm. "Let see, which option do I pick?"

Josh's expression remained hard. "You'd be giving the land to Gabe, too."

"He doesn't want it."

She had Josh there. Gabe was her staunchest supporter. He'd fought his half brothers tooth and nail, insisting she be allowed to continue using the five hundred acres August had granted to her in his will.

"Not yet." Josh arched one brow. "He may change his mind when we go broke."

"He'll sell off some of the cattle first. He's done it before."

"Cole and I weren't here then."

She tensed. "Are you threatening me?"

"I'm asking you to see reason."

"Ah." She nodded. "Your version of reason."

"Let's not argue. That's not why I came here."

"Why did you?"

"First we finish feeding." He hoisted a bale from the flatbed trailer.

She started to protest, again, that she didn't need help. The pain shooting up her arm from her sore hand changed her mind.

They labored side by side for several minutes and were almost done when he asked, in a far more amiable tone, "What got you started rescuing mustangs?"

She considered making an excuse about why she didn't feel like talking. Instead she said, "The Powells."

"The family who owns the horse stables up the road?"

She nodded. "We're friends with them. They rescued Prince a few years ago. He was the last wild mustang in the valley. Up until the 1950s, wild herds continued to roam the mountains. After Prince, the Powells began rescuing other mustangs from all over the state. Ones that were starving or in overpopulated herds or sometimes abused and neglected."

"But how did you become involved?"

"The Powells needed help, and I had time."

That was true. It was also true she'd started volunteering after things between her and Manuel had turned bad. Javier was a baby. The Powells hadn't minded that she brought him along, as they were simply happy for another set of hands. But Josh didn't need to know that part, and she wasn't about to tell him.

"When did you acquire the sanctuary and move it here?"

Leave it to Josh to ask the hardest question. "Three years ago. The Powells were running out of room and busy with—" She hesitated, not wanting to say "having babies and raising their children." That had been an activity Cara and the Powell wives once had in common. "With work," she finally said. "I started with a few mustangs. Then more. Eventually, they all came."

That was after her son died. Without the sanctuary, Cara was convinced she'd have gone quietly crazy.

A loud clattering made them turn around. They were met by twenty or so mustangs, their heads hanging over the gate and their tails swishing.

"Looks like the natives are getting restless." Josh

smiled at the horses ready to storm the feeding station and chow down.

Cara would have replied except she couldn't. Josh's smile, and the laughter lighting his eyes, literally captivated her. He was so handsome, more rugged than movie-star pretty despite his classic blond hair and blue eyes. Not that she hadn't noticed his looks before now. But their effects on her were new.

She and Josh didn't usually stand this close. That must have been the reason. If she moved her hand a mere inch, it would graze his shoulder. She wasn't tempted. More like curious. It had been a long time since she'd touched a man with anything other than innocent casualness.

Wait. Wait. *Wait!* This was seven kinds of wrong. Josh Dempsey was the last man about whom she should be entertaining romantic notions. Correction: she should not be entertaining such notions about *any* man. Her son had died two years ago in an entirely preventable accident. She wasn't entitled to feel anything but grief and guilt. She might never be entitled.

"Ready?" Josh's bright smile hadn't dimmed one small watt.

"Sure." Cara hesitated, worried her wobbly knees would buckle. "Can, um, you get the gate?"

He spared her the briefest of odd glances before doing as she'd asked. "Stand back," he called. "Here they come."

She had only enough time to duck behind the nearest feeder before the horses clambered through the gate and headed straight for the hay, pushing and shoving and nipping at one another in their haste.

The sight was a comical one, and Cara almost

laughed. She didn't, though. Like romantic attraction, happiness wasn't possible. The mechanism inside her responsible for manufacturing it had broken.

Josh did laugh. The sound, loud and rich and full, caused a pleasant ripple to course through her. She tried to tamp it down and failed.

Suddenly afraid and not sure of what, Cara cut a zigzag path through the horses toward her pickup truck.

"Wait," Josh called.

She reluctantly stopped. The next instant, he was beside her, and her awareness of him intensified.

"I want to talk to you about one of the horses." He waited until she met his gaze, which was hard to resist.

She steeled herself. "Which one?"

"The small, homely gelding. What did you call him?"

"Hurry Up."

"He'd make a great horse for my kids."

She knew Josh had recently won custody of his children and would soon be bringing them to Mustang Valley. It was something she tried not to think about.

"Please," he continued. "I haven't been the best dad before now. It's a situation I'm determined to change."

"Kids need more than a pet."

"I get that. But a love of horses is something I can share with them, teach them about, and I'm not above bribing them." He added the last part with a guilty grin.

Cara nodded. Speaking was difficult because of the large, painful lump lodged in her throat.

"You mentioned an adoption process. Can we start it? I fly out tomorrow to pick up the kids from their grandparents' in San Jose."

Young children. Underfoot. In the way. She wouldn't

be able to escape them and the constant reminder of what might have been if not for that terrible day.

"Look," he said. "If you won't let me adopt Hurry Up, maybe I can sponsor him. I'll pay for his food and care. In exchange, you let me use him for my kids. He can stay in the sanctuary. I won't move him to the horse stable."

He was being more than reasonable. To refuse him simply out of spite was unfair to him, his children and the sanctuary, which was always in need of extra money.

"All right, you win," she said, but it sounded like someone else talking.

Chapter Three

Josh had no idea how much room was needed for two little kids. Eight hundred square feet? Two thousand? The apartment above the horse stable seemed small to him, what with its one bedroom, living room/dining room, kitchen and bath.

Raquel had been kind, offering him use of the apartment and helping him move in. Okay, technically the apartment, along with all of Dos Estrellas, was one-third his. But she had been the matriarch of the ranch for over twenty years, and he didn't want to appear rude or ungrateful.

"If you ask me..." Raquel let the sentence drop.

"I am." Josh carried a crib mattress under one arm and a merry-go-round lamp under the other.

The remainder of his kids' furniture was in the stock trailer parked below, including a youth bed, dresser, changing table and toy chest. There was also a mobile, playpen, stroller, linens, nursery monitor and several dozen boxes yet to be unloaded. After six weeks in storage, everything was dusty and dirty.

"I'd put the crib and youth bed in the bedroom." Raquel pointed down the short hall. "You could sleep in the living room. The couch converts to a bed."

Josh expelled a long sigh. This, more than unpacking and cleaning, was exactly the help he needed. "Good idea."

He'd been spoiled. Living half of the last fourteen years on the road, he'd relied first on his mother, then his ex-wife, then his mother again to keep his home in order.

Maybe Cole was right to doubt his parenting abilities. Josh had a lot of growing up to do, and quickly.

After carrying the crib mattress and lamp to the bedroom, he returned to find Gabe lifting two large boxes. For every load Josh had carried up from the trailer, Gabe had carried one down. In recent years, the apartment had become a dumping place for odds and ends. Raquel was overseeing the clearing out.

"Take this, too." She added a shoe box to her son's load, though, from the bulging sides, the box didn't look to contain shoes.

Gabe peered around the stack in his arms. "Where do I put all this stuff?"

"The spare bedroom for now. I'll figure out what to do with it later."

As Josh watched Gabe and Raquel conversing, he was struck with a strange sense of surrealism. He'd often imagined having sole custody of his children, but never living with them in an apartment on his late father's ranch. Nor had he imagined his half brother and his father's longtime companion being the ones to help him clean and ready the apartment.

He blinked, but nothing changed. Raquel and Gabe continued to chat in the living room.

"What's in these, anyway?" Gabe pretended to buckle, as if the boxes were heavy.

His mother smiled. "Old clothes, mostly. From the hall closet."

"Feels more like bricks."

Raquel patted Gabe's arm as she sidled past him into the kitchen. "Be good, *mijo*."

She called him the endearment a lot. It was always accompanied by an affectionate touch. The two of them were obviously close.

Josh couldn't say the same thing about his own mother. She wasn't affectionate with anyone, not even her family. But then, she wasn't a happy person. She resented his late father to this day and had attempted to pass that resentment on to her sons. She'd succeeded with Cole, probably because he was younger and didn't have as many happy memories of his father as Josh did.

Whatever anger Josh felt toward his father had been pushed out, thanks to his ex-wife and her addiction. His heart had only so much room for bitterness and disappointment.

"Hey. How's it going?" Reese McGraw peeked inside, a smile on her face.

It was hard to tell who brightened more, Gabe or Raquel.

"Come in," Raquel beckoned to Reese. "Don't just stand there."

"Wow, you've been busy." She walked straight to Gabe and, standing on tiptoes, kissed his cheek. "Can I help?"

His eyes roved her face as if committing every detail to memory. "You already have."

Josh was happy for the two of them. His marriage and that of his parents may have tanked, but that didn't mean he'd lost faith in the institution. He liked to believe that with the right two people, anything was possible.

Unfortunately, his parents couldn't have been more wrong for each other. According to his mother, Raquel was the reason his father had left her. Josh had bought the story hook, line and sinker—at first. He'd been eighteen when his grandmother had inadvertently let it slip that his parents' marriage was in trouble long before his father had met and fallen in love with Raquel.

"The closet's all yours."

Raquel's remark returned Josh to the present. Good. He was weary of traipsing down memory lane and welcomed the interruption. "Thanks."

"If you don't need me anymore," Gabe said, "I'll see you later."

"Appreciate the hand," Josh said.

"Anytime, brother."

Brother? Another surreal moment. Who'd have guessed he and Gabe would ever act like normal siblings? They'd grown up apart, hating each other for different reasons, the product of their parents' animosity. Reese was mostly responsible for the changes in Gabe. She'd encouraged him to love and forgive.

Josh and Cole could benefit from some encouragement. They'd made considerable progress these past few months, learning to be a family with Gabe, but they still had a long way to go.

"Bye, Josh." Reese waved, then hurried behind Gabe, warning him to watch his step.

Raquel sighed with contentment, her hand resting on her heart as she watched the happy couple leave.

"Children are such a blessing," she said to no one in particular.

"Why didn't you have more?" Josh should have been heading downstairs. There was a lot left to unload and carry up. Something made him hesitate.

"It wasn't in God's plan." She turned a lovely smile on him.

For a fleeting moment, Josh saw a beautiful young woman, the one who must have captivated his father.

"I was lucky to have Gabe. And Cara."

"You and her mother were friends?"

"More than friends. Leena was like a sister to me. After her husband died in that terrible car crash, she and Cara stayed with us for a while."

Josh thought it interesting that he and Cara had both lost their fathers. Though, in her case, a beloved father.

"There was never a question where Cara would live when she and Javier's father separated," Raquel continued. "Or that she would remain after Javier's death."

"I can see why she's attached to the place."

"More than attached. Dos Estrellas is her home."

If Raquel was trying to make a point, she was succeeding. "I don't want her to leave," he said.

"Then why are you trying to take away her purpose?" she asked.

"Is the sanctuary really that important to her?"

Raquel drew herself up as if affronted. "If you have to ask, you can't possibly understand how she feels."

"Then help me understand."

She studied him for a moment, then resumed unpacking a box. "She and Manuel didn't divorce right away. They saw a marriage counselor twice a week up until Javier died. After that, Cara saw a grief counselor."

Josh hadn't heard this part of the story before. "Did Javier die in the apartment?"

"No, no!" Raquel crossed herself. "There is no reason for you to be afraid of living here. You and your children are safe."

"I'm not afraid."

"They were at her old house. Manuel stayed there during the separation, and Cara took Javier for a visit. Javier was climbing the shelving unit when he fell and hit his head. He never woke up and died four days later in the hospital."

"I'm sorry." Josh couldn't imagine something so horrible.

"Such a lovely little boy. My pain is nothing compared to Cara's. I had many wonderful years with your father. Her time with Javier was cut short."

Josh had been through a lot, between his ex-wife's addiction, their divorce and bitter custody battle. His two children were alive and healthy, however. He had much to be thankful for.

The closest he'd come to understanding Cara's loss was when his ex had taken off with the children. Those weeks of not knowing their whereabouts, if they were all right or lying dead on the side of the road, had been unbearable.

"It will be good for us, having children again." Raquel wiped at her eyes. "I am so excited to meet your little ones."

Josh was excited to see his kids, too. He'd seen very little of them recently. As much as he'd hated not being with them over the holidays, he knew he'd done the right thing by his former in-laws and his ex.

Josh didn't hate Trista despite the hell she'd put him through. But he didn't trust her, either. Running off with the children had been bad. Coming home and finding her in a drug-induced stupor, the children filthy, hungry, crying and neglected, had been too much.

He accepted some of the blame. He'd been gone a lot, competing. That wasn't going to happen again. He would be the best parent possible, better than he'd been so far. Better than his father had been to him.

"I'm excited," he admitted. "I'm told Kimberly is almost walking and Nathan can ride a tricycle."

Raquel's expression melted. "They sound like angels."

"Kimberly doesn't sleep through the night yet. Nathan does. Probably because he spends all day getting into trouble and tires himself out."

"Just like a boy."

He pulled out his cell phone. Raquel had asked to see pictures of the kids before, so he didn't think he'd annoy her by sharing the latest batch his former in-laws had sent.

She gasped with delight. "They're adorable. You are truly blessed. If you ever need a babysitter, you simply have to ask."

"I don't want to impose."

"If you don't ask me, I will be hurt." When he laughed, she insisted, "I am serious."

He had no doubt of it. "I am fortunate you built this apartment. Not sure what else I would have done or where I would have gone."

Her smiled dimmed. "Your father and I, we had hoped my parents would stay here during their visits. That is why we built it."

"They didn't?"

"No." She methodically wiped dry the baby bottles she'd just washed. "They preferred the inn in town."

Josh was admittedly curious and would have asked more questions, but footsteps sounded on the outside stairs. He expected Gabe and Reese might be returning or perhaps Cole, checking out the new digs. Instead, Cara entered the apartment, a look of horror on her face.

"What are you doing?" she demanded.

"Unpacking." Josh was unsure what to make of her reaction.

"Raquel?" She turned to the other woman, who swallowed guiltily.

"I offered Josh the apartment," Raquel said. "For his children. I was going to tell you…"

"When?"

"Wait a minute." Josh stepped between them. "Raquel hasn't done anything wrong. In fact, she's been very helpful."

"That's right." Cara directed her anger at him. "You're one of the owners. If you want to move into the apartment, no one can stop you."

"Why would you?" Josh genuinely wanted to know. "You aren't living here now."

Cara brushed at her damp eyes, then fled the apartment.

"I should have told her." Raquel tossed aside the dish towel. "I was going to. Then I didn't."

"This isn't your fault," Josh reiterated.

"She has so many memories of this place. Too many for her to continue living here after Javier died."

"She had to assume someone would move in eventually."

"Perhaps she chose not to think about it."

That was possible, he supposed. Then again, he specifically could be the cause of Cara's objections.

"I'm going after her," Raquel announced.

Josh didn't stop her. Better she speak to Cara than him. Whatever he said was bound to upset Cara, and no amount of wanting to change that would make a difference.

"Is it possible you overreacted?"

Cara studied her friend Summer Goodwyn, seeing only concern and not criticism in her eyes. "Maybe. A little," she admitted. "I was surprised. Raquel should have told me. Or Josh. Someone."

"Josh? Seriously?"

"Okay, not him."

"He might not have known you used to live in the apartment."

"I doubt that."

"You can't always think the worst of him just because you want to."

That was the thing about Summer—she didn't mince words. They'd been friends since after Javier's death. Cara had joined a support group that met at the Mustang Valley Community Church. Summer belonged to another support group, one for parents of children with special needs.

After talking several times in the hall between groups, they'd gone for coffee. Then, lunch. Eventually, they began meeting up at least once a week. Summer was one of Cara's biggest supporters, championing the sanctuary and volunteering with fund-raising.

"I wish I'd known," Cara murmured.

"Would it have made a difference?"

"I'd have been prepared. Not blindsided."

They stood inside the round pen, the late-afternoon

sun warming them on what would otherwise be a chilly day. The ranch was relatively quiet, as most everyone was involved with the semiannual equipment maintenance. Except for Josh. He'd gone to San Jose to retrieve his kids.

Summer's eight-year-old son, Teddy, was in the pen along with Cara, Summer and Hurry Up. The boy usually loved animals. For some unknown reason, he hadn't taken to the gentle horse.

"I think it's a good idea," Summer said, her gaze straying to Teddy, whose autism often caused him to behave unpredictably. "Someone moving into the apartment. It's been like a tomb these last two years."

The words hurt, but that didn't change the fact Summer was right. Cara had no claim to the apartment simply because she'd lived there for six months with Javier.

In many ways, those were the worst months of her life. The separation from Manuel. Their constant fighting. The lonely nights. And in some ways, they were the best months. Whoever said children were at their worst during their twos hadn't met Javier. He'd been a delight. The absolute light of her life.

Cara took a deep breath. "Having someone live in the apartment won't make me suddenly stop grieving."

"I didn't say it would." Summer put an arm around Cara's shoulders. "We can't halt time. We can only move forward."

Cara sniffed and bit down, her emotions dangerously close to the surface.

An odd strangled sound spurred Summer into action. Teddy crouched on the ground, his back pressed against the round pen railing. He stared wide-eyed as if confronted by demons.

"Teddy! It's okay." Summer knelt in front of him and tried to get him to look at her by putting her face directly in his line of vision. She didn't touch him, however. Teddy didn't like to be touched, especially when he was agitated. "It's all right, baby. The horse won't hurt you."

Teddy continued to stare at Hurry Up, who stood placidly by the gate, his nose to the ground, his breath blowing dust into the air and not the least bit interested in any of the humans.

"Garh, garh." Teddy waved an angry hand at Hurry Up in an attempt to shoo the horse away.

Cara unlatched the gate. "I'll get Hurry Up."

Whatever the horse had done—looked directly at Teddy, nuzzled his arm, snorted, swished his tail—had set the boy off. Best to just return Hurry Up to his stall.

Experiment a total failure, Cara thought as she led Hurry Up to the horse stable. Before she would agree to let Josh have the horse—make that *sponsor* the horse—she'd decided to see if Teddy wanted him. Obviously, he didn't.

Teddy's screeching reached Cara's ears even at this distance. She felt terrible for her friend. At the same time, she envied Summer. Her son was alive.

With Hurry Up happily munching on an oat and bran mixture, Cara sought out Summer and Teddy. They were at Summer's car, parked in front of the stable. Teddy sat in the rear seat, a quilt thrown over him and covering his face. Summer crouched inside the open car door, softly reciting a nursery rhyme.

Cara had seen this before. The weight of the quilt and the darkness, along with the sound of Summer's voice, calmed Teddy. After a few moments, he stopped struggling and quieted. Summer slowly stood, strain showing on her face.

"Sorry about that."

Cara dismissed her with a wave. "As if you have anything to apologize for."

"He'll be okay now."

"What can I do to help?"

"Nothing." Summer smiled weakly. "But thanks."

"Here." Cara tugged her friend around to the rear of the car. She also knew from experience that Teddy would remain where he was. "Relax. Breathe deep."

"He's been agitated more than usual lately."

"Any reason in particular?"

"Hal came by earlier this week."

"Oh." Cara nodded.

"He hasn't seen Teddy for months. Then, boom, he shows up out of the blue, deciding he's going to be a father." She pressed her hands to her cheeks. "I wish I'd never agreed to visitation."

"You could go back to court."

"No, thank you!" Summer lifted her chin, visibly composing herself, then promptly changed the subject. "At least Josh is trying to be a good father."

Cara made a face. Couldn't they talk about something else? "The man's impossible."

"He's taking responsibility for his kids and giving them a secure home. That says a lot about a person."

Cara waited until the pain in her chest subsided. "I hate it when you're right."

"Give him a chance. I get that it's hard for you to think about someone else living in the apartment you shared with Javier. Someone with children. But it really is best for them."

"I thought he'd keep the guest suite and his brother Cole would move out."

"You hoped."

"He wants Hurry Up for his children."

"Aren't they a little young to ride?"

"Yes."

Summer smiled. "But you're going to let him adopt the horse."

Cara shrugged one shoulder. "Sponsor the horse. For a monthly stipend. If it doesn't work out, I'll take Hurry Up back."

"Sounds like a good compromise."

"He wants the black stallion, too. He didn't tell me, but I overhead him talking to Cole. I'm less inclined to agree."

"Because?"

Cara groaned in frustration.

"Let him sponsor the horses, Cara. You're always looking for good homes. What better home is there than Dos Estrellas?"

Right again. This was getting old.

"Muh, muh," Teddy called from inside the car.

Summer glanced over her shoulder. "I'd better go. He's getting restless."

At the driver side door, the two women hugged. Summer tucked a lock of Cara's hair behind her ear in an affectionate gesture.

"You're stronger than you think," she said. "You can handle this."

Maybe. "I'll call you tomorrow."

Rather than return to the house, Cara walked through the horse stable. It wasn't Hurry Up that drew her, but the apartment stairs. The next thing she knew, she stood on the landing.

Her hand reached for the knob and turned it. The door wasn't locked, and she slowly entered, her boot-steps soft on the braided area rug. Josh and the children weren't due for several hours.

Like a ghost, she silently walked across the small living room, down the hall and to the bedroom. Her heart lurched at the sight of the crib set up in one corner and the changing table beside it. She'd furnished the room similarly. The only difference was the youth bed in the opposite corner.

Summer had been wrong. Cara wasn't strong at all.

She noticed the covers on the electrical outlets were still in place, as well as safety locks on the windows and doors. An inspection of the closet yielded a baby gate tucked in the back.

Josh would need that. Stairs were dangerous for toddlers, though that wasn't where Javier had fallen. After all her worrying and diligent watchfulness, something as seemingly harmless as the laundry room was the site of his fatal accident.

She rested a trembling hand on the crib railing. "Oh, *mijo*. I miss you so much."

Distant voices distracted her, and she quickly withdrew her hand. The voices were accompanied by the sound of someone climbing the stairs. Who was here? Her mind had barely asked the question when she heard the unmistakable sound of Josh's voice.

"Come on, buddy. That's it. Grab the railing."

"I firsty, Daddy."

"We'll get you some water in a minute."

Cara panicked and searched frantically for an escape route. There was none. Josh was going to catch her in the apartment. What would he think? What excuse could she offer?

She dashed toward the living room, preferring to be caught there than in the bedroom. Her mind emptied the moment Josh entered the apartment.

He held the hand of a young boy bundled in a warm jacket and knitted cap, and with the same striking blue eyes as his father. In his other hand, Josh held a baby carrier. From beneath the rainbow-colored blanket, a chubby face peeked out, rosy-cheeked and sucking on a pacifier.

Both children were incredibly beautiful, and Cara's heart lurched anew.

"I, ah, didn't mean to intrude," she stammered and brushed self-consciously at her damp eyes.

Josh strode forward. "Actually, if you don't mind, I could use some assistance."

"From me?"

He smiled, and she wished he hadn't. This was hard enough for her, and she didn't need him being nice.

"Can you hold Kimberly for a minute? Nathan's thirsty, and I promised him some water."

Without waiting for her answer, Josh handed her the baby carrier.

Cara watched as her hand, acting on its own, grabbed the carrier. She stood frozen in place while Josh went to the refrigerator, removed a jug of water and poured some into a plastic sippy cup he'd produced from…she had no idea where.

"Here you go, buddy."

The boy, Nathan, drank, never taking his eyes off

Cara. She couldn't meet his stare and instead gazed down at Kimberly, the baby's face that of an angel.

Suddenly, Cara's hand shook. Afraid she might drop the carrier, she set it down on the floor.

"Are you okay?" Josh asked.

She wasn't sure and stumbled toward the couch. The cushions dipped as she sat. She'd forgotten how old and uncomfortable the couch was. Josh would probably have trouble sleeping on the pullout bed. She had.

"I haven't been around little children much…lately." She wrung her hands nervously. Why wasn't she leaving?

Josh sat on the other end of the couch, balancing Nathan on his lap. "We'll try to keep out of your way as much as possible."

"You don't have to do that." It was her problem to handle, not his.

Nathan didn't want to sit and scrambled off Josh's lap. He walked over to his sleeping sister and set his sippy cup in the carrier at her feet.

That made no sense. Then again, he wasn't three years old yet.

"Daddy, I hungry."

"The kid eats like nothing I've ever seen." Josh got off the couch and headed to the kitchen. "Raquel put some hot dogs in the fridge."

"Hot dogs!" Nathan tumbled excitedly into the kitchen.

The boy grabbed the counter edge as Josh removed a perfectly good hot dog from the package, arranged it on a paper plate and put it in the microwave. Ninety seconds later, the pair of them stared dejectedly at a deformed hot dog.

"I guess I messed that up." Josh shot the microwave a dirty look as if it were responsible.

Nathan started to cry.

Cara pushed to her feet, fully intending to leave. Except, she didn't. Going into the kitchen, she automatically patted Nathan on the head before realizing her mistake. His hair was the texture of silk.

"Hot dogs take thirty seconds to heat," she said, examining her hand before brushing it on her jeans.

Josh placed a second one on the paper plate. "I have a lot to learn." He pressed buttons on the microwave. This time, when the buzzer sounded, the hot dog looked edible. He cut it into small pieces and then carried the plate to the table.

"Did you bring a booster seat?" Cara assured herself that the baby slept peacefully in her carrier on the floor. It was as good a place as any.

Josh shook his head. "I don't know. My in-laws and Trista did most of the packing."

"Daddy. Hungry!" Nathan complained impatiently.

"Wait." Cara hurried to the hall closet. The extra pillows were there, just like before. Back at the table, she set the pillows on a chair, then instructed Nathan, "Sit here."

He eagerly clambered into the chair, situated himself and began stuffing pieces of hot dog into his mouth.

Satisfied, she started for the door. "I'll leave you to your dinner."

"Before you go." Josh intercepted her. "I have a deal to propose."

Her suspicions flared. This must be about the horses. "What kind of deal?"

"Clearly, I need help with my kids."

"I'm sure you'll do fine."

He smiled. "I could use a teacher. I was thinking of you."

"No." She jerked back so quickly, she bumped into the door.

"Hear me out first." Josh continued speaking, ignorant of, or indifferent to, her distress. "You show me the ropes, and I'll help you with the sanctuary. Anything you need. And I won't pressure you to give up the land."

Did he not realize how hard this would be for her?

She glanced at Nathan, smashing the last bite of hot dog into his plate rather than eating it. Kimberly had started stirring and would whimper any second. Most babies her age cried when they woke from a nap.

Cara wanted to run and not stop until she was a thousand miles away. She also wanted to hold Kimberly. The two longings waged a war inside her. Eventually, one prevailed.

Going to the carrier, she undid the straps and lifted the baby into her arms. A splendid feeling washed over her. Cara cradled the baby close as tears filled her eyes. She wondered if they were tears of sorrow or joy.

"All right," she murmured and gently rocked the baby. "We have a deal."

Chapter Four

Nathan had decided to help Josh unpack. As a result, clothes and toys littered the bedroom floor. And now the boy was constructing diaper towers of varying heights.

"Come on, buddy." Josh tucked Kimberly in the crook of his arm. For once, she wasn't crying. "Time to clean up this mess."

"I almost done, Daddy."

Josh should have been grateful. Mess aside, the diaper project had kept Nathan occupied and out of trouble for the past thirty minutes.

Hold on. Making a mess *was* getting into trouble. Oh, well. It beat emptying the bottom cupboards, which was what Nathan had done when they first got up this morning at seven.

That was late for Josh. Typically, he rose earlier. But he'd been exhausted last night, falling into bed—make that onto the pullout couch—and sleeping poorly. Taking care of two young children was hard work. Not that he hadn't been alone with them for long stretches before now. But it had been a while ago, and he hadn't been in the midst of moving. Also, Nathan had become considerably more rambunctious and Kimberly more demanding, if that was possible.

Laying Kimberly on the changing table, he quickly nabbed the diaper at his feet. He was ready to put it on when he realized he had the wrong size. This was one of Nathan's diapers and considerably larger than Kimberly's.

"Son, what did you do with your sister's diapers?"

Kimberly started crying again, probably because she was cold, what with her bottom half-undressed. Darn, but the apartment was chilly.

"Here." Nathan patted the top of a crooked diaper tower.

"Can you bring me one, please?" Josh kept a hand pressed on Kimberly's stomach. She'd started kicking her legs, and he was afraid she might roll over the railing and off the table. "Hurry."

Nathan took his time selecting the perfect diaper.

"Any one of them will do, son."

Nathan handed him a diaper and Josh quickly put it on Kimberly. Aware that it sagged on one side, Josh nonetheless slipped his daughter into a pair of pink sweatpants and wrestled socks onto her feet. The kitten faces on the sock toes seemed to fascinate her. She stopped crying and lifted one foot for closer examination.

Josh cringed. How could she twist herself like that and not pop a joint out of place?

"Hungry, Daddy." Nathan tugged on the hem of Josh's white undershirt.

Somewhere in the messy living room was the shirt he hadn't had time to throw on yet this morning. "Give me a minute, okay?"

"Where's Mommy?"

Josh paused in the middle of cradling a now fully

dressed Kimberly in his arms. Nathan had asked this question at least five times in the past day.

"Mommy's gone to a special place, remember? She'll be there for a while. Until she feels better." Josh hadn't told Nathan about his mother agreeing to continued outpatient services along with residency in a halfway house. His son wouldn't understand.

"She's sick?"

They started walking toward the kitchen, Josh bouncing a whining Kimberly. He imagined she was hungry, too. "That's right, son. And when she's better, she'll come visit you. Or I'll take you to see her."

"I miss her."

Josh ruffled Nathan's hair. "I know."

Trista wasn't always the best mother. Frequently high on pain pills and lost in a haze, she'd neglected the kids. On the other hand, she had sober days. Trista with a clear head doted on her children and lavished them with affection. It wasn't any wonder Nathan missed her.

"I miss her, too, son."

Funny thing, Josh did miss Trista. Not the woman she was today, but the one he'd met and fallen in love with. Unfortunately, he'd lost that Trista years ago in the car accident.

He'd been at the Payson Rodeo. They'd celebrated their anniversary the weekend before. Sure, that first year had been tough, but didn't most newlyweds go through an adjustment period? Truth be told, they hadn't known each other long before eloping to Vegas. Just five months.

The call had come in right after he'd qualified for the calf roping finals. Trista had been driving home from work and was struck by a vehicle running a red light. The other driver was cited and, luckily, "No one was seriously hurt."

Josh could still remember the police officer saying those words to him during the phone call. He'd recall them during Trista's worst bouts with addiction and think, *not seriously hurt?*

She'd suffered a broken nose and fractured cheek from colliding with the air bag, in addition to a wrenched back and whiplash. Trista, it turned out, was slow to recover and in constant pain. Standard treatments hadn't helped. Pain pills were the only thing to provide relief.

Eventually, the doctor cut her off. She saw a different one, then another, changing her story each time. Maybe because Josh was on the road a lot competing, maybe because he didn't have much experience with addicts, it had taken him almost a full year to realize his wife had a problem.

He got her into a program, and she cleaned up. She stayed sober long enough to get pregnant and have Nathan.

Six months later, she was using again. Worse this time. A second stint in rehab also got her clean. Josh had high hopes she'd stay sober, especially when she got pregnant with Kimberly.

Then, one day, he came home from a particularly grueling rodeo and found Trista passed out on the kitchen floor. As if that wasn't bad enough, Nathan had been confined to his room with a baby gate, dirty, smelly and hungry. Who knew for how long? Six-week-old Kimberly was in her crib, in the same condition as her brother and wailing at the top of her lungs.

In that moment, Josh realized he needed to put his children first. Before his marriage and before his career.

After Trista woke up, he announced he was taking the kids to his grandparents' place the following day. It didn't happen. Trista sneaked off with the kids sometime during the night. Two weeks later, the private investigator he hired found them staying with a distant cousin in Louisiana. That spring, she did the same thing again. The PI located her and the kids in Nevada, and when Trista reluctantly brought them home, Josh served her with divorce papers and a demand for full custody.

"How about cereal?" Josh sat Nathan at the table, using the pillows Cara had made into a booster chair the previous afternoon.

"I want eggs."

"Eggs. Hmm." Did they have any?

Josh put Kimberly in the baby carrier, buckled the safety belts and placed her in the middle of the kitchen floor where he could keep an eye on her. She started fussing, and he grabbed a rattle and pacifier. She spit out the pacifier but accepted the rattle. That freed Josh to fix her a bottle of formula, warm a jar of strained bananas and scramble eggs for him and Nathan.

Thank you, Raquel, for stocking the kitchen.

The formula came out too hot—he really needed to get the hang of microwaving—and he burned the eggs. A second effort at both went better. He was even able to fix some toast.

Joining Nathan at the table, Josh gobbled down his breakfast while spoon-feeding Kimberly mashed bananas. They'd barely finished, and a glance at the clock caused him to jump to his feet. Eight fifteen. He was late. Very late.

He hadn't yet found his shirt when it became apparent Kimberly required another diaper changing. "Jeez," he said to no one in particular. "At this rate, I'll go broke in a month."

Josh headed with Kimberly to the bedroom. A knock sounded at the door before he'd finished changing her.

"Coming," he called and hurried to the living room, Kimberly bouncing in his arms. She liked that and laughed.

Cara stood outside the door on the landing, her half smile fading at the sight of Kimberly. "Morning."

"Come on in."

She did, and her glance went straight to the kitchen. "Oh, dear," she said, brows raised.

Oh, dear? Josh followed her stare. "Nathan, no!"

Without thinking, he shoved Kimberly into Cara's arms and bolted to the kitchen, where Nathan had dumped the remaining carton of eggs onto the floor and was "skating" across the slimy puddle in his bare feet.

How had that happened? Josh hadn't been gone for more than a couple minutes.

"Hey, hey. That's enough." He took Nathan by the hand and located his sneakers and socks where he'd dropped them next to the open refrigerator.

"I scrambling eggs."

"I see that." Josh closed the refrigerator door and looked over at Cara. "Do you mind watching her for a second?"

She appeared uncertain but answered, "No problem."

He took her at her word. "Thanks."

A second turned out to be five minutes. Josh and Nathan emerged from the bathroom—cleaner and dressed in Nathan's case, and more harried in Josh's. He surveyed the apartment and groaned. It looked as if a cyclone had traveled from one end to the other.

"Sorry about the mess." Relinquishing Nathan, he swiped a half dozen paper towels from the roll on the counter. He'd start with the floor. After that…

"It's all right." Cara sat on the couch with Kimberly, cleaning the baby's face and fingers with a wet towelette. "Two little ones demand a lot of attention."

"I'll never judge another mother again."

"Did you?" Cara observed him from across the room.

"Truthfully? No. But not because I'm some great guy who appreciates mothers. The complete opposite. I'm ashamed to admit, but I didn't give parenting much thought before becoming one."

"Even when you think you're prepared, you're not." She seemed sincere, if a little preoccupied.

Josh continued cleaning the mess with Nathan's "help." He was curious as to how Cara felt about his children and him as a father. She wasn't an easy person to read. While she competently handled Kimberly, she didn't coo or fuss over the baby like Josh noticed most women did.

Discarding the dirty paper towels in the trash, he peered at Cara over the counter. "You sure you don't mind helping me?"

"Not at all."

All right. It wasn't his imagination. Her voice sounded forced. He considered giving her the chance to opt out of their deal, then decided against it. He needed the help and the advice. There was also his plan of getting to know her better, and their deal provided the perfect means.

"What are you doing for child care? If you don't mind me asking."

"I haven't a clue." Josh dispatched Nathan to the

living room with a sippy cup of apple juice. "Raquel is helping me this week."

"I'm not surprised. She loves kids."

"I can't count on her permanently. It wouldn't be fair."

"Because she and I might not be living here that long," Cara answered flatly.

He forced himself to be patient. "That's not the reason."

"I forgot." She lowered Kimberly onto the floor between her legs. The baby started crawling after her brother, moving faster than some people walked. "We agreed not to discuss the ranch."

"We agreed to more than that."

"Right. A reprieve. For as long as you need my help."

"Why do you always want to argue?"

"Maybe because I'm worried."

That stopped him. Her future, like all of theirs, was uncertain. "You mind if I finish getting dressed?"

"Go ahead."

Josh didn't remember until he'd asked the question that his bedroom was, in fact, the living room. Specifically, where Cara sat. He rummaged through one of the suitcases he'd yet to unpack and found a clean work shirt. Donning that, he buttoned it on the way to the bathroom, where he quickly shaved, combed his hair and brushed his teeth.

Simple daily tasks he'd previously taken for granted. Like parenting.

When he finished getting ready and considered himself prepared to face the day, he returned to the living room—and came to an abrupt halt.

Cara still sat on the couch, one child snuggled on

each side of her, reading a picture book she must have found in one of the boxes. Her voice, flat earlier, rose and fell as she infused emotion into the simple story. Her eyes, previously dull, lit with delight. And her face radiated pure pleasure.

The children were completely captivated. Josh didn't blame them. He, too, was caught in her spell.

Here, at last, was the woman he'd suspected lay beneath the surface. The one who drew him to her like a siren. All it took was a single glimpse, and he was more determined than ever to bring her out of her shell permanently.

"AFTER THAT, RABBIT and Fox were friends forever, living happily together in the Wonderful Woods." Cara closed the storybook. "Did you like that?"

"Read again! Read again!" Nathan slapped a pudgy hand on the book page. "Rabbit and Fox."

She gazed down at Kimberly, who stopped sucking her thumb long enough to point and babble a string of nonsense syllables.

What a beauty. With those enormous brown eyes and dimple in her left cheek, she would break a lot of hearts one day. She was already breaking Cara's.

"I think your sister wants to go outside." Cara reached for Nathan's nose, hesitated and then tweaked it. He giggled.

There. That wasn't so hard.

Except it was. Quite hard. It required all her willpower not to fall apart. "Read Rabbit and Fox." Nathan insisted.

"I will later." Her voice cracked. "I promise."

"No." Nathan made a frowny face. "Now."

He didn't look a thing like Javier. Yet he reminded her so much of her son. His laugh. His silliness. His sweet nature. Even his obstinacy.

Josh materialized from nowhere and reached for Nathan, interceding before the outburst gained momentum. "Let's get ready, buddy. We're going to the house. Someone special wants to meet you. She's going to watch you while I work, okay?"

Cara tensed. How long had he been standing there? Seconds? Minutes?

"Sorry," she stammered.

"For what? Entertaining my children? I'm grateful." He set Nathan on his feet. "If not, I wouldn't have been able to finish getting dressed." He flashed her a dazzling smile.

Cara's face grew warm. She wasn't sure if it was from the smile, his praise or the reference to getting dressed.

Not the last. Oh, no, please. It couldn't be that.

"Say thank you for reading the story," Josh told Nathan.

Instead of doing what his father requested, Nathan jumped onto Cara's lap. "Want to stay with her."

"She's coming with us, buddy."

"It's okay, *mi*—" Cara bit her tongue. She would not call Nathan by the same endearment she had her child. *"Niño,"* she amended. Little boy. That was better.

"My name is Nathan," he said and stabbed himself in the chest with his thumb.

"And my name is Cara."

Leaning forward, he kissed her soundly on the cheek. "Cara."

Her name had never sounded lovelier. She wanted to cry.

"All right. Time to go." Josh grabbed Nathan under the arms, swinging him up into the air.

The boy giggled and squirmed. "Daddy, don't."

Of course, what he really wanted was for his father to continue. Manuel had played the same kind of game with Javier. She and her ex might not have gotten along, fighting almost constantly near the end, but he'd loved their son and suffered now, too, fighting his own demons.

"Where did you hide your jacket?"

It took Cara a second to realize Josh was talking to Nathan and not her. Suddenly self-conscious, she stood. "I'll pack Kimberly's diaper bag."

"That would be great." Josh deposited Nathan onto the floor, and he took off. "I have no idea what goes in it besides diapers."

"Maybe I should give you a lesson."

His gaze roved her face, then lingered as he moved closer. "I'd like that."

"Okay." She retreated a step. "Next time."

"I can't wait." His tone was teasing.

Uh-oh.

Cara suddenly remembered the reason she'd come up to the apartment in the first place. "If we have time, can we stop by the corral first? There's something I want to show you."

"Sure. What is it?"

She should tell him. There was no reason for her to keep it a secret. Yet she did, afraid he might misinterpret her motives. "Better I show you."

"All right," he answered in the same teasing tone.

Cara felt a spark illuminate a place in her heart that had been dark for a long, long time. Of all people, it had to be Josh Dempsey who affected her.

"Diaper bag, young lady." She lifted Kimberly into her arms.

The baby was easier for Cara to feel affection for than Nathan. Kimberly didn't remind Cara of Javier. She wasn't the same age. She was…safe.

In the bedroom, Cara set Kimberly down. The baby crawled between the diapers scattered across the floor while Cara packed the bag. She heard Josh's cell phone ring and him answer it. His baritone voice was pleasant to the ear. He didn't, she noticed, talk fast. Rather, he delivered his words clearly and articulately, as if he thought first before speaking.

It was a nice quality, and Cara admired him for it. She tended to blurt out whatever popped into her head. No filter, her mother often said.

Manuel had liked her spunk and frankness. At first. Later, he'd complained she was difficult to get along with and unwilling to compromise. He might have been right. At least she hadn't cheated on him.

As much as Cara loved Raquel and adored August, she'd struggled with that aspect of their relationship. The two of them had begun their affair when August was still married to Josh's mother. And while Cara believed Raquel and August were perfect together and true soul mates in every way possible, to her, adultery was wrong.

Eventually it didn't matter, as August and his wife divorced. But would they have stayed married if not for Raquel? Really, it was none of Cara's business and didn't matter now. But because of Manuel's infidelity, she could sympathize with Josh's mother and understand her anger.

What Cara didn't understand was her turning Josh and Cole against August. That was selfish and cruel to everyone involved. Cara thought it a shame that the brothers had lost out on the opportunity to know a wonderful man.

Josh's voice carried through the apartment from the kitchen. It sounded as if he was talking to Gabe and Gabe would be spending the morning at the Small Change, Dos Estrellas's closest neighbor and the ranch owned by Reese's father. Theo McGraw suffered from Parkinson's, and Gabe had been helping out more and more lately.

Cara collected the bulging diaper bag and Kimberly's jacket before lifting the baby into her arms. Grappling with her load, she returned to the living room. Josh washed dishes in the sink while at the same time talking on the phone. Nathan drove a toy truck in circles around the table, adding sound effects.

Cara set the diaper bag and Kimberly's jacket on the floor, then straightened. She instantly froze.

Displaying the same knack for mischief as her late son, Nathan had opened the front door and slipped outside, heading straight for the stairs. Cara was suddenly thrown back in time two years. Heart pounding and blood racing, she chased after Nathan, Kimberly squealing from being bounced about like a sack of potatoes.

"No! Nathan, stop!" Cara reached out a hand, her fingers grasping thin air. "Come back here now."

Thank God, the boy did.

"Don't ever go out there by yourself. You hear me?" She dropped to her knees on the landing and took him into her free arm, clasping him to her as if she'd rescued him from the ledge of a ten-story building. "It's dangerous."

"What's wrong?" Josh had hurried over.

Cara glared up at him, shaken to her core. "Nathan went outside. He could have fallen down the stairs."

"You okay, buddy?"

Nathan started to cry. Josh removed him from Cara's embrace, his expression stoic.

She'd done nothing wrong, yet she felt the need to defend herself. "I was afraid he'd get hurt."

"Come on." Josh patted Nathan's back. "Nothing happened. You're just scared. No need to cry."

Cara stood, holding Kimberly and ready to hand her to Josh. Clearly, he had no clue how dangerous seemingly innocent situations could be. "I'd better go."

"Don't. Please," he added.

"I made a mistake."

He put a hand on her shoulder. "I took my eyes off Nathan. I'm the one who made a mistake. I'm angry at myself more than anything."

His hand was strong and his touch tender as he moved his warm palm down to the center of her back. Her hands, however, had become damp and sweaty. In fact, she felt cool and clammy all over.

Josh unnerved her. No, that wasn't it. Completely the opposite. She was attracted to him. And unless she was mistaken, he was also attracted to her.

Dios mío! What a mess.

She couldn't let Josh know how she felt, not under any circumstances. Cara wasn't ready for a relationship. With any man, but especially Josh. He was tall and imposing and all male. He was also the father of two children.

That would be more than a romantic relationship. She wasn't ready to give her heart to a child. And that would happen. Nathan and Kimberly were too appealing. She could fall for them as easily as she could Josh. She had to protect her fragile heart at all costs.

"We'd better hurry," she said. There was nothing pressing, but luckily, Josh didn't dispute her.

A few minutes later, they were taking the stairs that Cara had been terrified Nathan would fall down. Josh carried his son and Cara his daughter.

As they passed Josh's truck, she asked, "Where's Kimberly's stroller? It might come in handy."

"Stroller? Hmm." His brows knit in confusion.

They found it buried in the truck bed beneath boxes, bags and suitcases. Cara loaded the baby, tucking her beneath a blanket she'd found in a sack of linens. Together, the four of them made their way to the small corral beside the round pen. Cara was in the lead, pushing the stroller and carefully navigating it over and around the many minor obstacles. It felt both familiar, like riding a bike, and alien, as if she had no business being here and doing this.

Amazingly, she didn't trip and inadvertently dump the stroller, what with her damp palms and wobbly legs. She probably should have left earlier when she had the chance. Forgotten all about this crazy, stupid idea.

"I've been wanting to ask you something." Josh's voice invaded her thoughts. "About my father."

"Oh?" Where was this going?

"And Raquel. Tell me about them." He kept an eye on Nathan, who ran ahead of them.

"Why the sudden interest after two months?" Cara asked.

"She's been kind to me and Cole, and she doesn't have to be."

"That's Raquel for you. There's no one nicer or more generous. And you're right, she doesn't have to be. But not for the reason you think." Cara avoided a pothole.

"Go on."

"Your mom wasn't the only one who gave her and your dad grief. Raquel's father is very religious and didn't approve of her involvement with your dad. That's why they never married. Her father told Raquel if they did, he'd cut her off from the rest of her family. But that didn't stop her and your dad from loving each other and Gabe from having a happy life. August's one regret was losing you and Cole."

"I hate to burst your bubble," Josh said, "but Dad chose not to have us in his life."

Cara stopped pushing the stroller. "You're wrong, Josh. He wanted to have a relationship with you and Cole. But your dad knew how close Raquel is to her mother and brothers. He refused to allow her to be cut off from them, which her father would have made sure happened if your dad let you and Cole visit."

"I've heard all this before. Raquel's father didn't approve of Dad because he was a married man."

"His religion was important to him and Raquel. Your father respected that and wouldn't come between her and her family."

"So, he traded two sons for a mistress." Resentment colored Josh's voice.

Cara shook her head. "Not a day passed that your dad wasn't in anguish about the loss of his sons. As his time drew to an end, it was all he talked about. He desperately wanted you, Cole and Gabe to reconcile. It's the reason he gave the three of you the ranch."

"Gabe wants to buy out Cole's and my shares. I may let him."

"Your dad anticipated that. Which is why he included a clause in his will that all three of you must be in agreement."

"In case we didn't reconcile."

Perhaps she'd been wrong. It wasn't resentment she had heard in his voice earlier, but hurt. "If it makes any difference, he was very good to Raquel and Gabe. Me, too."

Josh opened his mouth to speak, only to snap it shut and stare ahead. They were nearing the corral, and he'd spotted her surprise.

He turned to her, his earnest expression heart-tuggingly handsome. "You're not messing with me, are you?"

"I'm not. I decided to let you sponsor him. Hurry Up, too."

"Thank you."

Was it her imagination, or did he sound a little emotional? "You're welcome."

Cara found herself smiling. She'd made the right decision.

The black stood majestically in the center of the corral, head held high and tail flowing, every inch the king he was. As they approached, he broke into a slow gallop, circling the enclosure, his feet flying.

"Look, Daddy." Nathan pointed. "Horsey."

"Yeah, horsey." He turned back to Cara. "Do you mind watching the kids for a bit?"

"Not at all."

Josh crawled through the railing and attempted to acquaint himself with the black. Unfortunately, the stallion wasn't ready. Josh patiently persisted and, eventually, he was able to approach and lay a hand on the horse's whithers.

"Good boy," he cooed.

The horse bobbed his head.

Cara was impressed.

To the casual observer, the four of them might have looked like a family. That thought, more than their mutual attraction, more than seeing Nathan heading for the stairs, sent a jolt of alarm racing through her.

A mere twenty-four hours after striking a deal with Josh, and she was already in way over her head.

Chapter Five

Who would've guessed it? The black—Josh had named him Wind Walker—was not only intelligent and fearless, but gentle natured and affectionate, too. All the stallion had needed was a little guidance and a lot of encouragement to turn his rebellious nature into a hardworking mount eager to please.

Josh could hardly believe it. One solid week working with the horse and already he had gotten the stallion to accept a halter, respond to voice commands and allow Josh to put a saddle blanket on his back. Incredible progress. Soon he would try a lightweight saddle. Perhaps a bridle.

He couldn't wait to ride this fellow. What a kick that would be!

If he could just get Cara to respond to him with the same kind of enthusiasm. He might if she'd drop those damned barriers of hers long enough for him to try. Except she'd have none of it, or him. She much preferred him at arm's length.

Josh and Wind Walker were in the round pen practicing. Josh stood at the center, a long lunge line attached to the side of Wind Walker's halter. The stallion trotted in circles, his gait easy and rhythmic.

After forty minutes of steady exercise, he barely showed any signs of fatigue. The same couldn't be said for Josh. He'd shed his jacket earlier, sweat dampening his shirt front and back despite the cold weather.

"Atta boy," he murmured, admiring the horse's agility and power. The next minute, he commanded, "Whoa," while tugging firmly on the lunge line and sounding a clicker twice with his free hand. The technique, combining voice, physical cues and clicking, was working well. He had his brother Cole to thank for teaching him.

Wind Walker promptly slowed, then stopped. Josh walked over and patted the horse on the neck.

"Good job. Easy does it."

The horse rewarded him with an inquisitive sniff to his cowboy hat.

Thinking he should call it a day, Josh led Wind Walker around the pen, cooling them both down. It was barely noon, and he had a dozen chores waiting for him. He probably should have skipped the lunch-time training session, but the prospect of working with Wind Walker had been too tempting.

With Gabe spending more and more time lately at their neighboring ranch, the Small Change, Cole and Josh were picking up the slack. They were all happy to help. It was Reese's father who'd saved their hides when the newly purchased steer became sick with red nose. The highly contagious virus had created a shortage of available antibiotics. Theo McGraw had offered his supply. Without it, they'd have lost countless steer and potentially been bankrupted.

Busy as he was, Josh was more than happy to cover for Gabe whenever he was at their neighbors' place, though frankly, he should probably have spent more time on his parenting skills.

One week into single fatherhood, he was no more adept at it than when he'd started. Not that Cara failed as a teacher. Exactly the opposite. She excelled. Patient, resourceful and a wealth of information. Josh, for his part, fumbled and bumbled and stumbled through the simplest tasks, overwhelmed by all there was to learn.

He should have paid better attention during his marriage to Trista. Should have stayed home more. Maybe then she wouldn't have become an addict. Or he could have interceded while there was still time.

Then again, two small children needing her hadn't made a difference or stopped her from using long after the pain from her accident diminished.

Okay, he didn't understand addiction and wasn't very tolerant of it. Perhaps because Trista hadn't displayed the slightest desire to battle hers, not until Josh went after full custody. The only reason she'd consented to rehab was the chance to see the children if she stayed sober. The same children she'd sorely neglected while high.

Josh briefly considered going by the house when he was done with Wind Walker. Raquel had been a godsend this past week, and the kids really liked her but he felt guilty for imposing. Unfortunately, Mustang Valley wasn't a large community and had limited day care options.

He'd already scoured the bulletin boards at the community center, library and market, as well as visited the three churches and the grade school. All to no avail. A local woman had space for one child, but not two. The play camp at the community center didn't accept children under three years of age.

The peculiarity of his late father's longtime companion babysitting his kids wasn't lost on Josh. If his mother ever found out, she'd throw a fit. She'd been pestering him to bring the kids home for a visit. He doubted she'd come to Mustang Valley, but stranger things had happened. The fact that he was living at Dos Estrellas was proof of that.

He was nearly done with Wind Walker when he spotted three people approaching: Cara, another woman and a boy Josh guessed to be seven or eight. He thought he remembered seeing the woman before.

As they drew nearer, her face brightened. Not Cara's. But then, she always seemed to be battling for control around him. Josh liked to think the sparks that flared between them whenever they were together were the reason.

"What a handsome fellow," the woman gushed the moment they were within range. She smiled at Josh. "You've worked wonders with him."

Her praise implied she'd seen Wind Walker before. At the sanctuary, perhaps? "He's coming along."

Cara made the introductions. "Josh, this is my friend Summer Goodwyn and her son, Teddy."

Josh stopped in front of them and reached a hand through the railing to shake Summer's. As he did, a memory surfaced. "We met at my father's funeral."

"I'm very sorry for your loss." She was an attractive woman about the same age as Cara with an engaging smile that somehow didn't affect him. Not like Cara's did.

"Thank you." It seemed strange to Josh, accepting

condolences for a man he'd hardly known and hadn't liked most of his life.

It must seem strange to Cara, too, for she sent him an arch look.

"I hope you don't mind the intrusion," Summer said. "My son loves animals, especially horses. He wanted to come over."

Teddy stared avidly at Wind Walker while making low, guttural noises.

Josh thought the behavior a little strange, but didn't comment. "Would he like to pet Wind Walker?"

"Is that his name? I love it." Summer's smile widened. "And we would both like to pet him, if that's okay."

"Come on in." He started for the gate, gathering the lunge line and winding it into a coil as he walked.

"I'm not sure that's a good idea." Cara trailed after her friend.

Josh reached the gate first. "He's pretty gentle."

"You've had him barely a week," she insisted. "He's not even broke to ride yet."

Josh waited for Summer to object. She didn't, and he released the latch. He'd come to accept Cara's caution where kids were concerned. Nathan opening the apartment door and almost escaping outside hadn't been the only incident. The other day she'd panicked because Josh had turned his back on Kimberly for a mere minute and then lashed out at him for letting Nathan jump on the couch as if it was a trampoline.

Okay, that last stunt had been a little daring, but Nathan wasn't hurt. Boys would be boys, right? His son certainly took after Josh and Cole when it came to roughhousing.

He swung the gate open.

"Come on, Teddy." Summer entered the pen first. She didn't take her son's hand, though she did glance back to make sure he followed.

Josh found that interesting, as well.

When they were all four inside the pen, Summer reached out a hand to Wind Walker. The stallion didn't make a liar of Josh and reveled in the attention, standing calmly while she stroked his nose.

"You try, Teddy."

The boy mimicked his mother, touching oddly curled fingers to Wind Walker. "Hahs, hahs, hahs." The garbled words were accompanied by a crooked smile and guttural sound that might have been a laugh.

"That's right. Horse." Summer radiated joy.

Josh found himself caught up in the unusual interaction. When he glanced at Cara, she, too, was watching, a mixture of happiness and sorrow on her face.

"Teddy always responds better to animals than people," Summer said.

Josh reluctantly tore his attention away from Cara. "Like a lot of folks I know."

"He's autistic," Summer explained without a trace of apology.

Josh was the first to admit he didn't know a lot about special-needs individuals. "Tough break."

Hearing his casual tone, he worried Summer might take offense. Fortunately, she didn't.

"Yes, it is."

"We all have our challenges."

"We do." She nodded agreeably, her hand hovering an inch above Teddy.

For several more minutes, the adults watched as

Teddy delighted in Wind Walker. While the boy didn't speak, he communicated clearly through gestures and facial expressions. Josh couldn't have been more pleased with the horse's performance.

"Can you believe the difference?" Summer asked Cara. "He's so much better with Wind Walker than that other little horse."

"Hurry Up?" Josh hadn't known they were acquainted with his kids' horse.

"Teddy wouldn't go near that poor fellow. I don't understand why. The horse was a perfect lamb. Teddy gets that way sometimes."

Cara cut in. "I introduced Teddy to Hurry Up before I agreed to let you sponsor him."

"Ah." Josh nodded.

He wasn't angry. If anything, it showed what a good friend Cara was to Summer and gave him more qualities about her to like and admire.

"It's nice of you to let us pet the horse." Summer leaned in close to Teddy. "Tell Mr. Dempsey thank you."

He shied away from her and inched closer to Wind Walker.

"Come on, sweetie. Mr. Dempsey has to get back to work."

Teddy hid his face in the horse's neck.

"Wind Walker's hungry. He has to eat." When Summer placed a light hand on Teddy's shoulder, he flinched and cried out as if burned.

"I'm sorry," she said to Josh.

"No worries. Take your time."

He glanced at Cara and was taken aback when she mouthed, "Thank you." She'd never looked at him with such warmth before.

An echoing warmth built inside him. He smiled in return, and she quickly averted her gaze, bringing their moment to an end much too soon.

Eventually, after much coaxing on Summer's part and a promise of returning in the near future, Teddy was persuaded to leave.

"See you soon," Josh called after the boy.

Teddy stared at Josh for several seconds before grunting and walking away. He traveled a few feet before stopping to wait for his mother.

Josh shook Summer's hand again. "I'm serious. Please come back."

"Teddy will behave like an angel the rest of the day thanks to you."

"My pleasure."

"You're very nice. I can see why a certain someone likes you." She added the last part in a whisper behind the shield of her hand.

A certain someone? Was she referring to Cara?

"Truthfully, I have my doubts."

"You shouldn't." Summer winked at him. "I don't."

CARA ASSUMED SHE would leave with Summer and Teddy, but when she fell into step beside her friend, Summer stopped her with a gesture in Josh's direction.

"We'll be fine. You stay. I insist," she added when Cara opened her mouth to protest. "If only to gaze at that big, handsome fellow one more time."

"Wind Walker is pretty special."

"I wasn't talking about the horse, and you know it."

Cara did. "He's making my life difficult."

"And exciting. I've never seen you off your game like this. It's a nice change."

"What I am is pulling my hair out by the roots."

Summer bumped shoulders with Cara. "Which you wouldn't do unless you cared."

Did she? Care about Josh? No! The thought was preposterous.

All at once, Teddy ran ahead of them, his legs churning awkwardly.

"Not so fast, sweetie." Summer chased him clear to the car.

Cara should have gone, too. To say goodbye if nothing else. She didn't, however. Josh had intercepted her, leading Wind Walker.

"I like your friend," he said.

Cara briefly met his gaze. Sometimes—like now, for instance—it was too intense and she too vulnerable. "Summer's a good person. She's had a rough go of it."

"I can imagine. Well, actually, I can't." Josh absently scratched the horse between the ears.

Cara was impressed with how far he'd come with Wind Walker in such a short period of time. She didn't tell him, though. He might let it go to his head. "I need to run. See you later."

"Wait. Come with me while I take him back to his stall."

She stopped short. "Why?"

"I thought we could discuss the farrier I have coming out to look at the mustangs."

"A farrier?" she repeated. "We can't possibly shoe two hundred horses."

"Even I'm not that stupid, Cara."

She blushed, acutely embarrassed and feeling every bit as off her game as Summer had pointed out. "I didn't intend—"

"I noticed some of the mustangs' hooves need attention. Overgrown or cracked and chipped."

Because she refused to let him think he affected her, she continued walking with him.

"A farrier is expensive," she pointed out. "The sanctuary doesn't have that kind of money."

"He's a friend of mine. He owes me."

"That has to be some kind of favor you did him," Cara said.

"His son and I used to compete together. Once, in Salt Lake City, I pulled him out from under a bull."

"Was he hurt badly?"

"Bad enough he retired. But he lived."

"You took a chance. Jumping in with a bucking bull."

"Which is why his dad owes me."

Cara studied him from the corner of her eye. "Are you always that risky with your life?"

"I am when what's at stake is worth it."

If there was a double meaning to what he said, she refused to acknowledge it.

They reached the stable and entered the aisle. In the shade, the temperature abruptly dropped. On the plus side, they were out of the wind.

She hugged herself and caught Josh watching her.

"Cold?" he asked.

"A little."

What would it be like to have him drape an arm around her waist and pull her close, sharing his body heat? She tried to banish the image. Her mind stubbornly refused.

Wind Walker's head shot up at the sight and sound of the other horses, and he began to prance, eagerly dragging them toward his stall. Always the show-off.

Kind of like his owner.

Owner? How quickly she'd come to accept that the horse belonged to Josh. Much as she hated admitting it, the two were well suited. She should forget the sponsorship and let him have the stallion. Hurry Up, too.

"I might have told my friend you'd be willing to part with a horse or two. Besides being a farrier, he also has a horse rental business on the side and can always use a couple of reliable mounts."

Cara stopped in the center of the aisle, hands firmly planted on her hips. "You expect me to trade horses for farrier services?"

Josh leaned close, well over the line dividing their personal spaces. She licked her suddenly dry lips, unable to help herself. His gaze went straight to her mouth, where it stayed. Her heart rate quickened.

"Actually," he murmured silkily, "I do."

"I have to…have to—" She readied to flee.

He took hold of her arm, firmly yet coaxingly. His grip was that of a man who would protect her and keep her safe. A man comfortable with intimate contact.

Heaven help her, she was in much deeper trouble than she'd thought.

"It makes good business sense," he said, his tone coaxing. He might have been talking to Wind Walker.

"I haven't checked him out. There's an adoption process." She eased away from him.

"He's a good guy, Cara. Treats his horses well."

"He rents them to anyone off the street. How can I be sure my horses won't be mistreated?"

"I'll take you to see his setup. It's just outside Cave Creek. You can inspect his operation and the condition of his rental horses for yourself."

She supposed there was no harm in looking.

Josh smiled. "You don't want any of the mustangs to come up lame because their hooves went unattended after you had the chance to use a perfectly competent farrier."

"We'll see." She wasn't ready to concede.

"He'll give them a good home, Cara, and isn't that what you want? The more mustangs you place, the more room you'll have to take in others that might be suffering or worse."

Like headed to the slaughterhouse. "What's this farrier's name?"

"You going to research him on the internet?"

"Yes." If he thought she was joking, he had another think coming.

"Rusty Collins. His business is Big Sky Horse Rentals."

Simple enough. She could remember that.

"What about Saturday afternoon?" Josh asked. "If you're free. We could stop for lunch at Harold's Cave Creek Corral on the way back."

She pursed her lips. "I thought we were just checking out your friend's place."

"It's a long drive."

"Not that long. An hour max."

"Each way. We might get hungry."

Wind Walker—funny how easily Cara thought of the black by his new name—was getting restless again. She and Josh started forward as naturally as if they were a couple—which they definitely weren't.

"I'm not going on a date with you," she stated.

"No date. We're stopping for food."

Two people lunching together at a nice restaurant struck Cara as a date. Or... Wait a minute!

"Are you bribing me?"

He laughed. Wind Walker must have liked the sound, for he swung his big head to the side and nudged Josh's hat, almost knocking it off.

Cara liked the sound, too.

People didn't laugh around her much, not since Javier died. Perhaps they thought it was disrespectful or inappropriate. Perhaps she didn't inspire laughter in others. Except, apparently, in Josh.

They arrived at Wind Walker's stall. The horse obediently entered when Josh opened the door and headed straight to his feed bin. Discovering it was empty, he faced the corner in disgust.

"Here, boy." Josh produced a pair of carrots from his duster pocket, and Wind Walker chomped them down. "If I was going to bribe you," he said to Cara, latching the stall door, "it wouldn't be with an invitation to lunch."

Against her better judgment, she asked, "What would it be with?"

He propped an elbow on the closed stall door and contemplated her for a long moment with his compelling blue eyes. Suddenly self-conscious, Cara wanted to look away. Wanted to, but didn't.

"Something more personal." He removed his cowboy hat and hung it on the stall latch. During the process, he'd somehow managed to move closer.

"Personal." She squared her shoulders, as if that would give her strength in the face of his overwhelming allure.

"I think you find me intriguing. Even, dare I say it, attractive."

"My, my," she scoffed. "You have an incredible ego."

"That may be true, but it doesn't change the facts."

"I assure you, I don't find you the least bit intriguing or attractive. Annoying, yes. Frustrating, absolutely."

"Well, in that case." He lowered his head until their mouths were within kissing range. "You won't mind if I test that theory."

Every one of her senses went on high alert. Breathing became difficult. Speaking impossible.

Run! her brain hollered. Her feet didn't listen and remained rooted in place.

"Don't—" She couldn't finish.

"I won't."

His assurance gave her no comfort. Yet she continued to stand there, staring at him as if cast under a spell. "Josh."

"I like how you say my name."

Hadn't she just been thinking how much she liked his laugh?

"We can't do this." She shook her head numbly.

"What are we doing?"

"You're…you're…going to…"

"Tell me." He smiled, fully aware of the torture he was putting her through.

Dammit, she had to resist him. Needed to prove her previous claims about not being attracted to him.

Mustering her slim reserve of courage, she admitted, "You're going to kiss me."

"Am I?"

"You're not?"

Sparks lit his eyes. That she could handle. It was

the decidedly male hunger beneath the sparks that terrified her.

"Not unless that's what you want, too."

Josh's breath caressed her cheek. The sensation unnerved her, enough that she almost missed the last part of what he'd said.

"Too?"

A low, sexy rumble emanated from deep in his chest. "Yes, I want to kiss you. Haven't you figured that out yet?"

"I'm, um, kind of rusty at this stuff."

"Like riding a bike, Cara. A few seconds, and it'll all come back to you."

Would it? She and Manuel had met their first year at community college. They'd dated four years before marrying and were together almost that long before having Javier.

Cara hardly believed it. She was almost thirty-one and hadn't kissed a man other than Manuel since college. She hadn't kissed Manuel, even platonically, for almost three years. No wonder she was scared.

All at once, she wanted to kiss Josh with a need bordering on desperate. Experience the touch of his lips on hers, soft and yielding at first, then firm and demanding. Discover how he tasted. What he felt like, his muscles tensing beneath her needy fingers as she pressed them into his flesh.

Oh, how she missed being with a man. More than the sex, she missed the incredible connection two people shared. Humans weren't designed to be alone. They thrived on companionship. Love. A voice on the other end of the phone line that instantly lifted one's spirits.

A hand to hold. A cheek to cradle. A warm body to cuddle with at night.

Josh wasn't the one to give her those things. But a kiss from him could remind her, if only for a fleeting moment, of what she'd lost and, maybe, could one day have again.

Standing on tiptoes, she caressed the line of his straight, strong jaw. The bristles of his day-old beard tickled her palm in a good way. His lower lip was warm and responsive as the pad of her thumb skimmed its surface.

"No rush, Cara. Take all the time you need." His voice wrapped around her like a warm cloak.

She took him at his word and continued her exploration. His hair, in need of a trim, beckoned her fingertips to sift through the fine strands. The skin on the back of his neck was tanned and taut and when she touched him there, he closed his eyes and groaned with a mixture of agony and pleasure.

Heaven help her, it was thrilling. It was also not enough. When the world didn't end, she let go and gave in. Slowly, carefully, delicately she placed her lips on his.

The kiss was everything she imagined. Achingly tender, deliciously sweet and then, gloriously intense as Josh wrapped her in a possessive embrace.

"Cara," he uttered and slipped his tongue between her lips, his hand pressing into the small of her back.

Shock waves immobilized her as alarm bells rang in her head.

Too much, too soon! She wasn't ready. Not for this and not for Josh.

Cara broke off the kiss, extracting herself from Josh's

arms. Her feet suddenly working again, they carried her down the aisle and away from him. To her relief, Josh didn't follow.

Inside the house, her luck held. No one was home. Raquel must have taken the children to the park in town.

Good. No one to witness her meltdown or hear her sobs. Just seven empty rooms and one empty heart.

Chapter Six

"Been right fine to meet you, ma'am." Rusty Collins tugged on the brim of his tattered straw cowboy hat. His baggy denim overalls could have been a hand-me-down from his grandfather.

"Same here. And please, call me Cara."

"We'll be talking soon, I hope."

"Yes, I think we will."

She liked the owner of Big Sky Horse Rentals despite her determination not to. An hour in his company, a thorough tour of his horse rental and farrier operation and a meeting with his friendly and loyal employees had changed her mind.

Darn it, Josh was right. Any of her mustangs would have a good home here and be well cared for by the big and burly man with a heart of gold. She already had a few horses in mind that would make reliable, docile saddle mounts under Rusty's competent tutelage.

The trade of two horses for farrier services was also more than a fair deal. He probably deserved three, once he got through inspecting her entire herd.

"How 'bout this Wednesday? Will that work for you?" Rusty asked, stroking his bushy red-gray beard.

No doubt the inspiration for his name. "We like to start early. At the crack of dawn."

"I'm an early riser, too." Cara genuinely smiled for the first time since kissing Josh on Thursday.

Kissing Josh! She still had trouble accepting that disastrous lack of judgment.

Her smile dimmed, and she looked away, pretending an interest in the group of riders just returning from the nearby desert trails. Rusty's guide was in the lead.

"We can come another day," he said. "If that's more convenient."

He'd misunderstood her sudden mood change. "No, no," she insisted. "Wednesday's fine."

The reason for Cara's distraction ambled toward them. He was also smiling. From what she'd observed, he hadn't stopped since their kiss. It was pretty infuriating.

"You all have fun?" Rusty greeted Josh with an amiable clap on the back.

Josh carried Kimberly in one arm. With the other, he held Nathan's hand. "The kids would've stayed longer if I let them."

He'd taken them to visit a litter of month-old puppies one of the barn dogs had given birth to in an empty horse stall. Cara suspected he'd used the excuse to allow her and Rusty some private time to reach an agreement. She should have been appreciative. Instead, she was annoyed. More at herself than Josh. She had been the one to kiss him, not the other way around.

"Like them pups, did you?" Rusty cuffed Nathan playfully on the chin.

The boy promptly burst into tears.

"Hey, there. What's the matter?"

Was he hurt? Sick? Cara started for Nathan, only to restrain herself. He wasn't her son, and this wasn't her problem to handle even if Josh did rely on her advice.

"I want a puppy," Nathan blurted between sobs. "Daddy says no."

"Hey, pal." Josh patted the boy's ball-capped head. "I told you we'd come back in a few weeks. The puppies are too young to leave their mama."

Nathan refused to be mollified, and his sobs escalated to wails.

"I think our visit here's cutting into his nap time," Josh offered as apology.

"Tell you what." Rusty knelt in front of Nathan, who stopped crying and stared at the older man, visibly torn between fear and wonder. "You come back here in three weeks, and you can have whichever one of them pups you want. I'll give you first dibs."

Nathan probably didn't understand everything Rusty had said, but he'd gleaned enough to realize a puppy was in his future, just not his immediate future.

"Want a puppy now."

"Would if I could." Rusty stood. "But them pups aren't ready yet."

Nathan started sniffling. Cara sensed they were in for another big cry.

Josh headed his son off with admirable skill. "Why don't we take Cara to see the puppies, and you can show her which one you want."

Nathan's tears instantly dried, and he turned his beautiful blue eyes on Cara. "Come on!"

She hesitated, then followed the boy, unable to refuse. Or was it that she didn't want to appear surly in front of Rusty?

"Take your time." The older man hailed the trail guide. "I need to get these folks checked out."

The puppies were an adorable cluster of black-and-white fluff balls that yipped excitedly and nipped at their ankles. Cara picked up a fat bundle that was chewing on the hem of her jeans. The puppy lavished her face with kisses before going after her hair and chewing it.

"Hey, wait a minute!" Cara averted her face, only to have the puppy attack her ear. "Ouch!" She gave a short, quick laugh.

Of course, Josh noticed. And smiled.

Cara put the puppy down. Then, mad at herself—she wasn't about to let Josh Dempsey dictate her actions—knelt to give the mother dog a petting.

She honestly had no idea how Nathan could settle on just one. All of the puppies were sweet, cute and friendly. She and Manuel had owned a dog, a lovely spaniel mix that Javier had called Paw Paw. Cara had given Paw Paw to Summer and Teddy when she'd moved out of the apartment, unable to stop thinking of Javier each time she looked at the dog.

"This one, Daddy." Nathan held up a squirming bundle.

"Okay." Josh inspected the puppy closely. He'd been holding Kimberly by both her small hands, helping her "walk" through the mass of puppies. She giggled and wiggled as first one pup, then another crawled over her feet or jumped up onto her chest. "Good choice. My dad always said white on a dog's ears was a sign of intelligence."

Cara wasn't sure what startled her most, the silly statement about a dog's ears or Josh's casual mention of his late father. Perhaps—no, obviously—not every memory was a bad one.

With the puppy chosen and Nathan satisfied, the four of them met up with Rusty to say their goodbyes. They confirmed Wednesday morning and shook hands all around before leaving. While Josh buckled Nathan into his car seat, Cara attended Kimberly. Two weeks of her agreement with Josh hadn't made her any more at ease with Nathan.

Not his fault. The boy was adorable and usually good-natured. But every sticky finger pressed into hers, every sweet-scented skin fresh from a bath, or sleepy head resting gently on her arm was like slicing open an old wound.

Cara climbed into the front seat, and they drove the long stretch of road to Mustang Valley. The kids were sound asleep within minutes.

She didn't blame them. If not for Josh, she'd lean her head back and close her eyes. She hadn't been this relaxed in the company of others for a long, long time. Funny she felt this way with Josh. He usually had her walking on pins and needles. Only since their kiss…

The thought stopped there and caused her to bolt upright. Forget being relaxed.

"You hungry?" he asked, sending her a look.

She considered lying despite being starving. Stopping for food would prolong the trip. And besides, she'd told him the other day they weren't going on anything remotely resembling a date.

"The children are asleep," she said. That much was true and not a convenient excuse. "You don't want to wake them. They'll be cranky."

"We'll go someplace with a drive-through window."

Fast food. Her favorite guilty pleasure. "I can wait till we get home." Her traitorous stomach grumbled loudly.

"There's El Grande Pollo," he said a minute later. "They have great chicken tacos." Without waiting for her response, he swung the truck into the parking lot and maneuvered in line behind an SUV.

Cara's resolution faded the moment she read the menu. Everything looked scrumptious. And she was thirsty, too.

"What do you want?" Josh flashed her a dazzling grin.

Her heart instantly raced, and she silently chided herself. This nonsense had to stop.

"A chicken taco."

He raised his brows. "Just one?"

"And a diet cola."

"Okay." At the window, Josh placed their order. "Six chicken tacos, an extra-large root beer and a large diet cola."

"Small cola," she corrected him.

He didn't change the order. When she tried to pay for her share of the food, he dismissed her. They were hardly back on the road, and he dived into the bag, handing the first taco to her.

"Eat up."

She did. Two tacos. They went down fast. Faster than Josh ate two. She was planning on stopping there but Josh offered her a third taco. She consumed it in four bites. Losing all willpower and giving in to him at every turn apparently worked up an appetite.

This was absolutely, positively the last time she was going anywhere with Josh. Humiliating herself again wasn't an option.

"Tasty, aren't they?"

"Yes," she mumbled, not liking the satisfaction in his voice, and stared out the window for the next two miles.

"You ready to talk yet?"

She narrowed her gaze at him. "About what?"

"Really?" His dazzling grin turned wry. "You have to ask?"

"Okay." She sighed. "Thank you for suggesting Rusty swap farrier services for three mustangs. He seems like a nice guy, very competent, and I like his setup."

"Three mustangs? I thought we agreed on two?"

We? Hmph. He was actually talking as if they shared ownership of the mustangs.

"Checking two hundred head of horses will take days. Even with a full crew," she said. "He deserves at least three."

"I agree. Actually, I was suggesting we talk about our kiss. Which was amazing, by the way."

"I plead the Fifth."

"And here I thought you'd rail at me until my ears peeled off."

"I don't rail."

His raised brows implied different. "Talk to me, Cara."

He'd been good, keeping his end of their bargain. She was slow to trust people, but he'd done his best to earn hers. And he was right. They should talk about the kiss, set things straight.

Glancing over her shoulder at the rear seat, she assured herself the children were sleeping. "I'm glad you liked it, because it won't happen again."

"Did you?"

"Like the kiss? Absolutely not."

He chuckled. "Don't lie."

"It scared me." Her blatant honesty must have surprised him, for he sobered.

"Why?"

She didn't answer.

"Because *you* liked it?"

At his arrogance, she found her voice. "For the record, I was simply curious. I haven't kissed a man for quite a while."

"That's a shame. You're very good at it."

"Please, Josh. No teasing. This is hard enough for me." More blatant honesty. Strange for her. Cara didn't normally open up. Not with people who weren't close friends, like Summer and Raquel.

"Okay. Truce." They drove for another mile before Josh said, "If we're making disclosures, I have one of my own."

"I'm not sure I want to hear it."

"I'd say I didn't plan on us kissing, except that's not true. I've thought a lot about what it would be like. *A lot.* I saw an opportunity, and I took it. You should also know, I'll kiss you again if the opportunity presents itself."

She groaned. "We can't, Josh."

"Maybe we shouldn't, but we certainly can."

"I'm not ready for a relationship." If he couldn't see that, he was blind.

"And I'm not rushing you. We can go as slow as you'd like."

"What I want is to end things now."

"I admit, I can come on a little strong." Josh glanced at her and then back to the road. "I'll try to dial it down a notch."

"Forgive the tired old line, but it's me, not you."

"Because of your son." He said it softly.

She hesitated. "Because of your children."

He checked the backseat. "They don't misbehave that much, do they?"

She shook her head and waited until talking became less difficult. "They're perfect. And that's the problem. Being in a relationship with you means having your children in my life to some degree greater than they are now. I can't handle that. No way."

"Let me pull off the road so we can talk."

The sympathy in his face nearly undid her. "That's not necessary. And please, for both our sakes, let's not ever kiss again."

SPRINKLES. NOTHING BUT a few scattered drops falling from what had been a promisingly ominous gray sky. Mother Nature was playing a nasty trick, giving them hope one minute and taking it back the next.

All three brothers, Josh, Cole and Gabe, were assisting the vet, health checking the cows in section three. Next week, they'd begin the artificial insemination process. If all went well, most of the cows would become pregnant.

Before today, Josh had no idea what percentage of pregnant cows was considered good. He was learning, and fast. To his complete surprise, he liked the ranching business. He'd always assumed he'd follow in his grandfather's footsteps and breed horses for a living after he retired from rodeoing.

Now he supposed Cole would be the one to return to California and take over. God knew, his brother didn't want to stay in Mustang Valley. Plus, he was better with horses. Though, gauging by Wind Walker's progress, Josh could hold his own.

Maybe he'd train some of Cara's mustangs. Make them more adoptable. The idea appealed to him for many reasons. Top of the list—working more closely with Cara and seeing her smile with delight.

She'd been on his mind a lot lately, especially during those restless nighttime hours when the kids kept him awake. He'd often recall the feel of her soft lips as she'd surrendered to his kiss, which increased his restlessness all the more.

"You okay?" Cole asked. "You seem distracted."

"Tired is all. Kimberly cried half the night."

"Is she sick?"

How did Cole know enough to ask that? Josh hadn't. He'd ended up phoning Cara and waking her. She hadn't sounded angry at the disturbance. She'd simply spoken to him in that annoyingly neutral tone of hers. Three days since their trip to Rusty's and their conversation about the kiss, and the only emotions he'd seen her display were around his kids.

After instructing him to take Kimberly's temperature—which was normal—and check her for other signs of illness or discomfort, they'd decided she either had an upset tummy or was simply being a baby. An hour of pacing the small apartment had finally soothed his daughter back to sleep.

Fortunately, Nathan had slumbered through it all. Josh, however, had lain awake on his lumpy sofa bed for the next forty minutes until he had unwound enough to drift off.

"She's fine," he told Cole. "Happy as a lark this morning."

"Can't say the same for you."

He had been short-tempered, flying off the handle at every little thing.

"Any luck finding permanent day care?" Cole asked.

"No. And that won't solve the problem of my lack of sleep." Josh tucked the clipboard he held under his arm and scrubbed his face, unable to stop the energy from draining out of him.

They walked among the herd of cows, verifying the ear tag numbers against Violet's log. She'd have performed the task herself, but she'd left the day before and wouldn't return until Monday. Her parents were in the midst of a personal crisis. Since Violet rarely requested time off, no one had complained.

Cole moved slowly ahead, reading off the number of the next cow. It eyed them cautiously, but didn't abandon the small, dry patch of grass on which it munched.

"Why don't you just hire Raquel permanently?" Cole suggested. "She keeps pestering you to let her."

Josh studied his brother. "Can you honestly say you wouldn't mind if I did?"

"Can you honestly say I'm the reason you haven't made the arrangement permanent?"

"She was Dad's mistress. You have to admit, her watching the kids is…"

"Different?"

He'd been thinking *weird*.

"After a thirty-plus year relationship," Cole said, "and having a son together, she was a lot more to him than a mistress. In some states, she'd be considered his wife."

"You have a point."

Cole recited the number of the next cow, then said,

"Truthfully, I'm surprised Raquel didn't contest the will. The life insurance payout she got wasn't exactly a windfall."

"A lawsuit's expensive and can drag on for months." Josh had learned that firsthand during his custody battle.

"Do you believe that story about Dad and Raquel never marrying because of her father?"

"Yeah, I do." Josh had repeated his conversation with Cara a few weeks back.

"I'm surprised Dad went along with it. He was the kind of man who didn't let people push him around."

Memories Josh had avoided recalling for years suddenly surfaced. Hearing his parents argue. His mother packing up their belongings. His father saying nothing when Josh had asked why they couldn't stay.

In the past, the memories had been accompanied by a rush of anger or pain. Today, that didn't happen. At what point had he changed? More interesting, perhaps, what had caused it?

He flipped to the next page on the log. "For all we know, Raquel might have refused to marry Dad. She's a strong woman in her own right, and she loves her family. She talks about them constantly."

"I kind of hate to say this, but I like her."

"I like her, too."

Josh understood Cole's reluctance to admit his fondness for Raquel. Until recently, they'd blamed her for their parents' divorce. She'd been the home wrecker, a belief their mother had stubbornly clung to and had passed on to her sons.

"I get that Mom carried her anger to extremes," Cole said. "But Dad did cheat on her."

"They were separated when Dad and Raquel met and would have divorced if Mom hadn't guilted him into reconciling. Insisting he had a responsibility to his family."

Those critical pieces of information were something Josh and Cole hadn't learned until coming to Dos Estrellas. For Josh, the discovery had significance. Their mother withheld information in order to foster the estrangement between father and sons.

The knowledge had slowly altered his feelings, at times leaving him more confused than ever. At other times, he saw the situation with a brand-new clarity. Growing closer to Gabe had also affected him, as did his growing feelings for Cara.

"Separated isn't divorced." Cole's terse voice reflected the grudge he still harbored. "Happy or not, he was a married man."

"I won't argue that. But it should have been our choice to have a relationship with Dad. Not Mom's."

Cole didn't respond. Instead, he targeted another of their father's faults. "Did it ever occur to you that he was sleeping with two women at the same time?"

Josh wasn't sure about that. There was a year's difference between each of the brothers, with Gabe in the middle. He didn't dispute Cole, though, convinced that would be a waste of energy.

Another memory, long forgotten, crystallized. "I called Dad once."

"You're kidding." Cole faced him, his expression wary, but curious. "Mom refused to let us have any contact with him."

"I was eighteen. Getting ready to graduate from high school. Wanting to rodeo professionally while Mom insisted I go to college. We fought, and I stormed out of the house. I called him from a friend's phone."

"Why?"

"Rebellion. Trying to get back at Mom. Who knows? I was young and tired of her telling me what to do. Tired of her constant nagging."

A long paused followed. "What happened?" Cole asked. "How did it go?"

Josh hesitated. This wasn't the best time and was hardly the best place for a discussion bound to stir up bad feelings. Any minute, they could be interrupted. Gabe and the vet weren't far away, just on the next hill.

Then again, Cole was rarely in the mood to talk about their father. Josh decided to take advantage of the moment.

"I asked him if I could come here. For a visit. What I really wanted was to use Dos Estrellas as a cooling off place while I saved enough money to hit the circuit full-time."

"You must have been pretty mad at Mom."

"She could be relentless."

Cole bent and picked up a small rock, twirling it between his fingers. "What did Dad say?"

"Told me to stay away. We argued, and I hung up after calling him a few choice names."

"Didn't that make you mad?"

"Oh, yeah. So mad, I shut out half of what he said to me."

"What kind of father turns his son away?" Cole flung the rock aside. "For nothing."

"Not nothing. I didn't realize until now that if he'd let me come, Raquel's father would've cut her off from her family. Dad said something. Something I chose to ignore. About making sacrifices to save the family he had because he'd already lost you and me."

"And you think that's okay?" Cole demanded. "For him to choose Raquel and Gabe over you? Over us?"

"We chose Mom over him."

"He cheated on her."

"She's hardly the easiest person to get along with. Did you ever think she might have driven him away?"

"That doesn't make what he did right."

"Doesn't make what Mom did right, either. She had it out for Dad. Still does. Maybe she's justified, maybe not. Nothing's ever black-and-white. But poisoning us against Dad was wrong."

"Poisoning?" Cole scoffed.

"All right. Prejudicing us."

"Dad was no saint. I can't believe you're defending him."

"He wasn't so terrible, either. We left here when I was seven and you were five and never saw him again or, in your case, even talked to him. We have no idea what kind of man he was. People change."

"I don't care."

Josh struggled to be patient with his brother. "A lot of folks in Mustang Valley loved and respected him. I can't go into a single establishment without being stopped and having my ear talked off by someone who thought he was a great guy, and half of them are our competitors. Look how much Raquel loved him. And Cara. She considered him a second father. Violet worshipped the ground he walked on. Can all those people be wrong?"

Anger flashed in Cole's eyes. "If he was such a great guy, why didn't he try to contact us?"

"How do we know he didn't? Mom twisted the truth.

On more than one occasion. And Dad's not here to tell his side of the story."

"She had her reasons."

Josh blew out a breath. If he'd thought he was going to alter Cole's opinion of their father in one afternoon, he was wrong.

"Josh, Cole!" Gabe hailed them, his boots digging into the ground as he climbed the hill.

By silent agreement, Josh and Cole dropped the subject of their father. Prior to Christmas, they'd fought bitterly with Gabe. He was the one raised by their dad, the one he'd seemingly loved the best. Josh and Cole had resented him.

Since then, however, the three brothers had reached an agreement to work together for the good of the ranch. They were also, slowly, becoming friends. Cole might feel differently, but Josh didn't want to risk all they'd gained by dragging Gabe into a private disagreement.

"You two mind finishing up with Doc Benning?" Gabe asked when he reached them.

Josh and Cole exchanged glances. "Sure," Josh said. "Is there a problem?"

"Theo's having a bad day. A reaction to a new medication. Reese took him to the emergency room in Scottsdale."

Must be serious, Josh thought. The nearest hospital was a thirty-minute drive. Most people went to the clinic in town.

"You meeting her there?"

Gabe shook his head. "I'm heading to the Small Change. Their livestock foreman's tied up in Casa Grande. Theo asked me to take care of a few things that can't wait until tomorrow. Assuming he's out of the hospital by then."

"I'll get right on it," Cole said.

Gabe nodded. "Thanks."

"No problem." Cole started down the hill toward the vet.

Josh went with him, only to be stopped by Gabe.

"You got a second, Josh?"

At Cole's indifferent shrug, Josh remained behind. "What's up?"

Gabe pushed back his cowboy hat and wiped his forehead with his coat sleeve. He looked as tired as Josh felt. "Reese is worried Theo's bad spell is something serious."

From what Josh had gathered, when the symptoms of Parkinson's appeared to be under control, often new ones suddenly developed or old ones worsened.

"I'm sorry to hear that."

"It's a critical time at the Small Change. The spring sale is in March. If the livestock aren't in prime shape, Theo could lose money."

Same problem they had at Dos Estrellas, though the Dempseys wouldn't be selling nearly as many cattle as their neighbor. Still, every dime counted for both ranches.

"How can I help?"

"I'm glad you asked." Gabe expelled a long breath. "Looks like I'll be spending more and more time at the Small Change."

That made sense. Theo's daughter was likely Gabe's future wife, and Theo had been a good friend to the family.

"I need someone to cover for me here. I'd like that person to be you."

"Me?"

"You've got what it takes to manage this place, Josh. You're smart and competent and have a natural instinct for ranching. Plus, I trust you."

Trust. The one word Josh never thought he'd hear from Gabe.

It would be easy to say no, and Josh was tempted. Not because of their strained past. He simply couldn't imagine fitting one more task into his already-full schedule.

But he'd find a way. One thing he'd learned these past months was that the local ranchers looked out for one another. He liked that particular aspect about living in Mustang Valley, among others. Cara's face sprang immediately to mind.

Perhaps equally important, he'd made a commitment to Gabe and the ranch. To the whole family. Not just to stick around for a year, but to give his all.

"All right." He smiled affably. "You can count on me."

Chapter Seven

A day off at last. Sort of. Josh was spending a few free minutes in the small corral next to the round pen, taking a peek at the new foal born during the night to one of the mustang mares. Cara had told him about it earlier during morning coffee. Their first real conversation in days.

Josh supposed he should thank Raquel. She'd invited him and the kids to the house for a late Saturday morning brunch. Tired of his own pathetic cooking, he'd jumped on the offer, not knowing that Cara would be there, too.

She'd managed to avoid him pretty much all week. Even when Rusty showed up with his crew and spent two full days trimming countless hooves. Even when three of her most promising young mustangs were loaded into Rusty's trailer, headed for their new home at Big Sky Horse Rental. Even when she'd silently cried as the trailer pulled away.

Josh wasn't sure if Cara had told Raquel about their kiss. The two were close, and Raquel was astute. She'd no doubt made an educated guess.

At brunch, Josh had gobbled down the best egg-and-chorizo burrito he'd ever eaten, made better by the addition of homemade salsa. Nathan had devoured his scrambled eggs while Kimberly mostly played with hers. The brothers had chatted about the family meeting Reese scheduled for later in the week, debating what that might be about and if anything new had recently happened regarding the ranch finances.

It was during Josh's second cup of coffee that Cara had mentioned the foal. She'd moved the mare to the small corral the day before in anticipation of the birth. Though no complications were expected, she'd wanted to separate the first-time mother from the herd.

He thought his kids might get a kick out of seeing the newborn foal. Now that he'd arrived at the corral, the error in his plan became clear.

Kimberly was far too young to have much interest and fell asleep in her carrier. Nathan, excited at first, sulked and whined when he learned he wasn't riding Hurry Up—being led slowly around the pen was his new favorite pastime.

Josh had given himself several figurative pats on the back for his smart decision to sponsor Hurry Up. And Wind Walker. Now, there was a fine horse. Maybe later today he'd try putting a saddle on the stallion and taking him for a test drive.

"Daddy, Daddy, baby horsey." Nathan jumped up and down in place, suddenly excitedly.

They stood at the corral fence, looking in. The mare kept a safe distance, putting herself between them and her foal.

"Yeah, son. Baby horse."

The foal's natural curiosity was getting the better of him, and he peeked out from behind his mother. Josh considered going into the corral. In his opinion, foals benefited from human contact right from the start, making them friendlier and more receptive to training later on.

He decided to stay where he was. The foal wasn't his and, more importantly, he didn't have anyone to watch the children. A second glance at the mare and foal made Josh reconsider. The foal had ventured out from behind his mother and was tiptoeing toward them, his gait slow and awkward.

Josh paused. He'd seen this before. Once in a great while, foals were born with constricted tendons, a condition that could be serious and required immediate treatment.

After a quick check on the kids—Nathan played at his feet while Kimberly continued sleeping in the carrier—he retrieved his cell phone from his coat pocket. The display was blank. He'd forgotten to charge his cell phone again last night. No surprise. He'd fallen asleep on the couch, fully dressed and without bothering to pull out the sofa bed.

"Dammit," he muttered, then winced. Had Nathan heard him?

Well, he'd return to the house, locate Cara and let her know his concerns. She could handle the situation however she chose. Only, that wasn't what he did. The foal's odd steps were too worrisome.

He took Nathan's hand, set the carrier on the ground and made him stand beside it. "Wait here, son. I need you to watch your sister."

"Why?"

"I'm going to check on the baby horse."

"I want to go, too!"

"You can't."

Nathan made a face. He was going to start crying.

"Come on, buddy. I need you to be a big boy and help me, okay?" What he really needed was for both kids to stay out of the way and out of trouble. "We'll go for ice cream afterward." Bribing his son. That was probably wrong for at least a dozen reasons.

Nathan reluctantly agreed, and Josh entered the corral, approaching the mare and foal very, very carefully. Luckily, the mare was friendly and the foal unafraid. Reaching them, he extended a cautious hand. The foal sniffed his fingers.

He decided Cara must have worked with the foal earlier this morning already, right after it was born. Good. That would make treating the constricted tendons easier.

"Daddy, I wanna pet the horsey."

"Stay there, son." Josh spoke more sharply than he'd intended and softened his voice. "It's important. Please."

Nathan was short enough that he could peek through the lower two railings. He watched Josh's every move with avid fascination.

"Easy girl," Josh coaxed. "That's it."

Petting the mare first, he examined the foal's front legs, running his hand down the length of them. The foal flinched but didn't pull away and instead smelled Josh's cowboy hat.

He used the opportunity to massage the foal's legs. That was hardly enough to correct the condition. It did, however, give him an idea of what to tell the vet, who was scheduled to visit in the afternoon.

"What are you doing?"

At the sound of Cara's voice, Josh looked behind him but didn't straighten. "I think we have a problem. The foal was born with contracted tendons."

"He was?"

She wasted no time and, bypassing Nathan and Kimberly, hurried through the gate into the corral. Her quick movements startled the mare, and she nudged her foal to the far corner.

Josh pointed. "Look at him."

She did. Both of them watched the foal take dainty steps, almost like a dancer.

"You're right." Cara's hand flew to her mouth. "How could I have missed it?"

"What foal walks normally at first?" His assurance didn't appear to make her feel better, and she gnawed her lower lip.

"I should have paid better attention."

"I can come back when the vet gets here, if you want. Fill him in."

"You'd do that?" The look she gave him was the most sincere, most intimate one she'd given him since driving back from Rusty's last weekend. Finally, an emotional response. He'd breached her defenses.

"Why wouldn't I?"

"I, um, haven't been very…sociable lately."

"Do you think I'd refuse to help because you've been avoiding me?" He moved closer. It would be nothing for him to place a kiss on the top of her head. "I'm not heartless."

"No. You're anything but."

He let one corner of his mouth curve into a grin. "Was that a compliment?"

She shook her head, but the hint of a smile played on her lips. "Anyone ever tell you you're incorrigible?"

He took her hand. "I've missed you."

Before Cara could answer or pull away, Kimberly

started whimpering, a sign she was waking up. With the moment at an end, Josh and Cara exited the corral, leaving the mare and foal behind.

He shut the gate behind them and engaged the lock. Cara removed Kimberly from the carrier, holding her as naturally as if she were her own child. On closer inspection, Josh decided they could pass for mother and daughter, what with their matching brown eyes and dark hair. Nathan, too, who tumbled about nearby, alternately hanging on to the corral railing and crawling under it, could be taken for her son.

He promptly dismissed the notion. Trista was Kimberly and Nathan's mother. It wasn't fair to her to think of someone else in that role.

Then again, it was well within the realm of possibility that he and Trista might one day find someone else and their kids would have stepparents. Imagining Cara in that role wasn't too far-fetched.

Josh stilled. To think of Cara as his children's stepmother would also make her his wife.

No. It was too soon to get married or even think about it. He'd been divorced a mere six months, though his marriage had been over long before the papers were signed and filed. But it wasn't too soon to think about dating.

Cara appealed to him in ways no woman had for—he couldn't remember the last time. Unfortunately, she'd made it clear she didn't reciprocate his interest because of her inability to open her heart to his kids. But neither had she denied their mutual attraction. How could she when it was off the charts?

She turned to him. "Thank you again for helping with the foal."

"We make a good team." He moved closer. He couldn't help himself. "My kids like you."

"They like everyone. Raquel, Cole, Reese." Her glance cut to Nathan playing, then to Kimberly, asleep in her arms. "They're very affectionate."

"For the record, I like you, too. And I'm very affectionate." Josh couldn't resist brushing a strand of Cara's hair, enjoying the silky texture.

"We've been through this before, Josh. Kissing isn't a good idea."

"Who said anything about kissing?" He eliminated the small distance separating them with a single step. "But if you're making a suggestion——"

She rolled her eyes. At least she didn't outright refuse him.

Kimberly had the appearance of a dead weight in Cara's arms, all loose limbs and lolling head. She struggled to shift the baby to a more comfortable and less precarious position.

"Here, I'll take her." Josh smiled as their hands and arms brushed during the exchange. "Nice."

She uttered a small sound of distress. Or was it surrender?

Laying Kimberly in the carrier, he buckled the straps. Cara must have felt safe, for she visibly relaxed—until he leaned in for a kiss.

She jerked in surprise, causing him to miss her lips and land on the corner of her mouth. Lucky for him, the next instant she froze. Josh took better aim with his second attempt.

She didn't resist him, but neither did she participate. Then he circled her waist with both arms. Like that, she stopped resisting and melted into his embrace, giving in to him and over to the sensations that consumed them both.

Heaven. Somewhere between a minute ago and now, he'd gone straight there with Cara leading the way. Her incredible body fit flush with his as if created for that sole purpose. The taste of her tongue, the scent of her skin and her soft sighs of contentment mingled together and, like a potent shot of aged whiskey, went straight to Josh's head.

And like any shot of good whiskey, it made him crave more. Deepening the kiss, he explored every inch of her mouth as his hands pressed firmly into the small of her back. Her arms looped about his neck, pulling him closer.

Josh had been wrong. That wasn't heaven earlier, only the fringes. The merest promise. They had much further to go. Much more to experience. Many places in which to lose themselves.

He was suddenly curious what her neck tasted like. Or, her ear. Maybe the hollow at the base of her throat. Yeah, he'd like nothing better than to sample that delicacy. The next second, his mouth was investigating all the lovely dips and curves of her neck, including her throat.

Cara whispered his name. He felt more than heard it as her breath skimmed the fine hairs at his temples.

What he wouldn't give to have this kiss go on indefinitely.

"I want to see you," he choked out. "Tonight."

Her response was to squirm violently in an effort to escape. "Let me go!"

Was the idea of spending an evening with him so unappealing? She'd been kissing him like a woman hungry for a man.

"Josh, please." Panic filled her voice, and she smacked his arm.

What? She'd hit him? He hadn't gotten that carried away.

Releasing her, he started to apologize. "I'm sorry. I thought you were—"

"It's Nathan!" She broke free and started running.

JOSH SAW IMMEDIATELY what had alarmed Cara. His son—clever, nimble little fellow that he was—had scaled the corral gate and was prepared to swing his leg over the top. The aluminum structure wobbled beneath the stress. Josh didn't worry too much. He was confident the gate would hold.

"Come on, pal. Get down."

He didn't panic like Cara. Nathan was always getting into predicaments of one kind or another. But Josh had also seen Cara become anxious when Nathan explored or played rambunctiously.

More reason than ever for him to remain calm. Getting upset would only feed her anxiety and upset Nathan.

Before he could stop her, Cara pitched forward, catching Nathan by the arm. "Please, *niño*, get down. Now!"

Her fear must have transmitted to Nathan, scaring him, too. Or perhaps, given her sharp tone, he thought he'd done something wrong. Whatever the cause, he started to cry. Josh strode forward, intending to intervene. Kimberly chose that moment to wake up and begin crying. She kicked her legs hard enough to shake the carrier.

At that point, the situation turned from bad to worse.

Nathan either lost his grip on the gate or got confused and let go. Cara didn't have a strong enough hold on him, and he toppled to the ground, landing with a hard *thunk* on his hind end.

Josh didn't freak. The dirt in the pen was soft and Nathan wore a thick diaper. Unfortunately, on the way down, he smacked his head on a jagged piece of metal and erupted in loud, frantic wails. Kimberly's crying escalated to match her brother's.

Cara dropped to her knees beside Nathan. "Are you all right, *niño*?"

Josh could see at once that the cut on Nathan's forehead was shallow, though it did bleed. What had him truly concerned was Cara's reaction.

She'd gone motionless, her gaze riveted on Nathan. No, not motionless. Her hands trembled violently and her face had drained of color.

Giving Kimberly a quick glance—she was fine, if a little perturbed at being ignored—Josh bent down beside Cara and Nathan.

"Cara?"

She didn't answer him.

He concentrated on Nathan. Helping his son to his feet, he dusted off Nathan's backside. Dirt and debris flew into the air.

"Hey, buddy. You okay?"

"Owie, owie." Whatever Nathan said after that was distorted by his sobs.

"Let me see."

Josh examined the cut. As he'd suspected, it was

minor. A good cleaning, some antibiotic ointment and a bandage should do the trick. Digging into his jeans pocket, he pulled out a handkerchief and pressed it to Nathan's forehead.

His crying didn't lessen one iota. Neither did Kimberly's. They were both, however, fine, if not happy. Josh turned his attention to Cara.

"I'd feel better if you said something."

"I'm okay," she whispered.

"You sure?"

She stood. "It was the blood. There was a lot when Javier fell."

Josh also stood. He wished he had a third arm, one he could put around Cara. His kids needed him, but she did, too. He wanted to be there for her with a desire that, if things weren't so crazy, would have given him pause.

"He's fine. See, the bleeding's almost stopped." Josh lifted the handkerchief, showing her the cut.

"I hurt!" Nathan cried harder, as did Kimberly.

Cara held out her hand to Josh, her breathing uneven. "Your truck keys."

That struck him as odd. "You want to borrow my truck?"

"For Kimberly. To play with."

"Right." He'd forgotten. Cara had done that once before with her keys.

The distraction was effective, and Kimberly stopped her wailing. That seemed to quiet Nathan, as well.

"Can I have cookie, Daddy?"

"Now?"

"Mommy give me cookie when I hurt."

"That's right. She does." Trista had believed sweets

had the power to fix any problem. She'd thought the same thing about pain pills, too.

He glanced over at Cara. The agony reflected in her dark eyes was that of a wounded animal.

He reached for her hand. "It's just a cut."

She turned away before he could touch her. "I tried to stop Nathan from falling," she said.

"I know. It might have been worse and wasn't, thanks to you."

"What if we hadn't seen him?"

"You did. That's what counts."

"We shouldn't have been kissing."

"I disagree. I liked it a lot. And if I were to venture a guess, you did, too."

She spun to face him. "Doesn't make it right."

A strong reaction. And she was standing up for herself. Obviously, she felt better.

Josh reached for her hand again. This time, when she attempted to pull away, he was faster. Grabbing her fingers, he held hers tight. They were slim and soft and linked with his. Custom-made to fit.

"Granted, the timing's not the best," he said. "We can go slow."

"I don't want to go at all. At any speed."

Was that true? She'd yet to rip her hand away.

"I'm broken," she admitted in a choked whisper.

"We're both broken. We've been through a lot."

"I'm afraid I might never be okay. I wake up at night, convinced I'll always be miserable, half a person for the rest of my life."

"You won't."

"It's been two years. I should be better. Why am I

not better? I've seen counselors. I still attend a weekly support group."

Her anguish was difficult to watch. "There's no timetable for recovering from loss. It's different for each person." Josh picked up Nathan and balanced him in one arm.

Cara lifted Kimberly's carrier by the handle. "I don't want to be like this. I want to be the happy person I used to be. The one who woke up looking forward to each day, even when my marriage was falling apart. I was fine because I was a mother." She wiped her damp cheeks. "I'm not anymore."

Josh didn't know how to respond. Insisting "once a mother, always a mother" might come off as heartless or insincere. Especially as he had two small children demanding his immediate attention.

"I should go. Get Nathan's cut cleaned up." He took Kimberly's carrier from Cara and waited for her to open the gate.

"Bye-bye, horsey." Nathan waved at the mare and her foal over Josh's shoulder.

Outside the round pen, they stopped. Josh searched for something to say to Cara. "If you need anything…" God, that sounded trite.

"I miss him." Her voice broke. "Every day. Every moment. So much I can't stand it."

"Of course you do."

"It was a shelving unit. A stupid plastic shelving unit in the laundry room." She wrung her hands together. "Javier was always fascinated with heights. If I didn't watch him every second, he'd climb tables and chairs and bedposts. Once, he stacked crates in the garage and made a tower. I'd gone to Powell Ranch. Manuel was supposed to watch Javier. Later, when I got home, I found him on top of the crates. Manuel and I had a huge fight."

"Kids do that. They're adventurous by nature."

"I thought Javier was napping. I'd checked on him not fifteen minutes before that. He was sleeping soundly."

Josh said nothing, realizing she was talking about the day of the accident.

"He was a good boy. Most of the time. Always taking his nap and waiting for me to come get him when he woke up." She paused, swallowing before continuing. "Manuel and I, we were arguing. Again. We'd separated by then and couldn't agree on anything. Normally, I tried not to argue with Javier in the house, but Manuel insisted. He accused me of using Javier as an excuse to avoid dealing with our problems. He might have been right, to a degree."

Josh didn't stop her, even though the kids were restless, sensing her need to talk. "It's tough when a marriage is in crisis."

"We tried to reconcile. More than once. I wanted to try again. Manuel insisted on a divorce. He'd cheated on me. Twice that I know of. I'm pretty sure he was seeing someone new."

"I'm sorry."

"I…" She paused to compose herself. "I suddenly had this bad feeling. I can't explain it. I just knew something was wrong. I walked out on Manuel and went to Javier's bedroom. He yelled at me to come back, but I didn't. Javier wasn't in his bed." Tears spilled down her cheeks. "I heard it then. A loud crash. I'll never forget the sound. It haunts my dreams."

"Cara." If only Josh could hold her. If only a simple embrace would wipe away her grief.

"I ran in the direction of the crash. It came from the laundry room. When I got there…" Her trembling returned. "He was lying on the concrete floor, the shelving unit on top of him. He wasn't moving. I thought maybe he'd had the wind knocked out of him. I screamed for Manuel, and he lifted the shelves off Javier. Then I saw the blood pooling on the floor behind his head." Her voice lowered. "There was so much of it."

Josh wanted to say, "Stop. Enough. Don't put yourself through this." But he didn't. He wasn't sure she'd heed him. Some stories, once started, needed to be told in their entirety.

"Manuel called 9-1-1. The EMTs came and took us all to the hospital. I kept begging them to tell me something. *Anything.* They just repeated over and over that they didn't know. I'm sure they were lying to me. I remember the looks on their faces."

"They were trying to protect you. And they aren't doctors."

Seeming disinterested in the adults' somber conversation, Nathan played with the snaps on Josh's shirt. Cara studied the boy, but it was obvious from the sorrow in her eyes, she was somewhere else, reliving that awful day.

"He had a six-inch fracture running across the back of his skull," she said.

"My God."

"He lived four days. He never woke up. I told him repeatedly that I loved him. I don't think he heard me."

Josh started to say, "He knew you loved him," then stopped himself. He'd heard enough well-meaning but useless platitudes over the years from dealing with Trista's addiction. He refused to subject Cara to them.

Instead, he touched her arm. "You were with him at the end. You spoke the words, felt them in your heart and took comfort from them. That's the most you can hope for at a time like that."

"He wasn't gone ten minutes when the doctors approached us, asking if we would consider donating his organs. Manuel came unglued. He didn't like the idea of them cutting open our son. But I insisted. It was important to me that Javier's death not be entirely in vain. That some small amount of good came out of it."

"For what it counts," Josh said, "I agree. You made the right decision."

Nathan patted both of Josh's cheeks. "Daddy, want cookie."

His demand must have galvanized Cara, for she moved away. "I need to leave."

Like with the horse, Nathan waved. "Bye-bye, Cara."

She didn't wave back. She was too busy hurrying away from them.

Josh let her go. It was his guess she didn't tell many people about Javier's death. He was certain she hadn't allowed another man to hold her, much less kiss her, since her divorce.

He was glad he'd been the one. Whether she realized it or not, they'd taken a huge step forward in their relationship. Soon, when she was ready, they'd take another one.

Chapter Eight

Cara wasn't sure what upset her more, how much she'd enjoyed kissing Josh or how natural it had been talking to him.

For the first two months in her support group, she'd barely managed a "Hi, nice to meet you." Yet with Josh, she'd blurted the entire story of Javier's death.

There was no denying the man's effect on her. Whether he was kissing her or being kind, she came undone. If he were smart, he'd steer clear of her. But he hadn't and, she was starting to suspect, wouldn't.

Even now, he waited with Summer and Teddy in the backyard. Cara's friend had agreed to watch Nathan and Kimberly during the family meeting this afternoon. Cara suspected Josh had spotted her returning from the sanctuary and concocted a reason to linger. That would be just like him.

He wanted to see how she was doing. At least, that was what Cara told herself. He wasn't lingering for any romantic reason. He couldn't possibly still be interested in her after she'd walked away from him the other morning.

Except, as she neared—ignoring him and Summer would be rude—his eyes shone with concern. When he said hello, his tone implied a shared intimacy. As she joined them, he put a hand out and gave her arm the briefest of caresses.

No, it can't be!

Something quite unsettling occurred to Cara. Josh wasn't merely attracted to her. That she could handle. He liked her. Really, genuinely liked her. He was nice to her and made her feel attractive. His claim they were friends was sincere, and his hope they could be more than friends was written all over his face.

Whatever trouble she thought she was in before didn't compare to now. This was serious.

"Hey." Summer's grin hinted at mischief. Did she suspect?

"Glad you're here," Josh said. "Now we can go to the meeting together."

"Right," Cara mumbled. "Together." Thank goodness they'd be walking a short distance.

He turned away from her. "Thanks again for watching the kids, Summer."

Teddy wasn't interested in Nathan or Kimberly. He tolerated other children as long as they gave him his space. Sitting in the grass, he hummed to himself while watching Josh with the same fascination he'd shown Wind Walker last week. Cara couldn't remember Teddy ever having an interest in someone other than his mother and father. She'd have to ask Summer about it later.

"Anytime," Summer said warmly.

She loved children and, as Cara knew, hoped one day to marry again and have more of her own. Sadly, finding a man willing to accept Teddy and support his many needs wasn't easy.

Josh gave Nathan a hug. Kimberly had fallen asleep on the blanket Summer had spread out, an adorable little pile of baby.

Nathan broke away from his father and plowed into Cara, grabbing her leg. "Wanna hug," he demanded.

Clearly he'd forgotten about her meltdown, if he'd noticed at all. Cara hesitated. Either she looked bad in front of Josh and Summer or returned the boy's hug.

Leaning down, she pulled him close.

"Read Rabbit and Fox?" he asked, the bandage on his forehead giving him a comical, yet endearing, appearance.

He would have to tug on her every heartstring. "Maybe Summer can read to you," she said. The cherished book lay on the blanket near Kimberly.

"No, no, no." He shook his head vehemently. "Want you."

"Okay. We'll see." Hopefully, he'd forget about the book as quickly as he'd forgotten about her overreaction to his fall. "We don't want to be late," she said to Josh.

Since this was official ranch business, Cara thought it important she and Josh arrive on time.

"You and your sister be good for Summer, you hear me?" Josh said.

"I be good, Daddy." Nathan waved as Cara and Josh crossed the lawn to the house.

This time, Cara waved back, a part of her wishing she could stay behind.

"You're looking better," Josh commented.

Cara swallowed. She didn't want to talk about the other morning. "Have you heard what the meeting's about?"

"I'm guessing finances. Gabe's been spending a lot of time in the office lately, poring over the books."

"You're probably right."

"Cara."

There it was again, the sexy, honey-infused voice that weakened her knees. "Whatever you're going to say, don't."

"I'm concerned. I care about you."

"Don't care too much, Josh. You'll wind up disappointed. I told you earlier, I'm broken inside. A couple of intimate moments won't magically heal me."

He smiled. "At least you're admitting the moments were intimate."

They'd reached the house, preventing her reply, and entered the kitchen through the back door. Inside, Raquel prepared beverages and an assortment of goodies for the meeting. No one went hungry in her house.

"Hi, you two." She spoke as if Cara and Josh arriving together was expected.

"Can I help?" Cara desperately needed an excuse to separate herself from Josh.

Thankfully, Raquel took her up on the offer.

Josh's bemused expression suggested he saw through her ruse. Nonetheless, he headed to the dining room without her. A few minutes later, Cara entered, carrying a pot of fresh coffee and some mugs, which she set on the buffet. Her bad luck continued. One empty seat remained, and it was next to Josh. She refused to appear intimidated and took the seat. A short time later, Reese started the meeting.

Sitting at the formal dining room table was always an interesting occasion. For many years, Dos Estrellas had been a place of joyous gatherings. Family dinners, birthday celebrations and holiday feasts. Then, when August had become sick, the dining room had hosted somber gatherings about prognoses, treatment options and, ultimately, end-of-life care.

After his death, the dining room had again been used for family get-togethers, none of which had gone well. Josh, Cole and Gabe couldn't have been more at odds. Cara had joined in, siding entirely with Gabe. Eventually, the brothers had united in order to battle the red nose virus that could have destroyed the cattle herd and bankrupted the ranch.

These days, family discussions centered on the ranch, the state of which was a constant concern. Cara continued to participate, less as a support for Gabe and more as an advocate for the mustang sanctuary.

Reese oversaw the ranch's finances, which was her job as trustee of August's estate. No one interrupted during her report on recently discovered delinquent property tax bills gone unnoticed in the chaos surrounding August's illness and passing. For a ranch the size of Dos Estrellas, eighteen months' worth of tax bills amounted to tens of thousands of dollars.

Adding to the problem, medical bills continued to surface, many from the experimental cancer treatment center where doctors had made a last valiant effort to extend August's life.

In December, Cole had sold off his four championship roping horses. That money had gone to pay for the antibiotics to fight the red nose virus and all the costs associated with artificially inseminating the cows. Without healthy calves born this coming fall, Dos Estrellas had zero chance of surviving.

Needless to say, the mood of those seated at the table was glum. It worsened when Reese distributed copies of Gabe's income projections for the next six months and a list of the outstanding bills. Lines of fatigue bracketed her eyes. The strain of her workload and caring for her ill father was obviously wearing on her. Cara admired Gabe for spending more time at the Small Change to help run the large ranch.

She also admired Josh for agreeing to fill the void created by Gabe's absence. Yes, he had a duty to the ranch, but he also already had a lot on his plate.

"I've listed the bills in order of delinquency," Reese said. "Those that aren't delinquent and just pending are ordered by due date."

Cara felt a little like an intruder, reading over bills that were private Dempsey business. More paperwork was distributed. The feeling of intrusion passed as the exorbitant dollar amounts left her stunned. Dying of cancer was expensive and a lot of the costs weren't covered by health insurance.

"I suggest we pay the property taxes first," Reese continued, "then decide what's next on the list."

"I agree." Gabe nodded. "We can't let the taxes lapse."

Cara's gaze went from one to the other. She thought it must be hard dating and, potentially, being on opposing sides of ranch finances.

Josh pushed his coffee away in order to make room for the papers. Taking a ballpoint pen from his pocket, he made notes as the meeting continued.

"Has anyone attempted to negotiate with some of the doctors and the cancer treatment center?" he asked. "They might be willing to accept less."

"You think?" Gabe looked surprised.

"It's possible. Kimberly was born a few weeks early and had some minor complications that required she be seen by a specialist. The fees were exorbitant and not covered by my insurance. I called and got the doctor to grant a discount. It wasn't a lot, but it helped."

Reese nodded. "That's a good idea."

Kimberly born premature? Cara wondered if that was because of her mother's drug problem.

The talks progressed with Cara following closely. Once more, she was impressed with everyone's willingness to work together toward a common goal, as well as the sacrifices they were willing to make.

Dos Estrellas was her home, too. As much her home as anywhere she'd ever lived. Surely she could do more.

For the first time, she began to question if she'd been fighting the wrong battle. Had she been selfish, insisting she keep the sanctuary when it was clear that the ranch needed every resource available for the cattle? During the past year, she'd acquired more mustangs than she had adopted out.

Maybe Josh was right. She and Raquel could well be homeless in the near future.

During a break in the conversation, she spoke up. "I, ah, could talk to the Powells. See if they're willing to take back some of the mustangs. That would free up one parcel."

"No, Cara," Gabe objected.

Josh also vetoed her suggestion. "There are other options. You can step up adoptions. Advertise. Maybe generate interest outside the Phoenix metro area."

"I'd thought about that." But she hadn't acted on it.

"You're busy taking care of the horses. Maybe someone else can help. Volunteers." Josh contemplated a moment. "What about the high school? You could offer an afternoon work program. That would free you up to promote adoptions."

"That's a good idea. Except the students would need supervision."

"Could Violet help?"

"Let's save this for another day," Reese said and effectively returned them to the topic of finances.

The glum mood prevailed. How could it be anything else with the prospects so utterly dismal? The plan the brothers eventually decided on was temporary, relying heavily on the spring cattle sale—which could go either way, making or losing them money.

Cara tried to pay attention, but she couldn't stop thinking about Josh's suggestion. It was imperative the sanctuary cease being a drain on the ranch. That wasn't what August had in mind when he'd left her the use of the land. There had to be something else she could do. Something with lasting impact.

At the end of the meeting, the group filed out of the dining room. Cara found herself filled with purpose. It was the best she'd felt in two years.

Well, other than when Josh had kissed her. Then, for a few minutes, she'd been her old self.

"WHAT ARE YOU THINKING?" Summer asked, a glint of conspiracy in her eyes.

"I don't know. Yet." Cara blew out a breath. One small comment from her about doing more to increase donations, and Summer was all-in.

The two relaxed on the same blanket where Kimberly had slept earlier. Teddy sat cross-legged in the grass near them, rocking to and fro and twirling a twig between his fingers. He could do that for hours. Cara had seen him. Every few minutes, Summer glanced over but didn't touch or speak to her son.

How hard that must be for her, not being able to embrace the child she loved. In a way, she'd lost him. That commonality made Cara and Summer's friendship all the stronger.

"Can you really make a difference?" Summer asked. "From what you said, it sounds like the ranch is in serious debt."

Cara gazed in the direction of the horse stable. Josh had taken the kids to the apartment. He was probably letting them play while he fixed an early dinner. Nathan would be driving his toy truck around a makeshift obstacle course, Kimberly crawling after him. Cara could see the scene in her head.

"I have to try." She turned back to Summer. "I can't let the sanctuary continue draining the ranch's resources."

"All right." Summer smiled brightly. "I'll help."

Cara loved that about her friend. Summer supported her unconditionally. Now, all Cara had to do was come up with a plan.

"I'd like for the sanctuary to be completely self-sufficient, not relying on the ranch for supplemental feed and free labor when needed. If I can swing that, I'll return one section to the cattle operation."

"And you're going to do that how?"

The question wasn't intended to be snide or insulting. Cara and Summer had done this many times before, brainstormed solutions to difficult problems.

"Adopt out more horses. Josh suggested enlisting the help of high school students for a work program. What if I involved the students in another way?"

"Such as?"

Cara's mind raced a mile a minute as one idea after another came to her. "The school has a film club. The members came out to Powell Ranch a few years ago after Prince was first captured and made a short documentary about him." In fact, the documentary had become a successful tool for soliciting donations in the early days of the sanctuary. "What if I got the club to make a follow-up film about the sanctuary and how adopting is good for both the mustangs and their new owners?"

"Keep going," Summer encouraged.

"The Powells have some contacts with local media. TV stations that interviewed them about Prince. We could ask the stations to show a segment during their nightly news programs or morning shows. It's a great story. Lots of appeal."

"I like it."

"Yeah." Cara did, too. But it felt as if she could do more. "A documentary takes time. Assuming the school agrees, and there's no guarantee they will, we need to boost donations now."

"What's worked in the past?"

"The raffle for a carriage ride last Christmas raised several thousand dollars."

"Do it again."

"That was during the Holly Daze Festival. The next

community event isn't until Spring Fling." Three months away. "Besides, I need a lot more than a few thousand dollars. Ten, at least." Thirty would be better.

"Hmm." Summer scrunched her mouth to one side. "We could raffle off a horse."

"Of course!" She snapped her fingers.

The noise startled Teddy. He stopped twirling the twig and glared at his mother. Sometimes the most innocuous things set him off.

"It's all right, baby." Summer was careful to avoid direct eye contact. "Mommy didn't mean to startle you."

She and Cara continued their conversation more quietly. It was apparently a good day for Teddy because he settled down quickly.

"I have the perfect horse," Cara said. "A young mare. She shows a lot of potential to be a solid pleasure horse."

"Maybe you could coax Josh into training her."

"Maybe. Cole is supposedly the better horse trainer."

"But Josh is the one who…"

For an anxious moment, Cara thought her friend was going to comment on Josh's feelings for her. Were they that obvious?

"…is helping you with the sanctuary."

"True." Cara sighed with relief.

"I'll design the tickets and fliers. I'm sure my boss will let me use the office printer to run off copies. He's a big fan of the sanctuary."

"That would be great."

"We can ask the members of our support groups to help with ticket sales and distribute the fliers."

"Do you know anyone good at social media? I can set up a Facebook page and a Twitter account, but I have no clue how to use them for promotion."

"I'm sure the high school students can tell you how. Most of them are experts at social media."

Cara's best idea so far suddenly popped into her head.

"What if we had an event here at the ranch for the raffle drawing? Sell hot dogs and ice cream bars. Give pony rides. I'm sure Josh would let us use Hurry Up, and the Powells have a few beginner horses at their riding stable."

"Why stop there?" Summer's face glowed. "Turn the event into an adoption fair with the raffle being the highlight."

"Yes!"

"Invite the TV stations. Put those contacts of the Powells to good use."

Excitement coursed through Cara. She and Summer chatted for another fifteen minutes. Cara thought they were finally winding down when Summer made another suggestion.

"What if Josh put on an exhibit with Wind Walker? The horse is amazing and so beautiful. People will be able to see what a little work and patience can produce."

"Do you think he would?"

Summer grinned impishly. "He will if you ask him."

"He does want to help."

"That's not the reason, and you know it."

Cara lifted her chin. "There's nothing between us."

"Nothing at all," Summer said sarcastically.

Cara considered continuing with her denial, then broke down and confessed. If anyone would understand her struggle, it was Summer.

"We kissed."

"What!" Summer's jaw fell open.

"Twice."

"Tell me everything. Leave nothing out."

"There's not a lot to tell."

"What! He's a bad kisser?" Summer's shoulders sagged. "Oh, no."

If only that were true. "Actually, he's good." Incredible. Phenomenal. She'd never been kissed like that before.

"What's wrong? You're both single. Both available. Clearly, you like each other."

"I'm not ready for a relationship."

"Go slow."

Had Summer spoken to Josh? He'd said almost the same thing. "I'll disappoint him. He'll want more, and I won't be able to…to hold up my end."

"No one said you have to jump into bed with him right away."

"I'm not talking about sex."

"What then?"

Cara sighed. "I'm emotionally damaged."

"That's a bunch of bull—" Summer glanced at Teddy. "Of you-know-what. We're all emotionally damaged. Josh, too. What's the real reason?"

"My son died."

"You think that precludes you from ever being happy again?"

"Yes." Cara looked away. "The accident was my fault."

Summer gripped her arm firmly. "It wasn't. You were a good mother. Attentive. Careful. Loving. You did everything right. You couldn't possibly have known that Javier woke up and snuck into the laundry room. Not unless you could see through walls, which no one can."

"I should have put a lock on the laundry room door.

I shouldn't have argued with Manuel. I shouldn't have let him convince me to stay when I wanted to check on Javier."

"And I shouldn't have married Hal. Then I wouldn't have a son with autism."

"Summer!" Cara was shocked.

"I don't mean a word of that. I was trying to make a point. You can I-should-have or shouldn't-have yourself to death. It won't make a difference, except you'll feel worse rather than better."

"It's hard."

"Not to sound clichéd, but you're young and have your whole life ahead of you. Josh is interested in you. He's attractive. A hard worker. A great father. You have a lot in common."

"He has two children," Cara said on a ragged breath.

"Pretty nice children, if you ask me."

"I'm not ready to be a mother again."

"Huh." Her eyes narrowed. "Or, are you not ready to take on the responsibility?"

"Javier died because of me."

"You'd checked on him fifteen minutes earlier. Not two hours. You did your job. Sometimes, awful things happen to good people. People who don't deserve it."

Cara didn't break down and demand of God or anyone who'd listen, why her? Why them? She'd done that a thousand times already and gotten no answer. No peace.

"What if I fail again, Summer? Make a mistake. Then Josh's children would suffer."

"What if you find love and spend the rest of your life unbelievably happy?"

"Not very likely."

"You won't find out if you don't take a chance."

That sounded scary to Cara. She wasn't strong enough to survive another blow to the heart.

Chapter Nine

"Come on!" Josh shouted to Cara above the ruckus. "Move along. Time's a-wasting." Riding his horse Wanderer, he herded the thirty-four mustangs down the dirt road, swinging his coiled lariat over his head and nudging the occasional wannabe stray back into line.

Cara didn't think he'd use the rope. Rather, he'd brought it for emergencies and to ensure the mustangs stayed together, trotting in the same direction. They were making the mile and a half trek from the feeding station at the sanctuary to the corral behind the horse stable.

She had to admit, she liked the image of Josh swinging the rope in the air, and took her eyes off him only long enough to perform her job, which was bringing up the rear. The rest of the time, she watched his every move.

He could have been plucked right out of an old John Wayne movie about driving cattle across the plains. Her imagination was further encouraged by his canvas duster, weathered boots and faded cowboy hat worn low on his head. The two-day growth of beard didn't hurt, either, giving him a rough and dangerous appearance.

"Stop thinking about him," she mumbled and turned

her horse to the left when one of the mustangs veered in that direction. The horse, an orphan yearling Cara had taken in last fall and hand raised for its first six months, obediently rejoined the others.

Resembling their wild brethren, the small herd moved rapidly along, heads high, eyes alert and flowing tails arched. Also like in the wild, they followed the lead horse. Today, that was Wanderer.

So much for distracting herself. Not a minute later, Cara was once again staring at Josh. Nothing noteworthy had happened between them since the family meeting, except that they worked closely together on the adoption fair and she helped with his children.

Hard to believe, a mere eleven days had passed since she and Summer had brainstormed the event. Yet it was scheduled to start today at two o'clock. Six hours from now. Everything had come together as if by magic. The entire Dempsey family, the high school, Summer's and Cara's support groups and the whole community of Mustang Valley had pitched in. Each time Cara thought about people's kindness and generosity, tears sprang to her eyes.

Even her mother and stepdad had driven out from east Mesa twice and would be here again today. Mostly for moral support, but they'd pitch in whenever and wherever needed.

"How's it going?" Josh turned in the saddle and hollered at her. "You okay?"

"I'm fine."

He grinned. And like that, her heart pitter-pattered.

Now? Of course now. It was always the same. Out here in the wide-open spaces, with thirty-four horses separating them, she still fell under his spell.

"You're doing great." He gave her a wave.

She hesitated before returning it.

He faced forward, giving Cara a reprieve. The invisible vise compressing her lungs released enough for her to breathe again.

She rode one of her favorite mares. The pretty gray had come to the sanctuary as part of the first group of mustangs from Powell Ranch. Cara had considered either trading the mare to Rusty in exchange for more farrier services or putting her up for adoption today. In the end, she couldn't bring herself to go through with it.

"Look at the sky." Josh pointed overhead. "What do you think?"

Above them, large cumulus clouds gathered, white, fluffy and, at the moment, blocking the sun. At long last, rain was predicted for either tonight or tomorrow and continuing for two days. The local ranchers were ecstatic. The drought was finally at an end.

"I hope the rain holds until after the adoption fair," Cara hollered in return.

As much as she wanted rain, grass required weeks to grow, and the Dempseys didn't have weeks. Everyone was counting on the proceeds from today's event to purchase additional hay for the sanctuary. More hay, less dependence on the ranch. Hopefully, the delinquent property taxes could soon be paid.

Already Cara, along with her helpers, had raised more than two thousand dollars in donations from people wanting to contribute but unable to adopt a horse. As of yesterday, double that amount had been collected from advance raffle ticket sales. Unfortunately, it was a small percentage of what was needed to make the sanctuary self-sufficient.

Because it was nearly impossible to be heard above the pounding of so many hooves, Cara and Josh didn't converse for the remaining half mile to the ranch. She studied his back while they rode, liking the confident way he sat in the saddle and the skill he demonstrated in maintaining control of the herd.

"What a lie," she softly scolded herself. The truth was, Cara enjoyed the eye candy.

She didn't need to see him to know he reached down and absently patted Wanderer's neck every few minutes. After weeks of spending hours together each day, she'd become familiar with the many little details about him. The pine-scented soap he showered with. What brand of work shirts he preferred to wear. His craving for a second cup of morning coffee at around nine. His not-quite-secret affinity for old-school rock and roll.

The looks he often gave her when he thought she wasn't watching. Kind of like how she looked at him now.

Josh was also a talker. Unlike her, he had no trouble opening up about deeply personal feelings and difficult past experiences. The other day, when they had been riding sanctuary land and inspecting the horses, she'd learned about the hardships he'd endured during the agonizing weeks his ex-wife had taken off with their children. And about coming home to find her passed out and the children neglected.

Cara was a little ashamed of herself. She'd been quick to judge Josh when he'd first arrived at Dos Estrellas, assuming that because he was estranged from his father, he wasn't a good man or a loving father himself. She'd been completely wrong. Josh's rugged exterior hid the most tender of hearts.

To any other woman, he'd be a catch. To Cara, he was the guy who terrified her because he got under her skin unlike any other man.

As they neared the ranch, the dirt road beneath them became wider and harder packed from frequent travel. Despite the distance, Cara could clearly see the activity at the ranch as vehicles—some of them pulling horse trailers—drove onto the grounds. The area next to the hay barn designated for parking was already filled to capacity.

The mustangs, in high spirits from the trip over, instinctively knew they were reaching their destination. Tossing their heads in excitement, they whinnied and pranced. It became difficult to keep them bunched together, and Cara was forced to pay closer attention, ending her obsession with Josh. For the moment.

Deciding which ones to put up for adoption had been a joint project with Josh and another reason for them to spend time together. It wasn't easy narrowing their choices to just thirty-four, which they'd temporarily housed in the feeding station.

Cara had wanted to find homes for as many mustangs as possible and to raise as much money as they could. Josh was more realistic, insisting they limit the horses to those truly ready for new homes. Her sanctuary couldn't afford dissatisfied customers—or *horse parents*, as Cara preferred to call them. Rather, she needed horse parents delighted with their adoptees to send referrals her way.

Choosing the best mustangs wasn't all Josh had done to help with the event. In addition to the exhibition featuring Wind Walker, he was in charge of the pony rides with the Powells. Along with Cole, he'd also constructed a simple wooden auctioneer's booth.

He'd accomplished all that while working the ranch, putting in regular hours at the sanctuary and being an attentive father to his children. He was a machine. A robot. What other explanation could there be?

Cara was grateful, make no mistake. And pleased. The adoption fair would be a huge success, in large part because of him. She was also in a constant state of emotional turmoil. Right now, her heart had yet to stop pitter-pattering.

The ringing of her cell phone startled her. She dug it out from her coat pocket and, recognizing the number, answered.

"Hi, Summer."

"Where are you?"

"Almost to the ranch. We're bringing the horses for auction from the sanctuary."

"We? I like the sound of that."

"Habit. I meant nothing by it."

"Too bad."

Cara didn't rise to the bait. "I need to go. These horses are acting up." Talking on the phone didn't mix well with riding and herding horses.

"Me, too." Summer's office experience had made her the perfect choice to handle the administrative and financial duties of the adoption event. She'd be running herself ragged all day, completing paperwork and processing the money transactions. "Find me when you have a minute. I brought someone, and I want you to meet him."

"Him?" Had her friend made a romantic connection?

"Not that kind of him. Dr. Franklin Armstrong, Teddy's

psychologist at the new learning center where I've been taking him. I've been telling the doctor all about the exhibition with Wind Walker, and he wanted to see it."

Josh had a surprise in store for Teddy. They'd kept it under wraps in case Teddy was having a difficult day as he sometimes did. Fortunately, Summer had reported her son was the most engaged and alert he'd been in months. Maybe years.

"Okay," Cara said. "I'll try and find you."

"If not, I'll find you. This is important. See you soon. Oh, good," she said distractedly. "The McGraws have arrived. Bye!"

Theo McGraw had volunteered to be the auctioneer. Made sense. He'd been to a lot of cattle auctions and wanted to participate.

Cara insisted on obliging him after he'd used his position on the community center board to borrow their PA system. She'd assured a worried Reese that her father would be sitting the entire time and not physically stressing himself.

Josh's suggestion to reach out to the high school had paid off in more ways than Cara could count. To start with, the equestrian drill team members were waiting for them at the ranch. Their job was to speed-groom the mustangs and clean their hooves in preparation for adoption. The horses needed to look their best. Without the students, Cara didn't have a prayer of accomplishing such a huge undertaking.

The film club had jumped at the chance to make another short documentary about the sanctuary, agreeing to cover all the costs. They'd been out to the ranch several times this past week, filming routine daily activities and interviewing Cara, Josh and Gabe. They also planned to interview new horse parents after the adoption fair. Yet another reason for the event to go well.

At the ranch, Cara and Josh herded the mustangs to the corral, where the equestrian drill team members waited for them with buckets of soapy water, brushes, mane combs and hoof picks. It was too cold to bathe the horses with a hose, but a little washing up and grooming would work wonders.

Dismounting, Cara and Josh hit the ground running. Literally. Cara barked instructions to the drill team, the wranglers, the student film crew and the many volunteers. Josh left to set up for the pony rides and ready Wind Walker. She'd spotted the Powells' truck on the way in and guessed they were somewhere waiting for him.

Two hours passed in the blink of an eye. Cara's arms ached and her feet throbbed. She'd been awake since four. How would she make it through the rest of the day?

Josh found her finishing up with the Literary Ladies, who were running the snack bar in exchange for half the profits going to the library fund. Pushing the hair out of her face with the back of her hand, Cara greeted him with a wan smile.

"You'll need to do better than that," he said.

"What?"

He looked fantastic. Somehow, he'd found the time to shower and change into fresh clothes and don a brown suede jacket that fit his broad shoulders to perfection.

Great. Sweat and dirt clung to her every pore. Her clothes wrinkled as they stood there.

"The film students want to do a segment with the two of us," he said. "Before the adoption fair starts."

"I should freshen up first."

"You look fine."

She did?

"All you need is a smile."

He would have to be charming on top of handsome, nice, kind, movie-star sexy and a phenomenal kisser. No way was she doing an interview with him without changing clothes and repairing her hair and makeup.

"Give me fifteen minutes." She pivoted and caught sight of her grubby fingernails. On second thought… "Make that twenty."

"Wait."

"I'm in kind of a rush." A ton of work remained for her to do.

"I have an idea. For the adoption fair."

"Tell me." A small tension headache made itself known behind her right eye.

Saying goodbye to the head of the Literary Ladies, she walked across the open area toward the house. Josh joined her. They had to navigate between and around people, vehicles, horses and riders, dogs, a donkey, one pony cart, three bicycles and a teenager on a gas-powered skateboard.

"You're letting me sponsor Hurry Up and Wind Walker."

Cara shot Josh a sidelong glance. "We both know that's a technicality. They're your horses."

"I pay you a monthly stipend."

"You can have the horses, Josh." She'd been silly and stubborn, making him jump through unnecessary hoops.

"I'll take you up on that offer after today. And pay you a reasonable fee."

"I can't accept. You've worked your tail off."

"Let's get back to my idea. There are going to be a lot more than thirty-four people here today, which is all the horses we're putting up for adoption. Why not give the rest an opportunity to sponsor a horse? Perhaps one that's unadoptable. The sanctuary is nonprofit. Their sponsor fees would be a tax deduction. More than that, they would potentially save a horse that might otherwise… meet an unpleasant fate."

Cara loved the idea. It spoke to her heart. And it would create steady income. Granted, a small amount, but reliable.

"With the website, we could reach potential sponsors outside Arizona." Her excitement grew. "All over the country."

"I take it you approve."

"Josh." Stopping, she drew in a deep breath.

She would not throw herself at him. Not rain kisses on his face or stand on tiptoes and loop her arms around his neck. Not bury her face in the open V of his shirt and inhale the smell of the pine-scented soap he used.

"It's a wonderful idea," she said.

His eyes, brilliant blue in the sunlight, twinkled. "Glad you like it."

Oh, what the hell. "Thank you, Josh."

He caught her as she hugged him and laughed heartily when she squeezed him tight around his middle. "Whoa there."

It was heaven, holding him. Cara closed her eyes and, as she always did, gave in. She didn't care they were in the middle of a crowd and that countless stares were no doubt fastened on them.

She was sorry when he drew back, not sorry when he gazed at her with a look of tender longing. "Hey, there."

"I forgot myself for a minute."

"Maybe what you did was find yourself."

No. He had to be wrong. This was a mistake. A momentary lapse in judgment.

"Excuse me. Are we interrupting?"

The voice belonged to Summer. Cara stiffened, then separated herself from Josh, her face flushed. Of all people, of course it was her friend.

"Josh and I were discussing an idea he had to raise more money."

"I noticed." Summer cast her companion a glance.

The distinguished-looking gentleman wearing a startled expression must have been the psychologist from Teddy's learning center.

Cara could live with that. It was the camera operator from the school film club standing behind them, filming every moment, that made her wish for the ground to open and swallow her whole. Please, let that not wind up in the finished documentary.

DOS ESTRELLAS WAS a cattle operation, not a horse ranch or rodeo grounds. They didn't have a show arena and bleachers or even a public restroom. Josh had pondered the problem for a full week before the adoption fair. They needed a confined place to show the horses and exhibit Wind Walker, and somewhere for the people to sit, if possible, or stand.

Hosting the event at Powell Ranch was a possibility, and they were more than willing. The problem was relocating thirty-four head of mustangs. After debating the pros and cons, Josh, Cole and Violet opted to use one of the livestock pens for a makeshift arena. It wasn't fancy but, once cleaned and graded, plenty serviceable. The small corral would be used as a holding area for the mustangs awaiting their turn up for bid.

Volunteer wranglers would lead each horse the fifty or so yards from the corral to the livestock pen, showing off the horse's gait and sound temperament in the process. For the past two hours, potential buyers had been inspecting horses in the holding area and test riding a few of the more broke ones in the round pen.

Cole was already in the arena. He was in charge of the horses once they were brought to the ring, while Violet was overseeing the volunteer wranglers. Two spotters had been chosen for their outgoing personalities. Their job was to assist in the arena, pointing out bidders to Theo and enthusing the crowd.

Josh had spent hours grooming Wind Walker, whose coat shone like patent leather. Violet had offered to braid his mane and tail and tie his forelock with a ribbon. Josh refused. He wanted the stallion to remind people of the mustangs' wild heritage. That was better accomplished without any frills.

He stood with Wind Walker at the entrance to the makeshift arena. The horse wore only a show halter with engraved silver hardware. Josh had won the halter years ago when competing on Wanderer. He and Nathan had polished the silver nose and brow band plates last night while Kimberly played with the lead rope. Josh wished the kids were with him now. He'd have to satisfy himself knowing they were watching from the sidelines with a new babysitter—a woman he'd found by chance in the Cowboy Up Café the other morning while he and the kids were having breakfast.

Theo McGraw's voice blasted through the PA system making preliminary announcements.

Josh glanced at his phone display. It was almost time for the fair to start. The exhibition with Wind Walker would kick it off. He cast about for his partner and caught sight of Teddy and his mother approaching.

Somehow Summer had managed to dress the boy in a pair of jeans, a Western shirt, a vest and boots. He and Josh had practiced twice during the past week. Between Wind Walker's desire to please and Teddy's positive response to the horse, Josh was reasonably confident their exhibition would go off without a hitch. He had one more surprise he hadn't told anyone about, including Teddy, which he hoped would boost adoptions.

"You look ready, pal." Josh pointed to the boy's shirt and vest when he and his mother neared. "I like the duds."

"Duhs," Teddy said and patted his chest, making the garbled sound Josh had come to recognize as his laugh.

"Just like a real cowboy."

Teddy laughed again.

Good, thought Josh, he wasn't nervous. Then again, did Teddy really understand what performing in front of an audience meant? Possibly not.

"I thought he should wear a jacket," Summer said, "but he refuses. He loves the vest."

"It suits him."

She glanced up at the clouds. The mild breeze had grown stronger the past hour, but didn't smell of rain. Yet. "I hope the weather cooperates." She raised her hand, the index and middle fingers crossed.

Teddy copied her, waving his hand in the air. Summer smiled lovingly at her son, though her eyes remained sad and her arms hung loose at her sides.

Before his divorce, before losing his kids for weeks

on end, before meeting Cara and learning about her late son, Josh might not have given Summer and Teddy much thought. The events of this past year had taught him a lot. Softened the hard edges of his heart. Enabled him to notice the pain a mother who couldn't touch her child endured.

"Thank you again for including him," Summer said.

"Are you kidding? Teddy's going to be the star of the show."

She patted Wind Walker on the side of his large head. The horse snorted, more interested in all the activity than receiving any spoiling. "I think this big guy's going to be the star of the show."

"Hahs, hahs." Not to be outdone, Teddy flung an arm around Wind Walker's neck as if they were old pals.

Josh had to admit, they were cute together.

"I'm very proud of you, Teddy." She leaned as close to her son as he'd allow. "Can I take your picture?"

He nodded vigorously. Summer snapped several shots with her cell phone. Teddy bared his teeth in his version of a smile.

The more Josh got to know Cara's friend, the more he liked her. Summer didn't have an easy life, yet she was always optimistic, upbeat and outgoing. Quite the opposite of Cara. Then again, maybe not. Cara was a passionate person. He'd had the pleasure of seeing her passion spring to life and had the excitement of holding her in his arms as it burned hot.

For many nights now, he'd imagined how it might be to lie with her in the dark, her bare limbs draped over his, her soft moans filling his ears as he stirred that incredible passion to even greater heights.

Damn. He gave himself a mental shake. Wrong time,

wrong place. He needed to stay focused. One misstep and the adoption fair would be a disaster.

"Do you mind if I stick close?" Summer asked. "I'm sure Teddy will be fine, but…"

"Why don't you wait by the gate?" Josh understood and agreed it would be better for Teddy if she was in the immediate vicinity should something go wrong.

She nodded gratefully. "I'll try to stay as much out of sight as possible."

Josh checked the time, then surveyed the crowd. Some people had brought lawn chairs, but most stood three-deep along the fence, studying the program Summer had put together that included a picture and background story of each mustang. Card stock bid numbers, courtesy of Summer's boss, were stuck in hat bands or protruding from front pockets.

"I'm guessing there are about a hundred and fifty people here," Summer said.

"I was hoping for more."

"No fooling? And here I was thinking this is a great turnout for a first time."

First time. He liked the way she thought. The event could become an annual occurrence. Bigger and better with more time to plan, prepare and promote.

Would he be here next year? There were many variables to consider. If the three brothers didn't find a way to pay off this latest batch of bills, the next family meeting might be about the best approach to selling the ranch.

"What matters most," Summer said, "is not how many people are here, but how much money we raise."

"That's right." Josh turned to Teddy, who still clung to Wind Walker's neck. "We need to show these people the kind of quality horse these mustangs will make. You ready?"

"Yah, yah."

"All right." Without thinking, Josh put a hand on Teddy's shoulder. Realizing what he'd done, he quickly withdrew his hand. Except Teddy hadn't reacted in the slightest. He glanced at Summer. "Sorry. I didn't mean for that to happen."

"Are you kidding?" She broke into a delighted smile. "That's great progress."

Josh promptly lost his train of thought, distracted by the sight of Cara heading across the makeshift arena toward the auctioneer's booth. He stared, admiring her determined yet graceful stride. Summer obviously noticed.

"You're good for her," she said. "Not that it matters, but I approve."

"She claims she isn't ready for a relationship." Josh wasn't 100 percent sure he was, either.

"An excuse. Trust me."

"You think I should try?"

"Answer me this. Who initiated the hug earlier?"

"Cara."

Summer's smug expression spoke volumes. "I rest my case."

Josh intended to consider her remarks at length when he had more time. Right now, Cara signaled them from the auctioneer's booth.

"Looks like it's showtime," he said to Teddy. "You ready?"

"Break a leg," Summer called after them as they entered the arena.

Josh and Teddy walked side by side with Josh leading Wind Walker. Theo made an announcement on the PA system, welcoming everyone to the auction. He reminded them to read the rules and regulations on the back of the program, to register at the welcome table if they hadn't done so already and, lastly, to note the very important locations of the portable restrooms and snack bar.

"Ladies and gentlemen, boys and girls." Theo's voice boomed loud and clear with only the slightest tremor, a side effect of his Parkinson's. "Before we officially get under way, we have a little something special for you."

He proceeded to talk about Wind Walker, the stallion's history, how he arrived at the sanctuary and how Josh had handpicked the horse for his own, recognizing Wind Walker's potential.

"What you are about to see will amaze you," Theo continued. "This is a horse that, up until a month ago, hadn't known the touch of a human hand. Barely had any human contact other than when he was captured last fall on the reservation near Tuba City after living his entire life in the hills."

There were a few oohs and aahs from the audience.

"Josh Dempsey is about to show you fine folks what a few weeks of intense training can accomplish. He will be helped by his young partner, Teddy Goodwyn. Teddy lives here in Mustang Valley and attends the Learning Center for Autistic Children in Scottsdale."

A small round of applause followed.

Summer had insisted on including the last part in the introduction. She thought people would be more impressed with Wind Walker's accomplishments if they knew Teddy had special needs.

"Now, Wind Walker hasn't been broke to ride," Theo

said. "Going to take a few more weeks of training for that to happen. Nonetheless, we're pretty sure you'll be impressed. So, Josh and Teddy, as the saying goes, take it away."

Josh led Wind Walker to the center of the arena, Teddy at his side. He let out the lunge line and cued Wind Walker to trot. Luckily, the horse didn't appear bothered by the people and noise. Josh marginally relaxed. After a few circles, he cued the stallion into an easy lope. When the moment was right, he handed off the lunge line to Teddy.

The crowd showed their appreciation. With Josh standing beside him and coaching him along, Teddy put Wind Walker through his rehearsed paces, including stopping and backing up. Neither of them could have performed better.

"Tell him to stand," Josh said.

The stallion responded to Teddy's cue. He and Josh approached Wind Walker and, as rehearsed, Teddy petted the horse. More applause followed and some cheers.

That was as much as they'd practiced. Josh, however, wasn't done. He still had his surprise.

"Teddy, I need you to listen carefully. This is very important." He waited until the boy looked at him, placing his hands over Teddy's and the lunge line. "When I tell you it's okay, you give Wind Walker the cue to walk. You understand me?"

He nodded.

"You sure? This is important." Josh didn't think he was taking too much of a risk, but things could, and sometimes did, go wrong.

"Shoor, shoor," Teddy said.

"Good boy." Josh smiled. "I knew I could count on

you. Now, go stand where we were." He pointed to the center of the arena.

Teddy did as Josh instructed.

"Well, folks," Theo improvised, as if he'd known Josh's plan the whole time. "It appears the exhibition isn't over."

Josh could sense the crowd's interest, and he tried not to let his nerves get the better of him. When Teddy was in place, he faced Wind Walker and stroked the stallion's sleek neck.

"I'm counting on you, too, boy. Don't let me down."

Wind Walker bobbed his head. They had practiced this only once. Yesterday, in private, and it hadn't gone great. Josh truly had no idea how the horse would behave today.

Retreating a few steps, he ran at the stallion, and then grabbed the mane with his left hand as he swung himself up onto Wind Walker's back. The stallion flinched, tensed and danced in place.

"Okay, Teddy. Now."

The boy cued the stallion. Josh applied a gentle pressure to Wind Walker's sides with his calves.

One step. Two steps. A quarter circle and no blow-ups. At the completion of the circle, Josh nudged Wind Walker into a trot, then an easy lope.

The crowd's applause was drowned out by the roar in Josh's ears as his pulse soared. They'd done it! And riding this magnificent animal was every bit as exhilarating as he'd imagined.

After several more rounds, Josh brought Wind Walker to a stand. "Whoa, boy."

Theo's voice burst from the speakers. "Look at that horse, folks. Just like we told you. Mustangs are smart, gentle and eager to please. You're going to have to put some effort into training them, but here is a perfect example of what you'll get in return."

The crowd applauded and hooted with excitement. Josh dismounted and let Teddy lead Wind Walker from the arena. Summer waited at the gate, her hands clasped to her chest and tears of joy in her eyes. She couldn't stop looking at Teddy, who flashed his funny grimace-smile.

"You were wonderful, honey."

Summer wasn't alone. Cara had come over during the exhibition. She was looking, too, but at Josh.

For the first time, she put up no barriers between them. Every emotion was there in her face for him to see.

She hurried forward to meet him and, like earlier, hugged him around his waist. "That was incredible."

When she finally let go and lifted her gaze to his, Josh couldn't stop himself from saying, "I'm falling for you, Cara Alverez."

He expected her to make a dash for the nearest hiding place. She didn't.

"Maybe we can talk later," he said.

Her answer, one simple word, gave him hope.

"Yes."

Chapter Ten

They met in the dining room, the Dempseys and Mc-Graws both. Summer, too, as she'd handled the book-keeping and paperwork for the adoption fair. The last truck and trailer had left the ranch an hour ago. After catching their breaths and grabbing a quick dinner of leftovers from the snack bar, the families were regrouping to review the results of their efforts.

Cara, not normally a nail-biter, sat next to Summer and chewed on her thumb as her friend tallied the proceeds. Cara had paid close attention during the bidding, mentally adding the final sale prices for each horse. With so many interruptions, she'd eventually lost track and now had no idea how they'd done.

A leaf had been added to the dining table to accommodate everyone and allow space for beverages. The guys were having a beer. Cara was too anxious to drink or eat.

Only Josh's two children and Teddy were missing. The babysitter Josh had hired watched all three in the family room. They'd wanted to play outside but, judging from the loud rumble of thunder every few minutes, rain would fall soon. Yet another reason to celebrate.

Cara alone fretted about the final total. Everyone else remained confidently optimistic.

Finally! Summer finished adding the credit card receipts and cash. Twice. She hit the total button on the calculator, an old-fashioned desktop model from August's former—Gabe's current—office.

"Well?" Cara demanded when Summer took too long revealing the results.

"Including the pre-event raffle ticket sales, what we took in today, sale of the thirty-four mustangs and donations collected both from the website and at the booth today…"

"Quit stalling," Cara begged.

Summer tore the tape from the calculator and held it up for everyone to see. "Thirty-seven thousand seven hundred and sixty-four dollars and change."

Cheers went up from the men. Raquel burst out crying. Reese and Gabe hugged.

"That's wonderful," Violet exclaimed. "Oh, Cara. I'm so glad. Good job. Good job, all of us."

"Congratulations." The quiet voice on Cara's other side belonged to Josh.

She heard the smile in it and was deeply touched. "Thank you. We wouldn't have raised anywhere near that amount without you, Teddy and Wind Walker."

"You put on a fine exhibition," Theo added. "Very impressive. If you're ever looking for a job, I might have an opening for a horse trainer."

Cole slapped Josh on the back. "Appears I have some competition."

"No worries," Josh said. "I'll never be as good as you, brother. And I'm starting to like cattle ranching."

How would August feel to hear his oldest son?

Raquel must be wondering the same thing as Cara, for she pressed a hand to her heart and closed her eyes.

Talk continued for several more minutes, swirling around Cara. She heard the words but nothing made sense. Her thoughts were too hectic, blending one into the other.

Thirty-seven thousand dollars! What she could do with that sum of money. With careful budgeting, who knew how long she could sustain the sanctuary? Months? A year? And once she implemented Josh's idea for a sponsorship program, she'd be bringing in more money. Hundreds, if not thousands, of dollars a month.

"Here. Keep this as a souvenir." Smiling, Summer pressed the calculator tape into Cara's hand.

She stared at the total, rereading the amount she'd memorized. It was huge, and without the help and support of the Dempseys, the sanctuary might have gone under.

"I want to pay you," she blurted.

"Absolutely not." Summer shook her head. "I refuse."

"No. You." Her glance traveled from one brother to the next. "Ten thousand dollars."

"What!" Gabe pushed back in his seat. "No."

"Yes. I owe you. The sanctuary does. For the land."

"Dad gave that to you."

"He allowed me to use it. That's not the same as owning. Now that I have funds, I should start paying a portion of the expenses. Rent, if you will."

"Cara, no." Josh touched her arm. "None of us expects you to contribute."

"Yes, you do," she argued. "Last month you were pressuring me to turn the sanctuary land over to the ranch in order to save the cattle operation."

"Not anymore."

"Nothing's changed." She laid the tape out in front of her, smoothing the crumpled paper. "The sanctuary takes up almost a quarter of the ranch. It's only fair that it pays for twenty-five percent of the property taxes."

"Ten thousand dollars is more than twenty-five percent," Reese said, donning her estate trustee hat.

"Consider the rest room and board." Cara turned to Raquel. "Since August died, I've contributed almost nothing to the household."

"You're family," Raquel insisted.

"Even family doesn't get to live here for free."

"You help out."

"I want to help out more." Cara indicated the pile of money and credit card receipts in front of Summer. "Is there ten thousand in cash?"

"A little more than that."

"Count it out."

Summer did, secured the thick bundle of mostly large bills with a rubber band and handed it to Cara, smiling in approval.

"Here." Cara passed the bundle to Gabe.

"Are you sure?" he asked.

"We all know how desperately Dos Estrellas needs money."

Gabe tapped the bills on the table top, some of the tension visibly leaving him. "I'll deposit this in the bank on Monday."

"I also want you to take back section six."

"That's too much, Cara," Josh objected. "Pick the smaller section."

"I have enough money to buy supplemental feed for the next six months, at least. I don't need the land."

"You might in the future."

"If that happens, we'll talk then."

"Well?" Gabe shot his brothers a look.

"I vote yes," Cole said.

Josh nodded. Beneath the table, his hand found Cara's and squeezed.

"Okay." Her sigh of satisfaction ended with a tiny burst inside her, strange at first, then familiar.

Joy. The emotion was tiny and fragile, like a seedling newly breaking the surface of the ground. With careful nurturing, it might grow. Might flourish and fill the hollow spaces within her heart.

Everyone else had started talking again. Cara, however, sat in silence, sending a prayer of thanks heavenward. Her first since Javier's death.

"I'm sorry," Josh said, his voice penetrating the din. "I was wrong about a lot of things."

Cara turned in her chair to face him. "You were right about a lot of things, too."

Caught up in celebrating, no one appeared to be paying the two of them any attention. Especially when Raquel returned from a trip to the kitchen with a tray of sweets.

Josh leaned in close to Cara and spoke softly. "I'm looking forward to our talk later."

Oh, heavens. She'd agreed to that, hadn't she? Simply because he'd said he was falling for her. Really? The heat of the moment was probably responsible.

"Um...yes." She removed her hand from his.

He chuckled. He must like seeing her frazzled, since he was always saying and doing things to unsettle her.

"Cookies?" Raquel sidled over with the large tray.

Cara refused, her stomach remaining in knots. Josh, however, plucked up two cookies.

Surprising Cara, Raquel bent and kissed her cheek. *"Te quiero, mija."*

"I love you, too."

"The money's a good sign. We won't lose the ranch."

Maybe. Dos Estrellas was hardly out of the woods. A mountain of bills resided on Gabe's desk, awaiting payment. But, for now, there was hope.

"Muh, Muh, Muh!"

The revelry halted abruptly as Teddy burst into the dining room, stumbling and almost losing his balance. He dashed straight to Summer, stopping short directly in front of her. His features were twisted in anger or frustration. Cara wasn't sure which.

"What's wrong, baby?"

Teddy answered his mother with a string of garbled words that made no sense.

Summer stood. "He's upset. I'm not sure what happened, but I think we should go. He'll only get worse."

The next instant, Nathan ran into the room. Like Teddy, he made straight for his parent and thrust himself onto Josh's lap. "Daddy. He stole my truck."

Josh glanced at Teddy, whose sobbing sounded like a rusty machine. "He didn't mean it, buddy."

Cara noticed Teddy held Nathan's truck behind his back. Summer noticed, too.

Getting anything back from Teddy once he had it in his possession was no easy task. Summer nonetheless tried. "Teddy, that truck belongs to Nathan. You can't have it."

Teddy grunted and ducked behind Summer's chair, preventing anyone from taking the truck. The next instant, the babysitter appeared, Kimberly balanced on one hip, issuing an apology for letting the squabble escalate out of control.

"It's all right," Summer and Josh said almost simultaneously.

Resolving the minor crisis took several minutes and a lot of coaxing. Ultimately, Nathan's truck was returned to him. Teddy, unfortunately, suffered a meltdown, yelling, thrashing and refusing to be mollified. When he ran out of the house, Summer chased after him. Raquel checked on them, returning a few minutes later to report that Summer and Teddy were heading home.

Regaining possession of his truck didn't appease Nathan, and he continued to whine. For whatever reason, Kimberly added to the fray with her earsplitting cries. Josh settled up with the babysitter, and the four of them left. Josh took his tired children to the apartment.

With the celebration at an end, Cara collected the credit card receipts and remaining cash, placing them and the adding machine tape in a plastic zippered food storage bag. She held the bag up to the light on the side table. She'd never seen this much money all in one place before. Keeping it in such a flimsy bag seemed silly. On the other hand, the clear plastic allowed her to see the money, and holding it gave her a rush of excitement.

In the kitchen, she asked Raquel, "What's left to do?"

"You must be exhausted," the older woman said, loading the dishwasher.

"Actually, I'm not." Cara hadn't felt this invigorated in ages.

"There aren't many dishes left." Raquel waved her away. "You go relax."

What Cara did was put the money and receipts in a

safe place—the bottom of a dresser drawer. Outside, sprinkles had started to fall and dot the glass windowpane. Against the backdrop of a dark evening, the drops glittered like diamonds.

It was still early, and plenty of work needed to be done in the wake of the adoption event. With the rain, most of it would have to wait. She supposed she could take down the temporary canopies they'd set up before the wind swept them away.

"I'll be back in a little while," she told Raquel and grabbed her rain poncho on her way out the door.

Taking down the two canopies was a simple enough job and over quickly. No one else was around. Josh, she knew, was with the children. She assumed Gabe had returned to the Small Change with Reese and her father. Cole had disappeared, and Violet had left earlier, stating she had a date with a hot bath. Weather permitting, a crew of volunteers was returning tomorrow afternoon to assist with cleanup.

Cara wasn't sure what to do with herself next.

Stowing the last canopy on a shelf in the storeroom behind the hay barn, she waited beneath the tall awning. In a short time, the rain had increased from a light drizzle to a steady downpour. While debating whether to make a run for the house or wait for a break, her cell phone rang.

"Hi, Summer. How's Teddy?"

"Fine. Resting. Say, listen, Dr. Armstrong is here. He stopped by on his way out of town."

The psychologist from Teddy's learning center. Cara had spent several minutes talking to him during the event.

"He has a proposition for you," Summer said. She

sounded harried. Or was she excited? Hard to tell with all the noise.

"A proposition?"

"I think this is something worthwhile. Good for the sanctuary and a lot of children."

Cara plugged her other ear with her finger to hear better. "I'm listening."

Fifteen minutes later, she leaned against a column, having just hung up from her conversation with Dr. Armstrong. Earlier, she'd thought her day, her whole future, couldn't have looked brighter. She'd been wrong. It was very possible the doctor was about to change her life and the future of the sanctuary.

She couldn't keep this news to herself and wanted to shout it to anyone and everyone who'd listen. What she did was run from the hay barn to the horse stable, up the stairs to the apartment landing, completely mind-less of the pouring rain.

Josh opened the door in answer to her frantic knock-ing and gave her a head-to-toe once-over.

"You're soaked."

"Can I come in?" she asked breathlessly. "I have something to tell you."

JOSH COULD HARDLY hear himself think over the sound of rain hammering the apartment roof. He was amazed his kids could sleep through the noise. But they had been tired, having missed their regular afternoon nap because of the adoption event. Cara's frantic knocking on the apartment door hadn't disturbed them, either.

"Here." He handed her a towel from the bathroom, insisting she needed one after taking her poncho and draping it on the landing railing.

"Thanks." She wiped absently at the long, dark hair lying in thick, sodden hanks against her neck and back. Between her flattened hair and sculpted cheekbones, her dark brown eyes appeared enormous.

"Are you cold?"

"I'm fine." She wiped her face and neck. Rain had soaked the collar of her blouse, and it clung to her skin. "Too excited to be cold. Where do I...?" She held up the towel, which he took from her.

"I have a very sophisticated laundry collection system." He tossed the towel into a half-full wicker laundry basket sitting beside the coffee table.

Cara's laugh caught him off guard. She really was excited.

They stood in the center of the living room facing each other. When she'd first arrived at his doorstep, he'd been watching TV and had promptly turned it off. Letting go of her after their hug—the third one today— hadn't been easy. She'd felt incredible in his arms, soft and yielding where it counted, firm yet pliant where it mattered most.

She was also bursting at the seams and not able to stand in any one place for long. What had put her in this state?

Having finished drying herself, she flitted away from him, unable to contain her nervous energy. Damp footprints appeared on the wood laminate floor in her wake. He'd mop later. Now his entire attention was centered on Cara.

"You'll never guess what happened!" she said.

He didn't even try. "I give up."

"Wait." She spun. "Where are the children?"

"Asleep."

"Already? It's only seven thirty."

"They were pooped. Kimberly nodded off in her high chair. Nathan lasted maybe another fifteen minutes."

"I don't want to wake them." She glanced down the hall.

"We won't. Trust me."

"Okay." She resumed pacing. Josh leaned against the counter to watch her. "Anyway, Dr. Armstrong called me a little bit ago. He's the head of Teddy's school. You met him this afternoon."

"Yeah." Josh recalled a gentle-mannered, middle-aged man with Summer.

"Anyway, he was impressed with you, Wind Walker and Teddy."

"Nice." Josh tried to listen. He was more interested in how to get Cara back in his arms or, at least, to stand in one place long enough for him to drink in the sight of her, slowly and leisurely.

"He's interested in partnering with the sanctuary and had a proposition for me."

Partnership? Proposition? That was enough to bring Josh back to the topic at hand. "What for? What can the sanctuary offer the school?"

"An equine therapy program." Cara's smile was as blinding as it was beautiful.

Josh had never seen her like this before, bursting with energy and brimming with happiness. He doubted anyone else had seen her like this, either. Not for the past couple of years.

It was a potent combination. He didn't care if this Armstrong guy wanted to partner with the sanctuary for the next deep space mission. He'd go along with it just to bask in her smile again.

"Come on." He drew her to the couch and sat her down. "Tell me all about it."

She did, the story pouring from her in a rush.

"He said animal programs have been proven to help individuals with special needs, especially young children. They improve social and communication skills, teach them how to take direction and build confidence. Plus, the physical activity is good exercise. And horseback riding is fun."

"Always the best part."

"Dr. Armstrong also said animal programs can be successful when other types of therapies have failed. I believe it, too. You heard Summer. That first time Teddy met Wind Walker, she thanked you and said how well Teddy would behave the rest of the day."

"I remember."

"Horse therapy programs are some of the most sought-after ones, and there are relatively few in the Phoenix metropolitan area. None to speak of this far northeast. And here's the best part." She twisted sideways on the couch to face Josh. "Parents will pay lots of money to enroll their kids in a qualified, reputable program."

She named an amount, and Josh whistled. "You weren't kidding."

"With income like that, the sanctuary could be completely self-sufficient. Indefinitely. No drain on the ranch whatsoever."

She rested her palm on his thigh, which made concentrating difficult. Josh took a deep breath, focused and recalled something she'd said about qualified, reliable programs.

"Don't take this wrong, but what do you know about teaching children with special needs?"

Cara didn't appear insulted by his question. "Almost none. Which is why I would partner with the learning center. They know very little about horses. We'd combine our different areas of expertise."

Josh jumped to a conclusion, but he felt safe doing so. Most businesses required an initial investment. "How much money, if I can ask, are you required to put up to fund the program?"

"I'll have to provide the safety equipment, harnesses and helmets. The round pen will suffice for now, but we'd eventually need to construct a small riding arena. I was thinking of using the open area behind the horse stable for that and six or eight outdoor stalls to house the program horses. It'll take time. I can't do everything at once."

"What about the institute? Are they contributing?"

"They'll bring in the clients, of course. That's a given. They'll also handle the marketing and secure appropriate licensing and any certifications required. Dr. Armstrong's looking into it this week and will call me. I won't order the equipment until the licenses and certifications are in place."

Josh was glad to see she was proceeding with caution despite her excitement. He would have hated for her to lose the money she'd earned today. But if people did pay as much as this doctor said, the risk wasn't too great.

"If all goes well, I might even be able to draw a salary eventually." Cara sat back. "Not a lot, of course. The sanctuary operates as a nonprofit organization. But something."

"I'm glad for you, Cara." He tucked a lock of her damp hair behind her ear.

"Are you?"

"It's obvious you want this."

"I do. I realized earlier, after Summer gave me the money, that for a long time, the sanctuary was a means to an end for me. I'd needed an outlet for my grief, and it gave me one."

Josh was impressed. "You found a way to cope and have done a lot of good at the same time."

"But I've changed. I'm not sure when. During the adoption event, I guess. Or the last few months. All I know is, I want the sanctuary to be more than a place for abandoned or abused mustangs. With the equine therapy program, I can really make a difference."

"You already do."

"I can make a bigger one, and not just with horses, either." Her eyes shone, pulling Josh further and further into their depths. "I can help children like Teddy. Improve the quality of their lives and those of their families. Only a little, but still."

"Maybe a lot."

"You think?"

"Honey, I think it's an idea that's tailor-made for you."

"With the sanctuary being self-supporting, Dos Estrellas will have a better chance of recovering."

"That's not why you should do it."

"It isn't." Her voice grew stronger. More certain. "I feel like this is what I've been waiting for. I'll get to save and rehabilitate wild mustangs and help children at the same time. I can't imagine anything more rewarding or satisfying."

Her enthusiasm was contagious. He tucked a finger beneath her chin and tipped her face to his. "Finding your passion. It's a wonderful thing."

"What's your passion?"

He considered a moment before answering. "For a long while, I thought it was rodeoing."

"And now?"

"Those two kids sleeping in the other room have become pretty important to me."

"I can tell."

"They're why I want, why I need, this ranch to get back on its feet and operate at a profit. So I can provide a secure home for them and a future."

She searched his face, her expression softening. "You're not at all what I expected."

"What did you expect?"

Her smile returned, more captivating than before. Josh couldn't take his eyes off her mouth, not even if he tried. He wanted to kiss that smile, discover for himself how sweet it tasted. How soft it felt. How easily her lips parted to let him in.

"You're not the same person you were when you first arrived here," she said. "You're different. You don't have a chip on your shoulder anymore."

"Can you blame me? For having a chip? My dad wanted nothing to do with me and Cole."

"It wasn't like that and not entirely his fault."

"If you're referring to my mother, I agree. But she had good reason to be angry at him."

Cara nodded. "I know what it feels like. Manuel cheated on me. Twice, maybe three times."

"That must have hurt."

"It did. In hindsight, the marriage was over and done with, though I refused to admit it."

"Kind of like my parents, when Dad met Raquel. But that didn't make his cheating on Mom right."

"Manuel asked me to forgive him. I did. Unfortunately, as the saying goes, I couldn't forget. I knew the second woman. Not well. She worked with him. How unoriginal is that?"

"It probably happens more than we think," Josh agreed.

"I met her at a company function. Thought she was nice. I was wrong."

"Manuel's the one who was wrong."

"We separated after I found out. I wasn't being nosy. I didn't go snooping through his desk or phone or hack into his email and Facebook accounts. I had no idea. It honestly didn't occur to me. I would never have cheated on him, so why would he cheat on me?"

"We tend to judge others by ourselves."

"I took Javier to Mesa to visit my mother. We no sooner got there than he started running a fever. Within the hour, he was vomiting, and I decided we should go home. Manuel didn't answer his cell phone. I figured he was working and shut it off. He did that sometimes. Imagine my surprise when I discovered him in bed—*our* bed—with his coworker. I turned around and walked out with Javier. We came here. August and Raquel let us stay in the apartment. I don't know what I would have done without them."

"I'm glad they were there for you."

"Me, too. It was important for me to give you and your brothers the ten thousand dollars today. If the equine therapy program takes off, I'm planning on making regular monthly payments."

"I hope it does take off. And not because of the money," he added, wishing she'd move closer.

"This is the first time I've felt optimistic about the future since losing Javier. I didn't think I ever could, or would, again." She met his gaze. "You're the one responsible. You and Wind Walker."

Him and Wind Walker. Not him, the man she'd fallen for like he had her.

"A lot of people are responsible," he said, striving to hide his disappointment. "Summer and Teddy, the student volunteers from the high school—"

"Hush, Josh." Cara placed a finger on his lips and let it linger.

He hesitated. If he talked, she might remove her finger. But then, her lips would be free to…

"I'd like to kiss you, Cara."

She tilted her head at a very appealing angle. "I'd like that, too." He dipped his head, and she stopped him. "The way I feel when I'm with you, it scares me. I've been hurt. Badly hurt. I'm too fragile to suffer another blow."

"You may be stronger than you think."

"Perhaps." She raised her eyes to his while tracing the line of his jaw with her fingertip. "Kissing you also makes me believe in things I thought were impossible."

"It's the same for me."

"That scares me more than the fear of being hurt. You're…you're the kind of guy I could…learn to love."

"You're that kind of woman for me, too."

"Good." Her smile returned and blossomed. "Being in love is much better with two people."

Josh had tried. Really, he had. Holding off any longer was simply impossible. Slipping one arm around Cara's waist and the other beneath her knees, he lifted her up and onto his lap.

"I'm glad we agree," he said and lowered his mouth to hers.

Chapter Eleven

Cara could have kissed Josh forever. He went slow, waiting until she relaxed before increasing the pressure and his demands. She acquiesced, and it wasn't hard at all. Actually, it was the easiest thing she'd done in years.

"You're beautiful," he said, his mouth leaving hers long enough to taste her neck, the base of her throat, the rounded curve of her breast at the opening of her shirt. "I thought that from the first moment I saw you."

Corny, maybe, but she loved hearing it.

"When was that?" Her voice sounded light and playful. Strange. She was so used to hearing the raw edge of grief.

"The first day Cole and I arrived. We got out of the truck. You were in the backyard, standing near the fence, staring at the mountains."

"I don't remember." The day had been a blur. Everyone had been reeling from August's death.

"Your hair was loose." He threaded his fingers through her long locks. "Like now. And blowing in the wind. You didn't turn, though I was sure you must have heard my truck."

"I was so sad. Missing August and hoping he'd finally found peace." The last few months had been an ordeal with August in constant, excruciating pain.

"I figured you were angry at me and Cole for not visiting Dad before he died."

"I was angry, but that's not the reason I didn't turn around."

He stroked her cheek. "Did I ever tell you I find prickly women a turn-on?"

"I'm not prickly!"

"You can't seriously be trying to deny it?"

She laughed with him, only to sober as memories returned. "I saw you for the first time when Raquel called me in from the yard. I'd already made up my mind not to like either you or Cole."

"Which changed the moment we met."

"Ha! You were every bit as aloof and cool as I expected. I didn't like you for a long time."

"Lucky for me, you came to your senses."

"Your children had a lot to do with it."

"So, it's Nathan and Kimberly you really like. Not me."

"I like you, Josh." She cradled his face in her hands. "You know that."

"*Liking* doesn't come close to describing what I feel for you."

She sighed. "This won't be easy. Whatever it is we're doing, wherever it is we're heading."

He searched her face. "Nothing worthwhile is."

"I'm worried."

"About?"

She shifted, wanting to, needing to, get off his lap. If she didn't, she'd lose her courage or he'd distract her.

He helped rather than hindered her. She liked that

about him. That he always allowed her to set the pace and was patient when a lot of men wouldn't be.

"Where do I start?" she said once she'd settled in beside him.

Her shattered heart, not yet healed and very vulnerable? Manuel's betrayal and her trust issues? What the people she cared most about in the world would think of her and Josh as a couple? His children and her fear of loving them only to lose them?

Taking her hand, he brought it to his lips. "Start with whatever worries you the most."

"This." She pointed to him, then herself. "Us. Together."

"Our relationship?"

"Yes. No." How to say it? She supposed the best way was straight to the point. "Intimacy."

"You think it's easy for me because I'm a guy?"

"I haven't dated since my divorce. At all," she emphasized.

"Me, either."

"I've been divorced longer."

Josh's brows rose. "Is that the problem? I haven't been single as long? Because my marriage was over well before—"

"It's not that." Not entirely.

"My friends tell me, don't ever talk about your past relationships with a woman. You'll never say the right thing, and she'll end up mad, hurt or jealous."

Cara raised an eyebrow. "You believe that?"

"Kimberly will be a year old at the end of next month. For the record, she was conceived during a very brief few weeks when Trista and I attempted a Hail Mary reconciliation. That was also the last time I had sex."

Cara hated admitting it, but hearing his confession made her feel better.

"How about some hot chocolate?" He stood.

"What?"

"You're not ready yet, and I refuse to force myself on a woman." He hauled her to her feet. "But make no mistake, I want you, Cara." The hunger in his eyes left no doubt.

"Okay." She was…flattered. Men didn't normally pursue her. At least, they hadn't for a long time. And— this was crazy—she wanted Josh in return.

"All I have is the instant hot chocolate from an envelope," he said from the kitchen.

Whew! They were back to making small talk. "Sounds great."

He'd just put two mugs of water in the microwave when the sound of crying traveled from the bedroom. Nathan, not Kimberly. Cara could easily distinguish between the two. She started to tell Josh, but then hesitated. Enough was enough. She wasn't going to keep avoiding Nathan simply because he reminded her of Javier. He was only a boy, for crying out loud, and, at the moment, distressed.

"Nathan's up. I'll check on him."

Josh glanced at her over his shoulder. "Hey, thanks."

Feeling good, she padded quietly down the hall. Rain still fell in torrents, giving no indication of letting up. A glance at her watch told her it was after eight. Nathan must have woken up, refreshed from his short rest. He might not go back to sleep.

"Shh, *mijo*." She entered the room, speaking softly. A grinning quarter-moon night-light provided enough illumination for Cara to see. "What's wrong?"

In the crib, Kimberly slumbered peacefully, undisturbed by her brother's cries. Nathan, however, was on his hands and knees, ready to straddle the guard and climb out of the youth bed.

Her heart jumped. Javier had done the same thing. That was how he'd escaped his bed on the day of the fall.

"No, no, *mijo*." Rushing forward, she grabbed Nathan by the waist and lifted him into her arms.

He stared at her with wide blue eyes identical to his father's. She was momentarily taken aback. "What a handsome young man you are."

Cara braced herself, anticipating ear-shattering wails. Instead, Nathan hugged her around the neck and laid his head on her shoulder.

"There, there." She patted his back and automatically began swaying.

He was heavy. No, not that heavy. Really, she didn't mind. Without realizing it, she began humming a lullaby. It was the same one she used to sing to Javier.

Cara waited for the onslaught of grief to hit her. The stab of a thousand invisible spears that made her drop to her knees and clutch her middle in agonizing despair.

And waited. A full minute passed with nothing. *Nothing.*

"You doing okay now, *mijo*?"

Tilting her head, she could see Nathan's open eyes. He seemed to be staring into space.

"Tomorrow is my son's birthday. He'd be five." Again, Cara braced for the debilitating grief and, again, it didn't come. "You'd have liked him. Javier was a good boy."

She continued her one-way conversation while Nathan sucked his thumb.

"He's asleep." Josh stood in the darkened doorway, his tall, broad-shouldered silhouette cast in shadows.

"That was quick," she whispered, continuing to sway. "I thought for sure he'd be awake for a while."

"You have the magic touch."

There were so many things she missed about Javier. This was one of them. A sweet, sleeping weight in her arms, little hands clutching her, soft sighs in her ears.

Being needed. It was more than simply satisfying for Cara. It was one of the vital components that made her whole.

No one would ever replace her beloved boy, and she wasn't Nathan's mother. But Cara and Nathan could, every now and then, be there for one another.

"You're a lucky man, Josh."

He stepped into the room and approached her, this larger than life man who had filled the doorway now filling every inch of the space surrounding her.

"I am lucky. For a lot of reasons."

Cara waited for a flood of emotions to drown her and cut off her air supply. Fear. Uncertainty. Inadequacy. Regret. As before, nothing happened.

What had accounted for this change in her? Was it Josh? His children? The adoption fair and the equine therapy program? So much had changed in her life from four months ago. From last month.

She gently laid Nathan down in his bed and covered him with the comforter. She thought of adding a second blanket, then decided against it. His footed flannel pajamas would keep him plenty warm. Besides, Josh would probably check on the kids before going to bed himself.

"The hot chocolate's ready," he said in the same tone she imagined him using when inviting her to undress and slip into bed with him. "We don't want it to get cold."

One last look at the two slumbering children, and Cara left the room, shutting the door partway so the light from the living room wouldn't disturb them.

"I should get going," she said. "It's late."

"Eight forty-five isn't late."

The two mugs of hot chocolate waited for them on the coffee table.

What would Josh do if she casually picked up her mug and relocated it to the dining table? Ultimately, she lowered herself onto the couch and patted the cushion beside her.

Josh wasted no time and sat down. What he didn't do was try to kiss her again. Soon, Cara relaxed.

They sipped hot chocolate and talked children, mustangs, cattle and weather. Long after their mugs were empty, they continued talking. Josh caught her peeking at her watch.

"Leaving?" he asked.

"Thinking about it."

At some point, he'd slung his arm over her shoulder. He now let his hand brush against her hair with the lightest of touches.

"You don't sound convinced."

"It's wet out there." She glanced at the window behind them, though she couldn't see through the closed blinds.

"Is that the only reason?"

"I've enjoyed myself tonight. Probably more than I should."

"I told you, we can go slow."

More like a standstill. "I'm not ready to jump into bed with you."

His fingers continued their featherlight dancing over her hair. "I'm not asking you to. We'll take that step when you're ready."

He spoke confidently, as if her being ready eventually was a given. Cara was less sure.

"There is something I'd like, if you're willing." She was almost afraid to ask.

"Anything."

"Hold me."

"Gladly." He opened his arms.

She didn't ease into them. "Not a hug." This was the potentially awkward part. "I want you to lie next to me. I've missed that lot."

He smiled. "Nothing I'd like more."

Arranging the two throw pillows at one end of the couch, Josh put an arm around Cara's waist. They stretched out side by side, him on the inside, her on the outside, her back to his front.

Spooning. That was what her parents used to call it. Manuel had obliged Cara if she asked, but for him, spooning was always a prelude to sex. What she'd craved was an emotional connection.

Less than a minute spooning with Josh and Cara knew she'd be safe and her wishes respected for as long as she remained with him.

That, more than anything else, was what finally won her over and lowered her defenses.

JOSH USUALLY WOKE up to the sound of Nathan hollering "Daddy" or Kimberly's crying. Neither was the case this morning. A loud banging on the apartment door made both him and Cara jackknife to a sitting position. They stared at each other in shock and confusion.

The banging resumed. "Hey, Josh. You there?" Cole shouted.

Josh scrambled past Cara, inadvertently elbowing her in the side.

"Ow!" She winced and rolled off the couch, then promptly banged into the coffee table.

"You okay?" Josh took hold of her arm and steadied her.

He let go when the doorknob rattled as if being shaken from the outside. "Josh, wake up."

Thank goodness he'd had the foresight to engage the lock the previous night. Cole had no manners and no compunction and thought nothing of barging in on Josh.

"You in there?"

"Yeah, yeah." Josh met Cara's nervous gaze. "Give me a second, will ya?"

"Hurry," Cole insisted. "We got a problem."

"I am hurrying."

"Any reason you can't let me in?"

"I don't want to wake the kids."

It was a minor miracle the pair wasn't up now, what with all the racket.

He and Cara had nothing to feel guilty about. Other than a few heated kisses, they'd passed the night cuddled—make that, crammed—together on the couch. They were without question the most crowded and uncomfortable conditions under which he'd ever slept. Also, the best.

Cara had been pure ecstasy to hold, lush and soft and smelling like heaven. Her curves had tempted him, their allure hard to resist. Josh had refrained—barely—having no intention of ruining a good thing. She'd fallen asleep in his arms and stayed all night. He intended for that to happen again, and it wouldn't if he moved too fast or made a wrong move.

"Go to the bedroom," he told her in a low voice. "I'll get rid of Cole."

She hesitated a moment before doing as he'd instructed and scurried down the hall, hurriedly straightening her rumpled clothes and disheveled hair. There was no need. In his opinion, she'd never looked more beautiful or sexy.

Hearing the bedroom door shut, Josh swung open the front door to find his brother on the other side. "What's up?"

Cole wore a rain poncho over his coat and a fitted plastic cover on his cowboy hat. He had yet to shave and was drenched from head to toe. Water poured off the brim of his hat in steady rivulets, pooling on the landing at his muddied boots. Above them, rain pummeled the stable's tin roof.

"We've got about a dozen cows trapped at the bottom of a flooded ravine in section two." Cole practically shouted to be heard over the rain. He didn't step inside despite his earlier insistence. "If we don't act fast, we'll be lucky to get any of them out alive."

"Let me change."

Cole looked him up and down. "Why? You're already dressed."

"I need a fresh shirt."

"It's pouring rain. No one will notice."

"Give me a second." Josh wasn't leaving without talking to Cara. "I'll be right back." He stared pointedly at Cole's muddy boots. "Stay there. I just mopped and vacuumed yesterday."

"You're Suzy Homemaker now?"

"Shut up."

"Who is she?" Cole called after Josh.

He ground to a halt, adrenaline flooding his system. "What are you talking about?"

"The woman you're hiding."

"You're crazy." He didn't stay, hoping a good defense was a strong offense.

"Take your time," Cole taunted him.

Dammit. Josh had wanted to protect Cara, had *tried* to protect her. Instead, he'd allowed Cole to humiliate her, though it was possible his brother hadn't guessed her identity.

Josh had made every effort to keep his and Cara's growing attraction a secret. He did it for the same reason their night together had been chaste. He refused to ruin a good thing.

Entering the bedroom, he stopped and did a double take. Cara, it seemed, had been busy, tidying up while Nathan and Kimberly slept.

"Cara, I'm sorry," he whispered. "I had no idea Cole was coming. There's an emergency. A dozen cows—"

"I heard."

From her abrupt interruption, he assumed she'd also heard the remark about Josh hiding a woman. "He doesn't know it's you."

"I don't mind."

"Seriously?"

She looked directly at him. "It's all right. We have nothing to be ashamed of."

Catching her by the waist, he planted a light kiss on her cheek. "I'll be right back. I need to tell Cole to go ahead without me. I'll meet up with him later when I figure out what to do with the kids."

He hadn't been thinking earlier, thrown off guard by Cole's unexpected appearance. No way could he leave without making sure the kids were in the care of a competent babysitter.

Calling the woman he'd used yesterday at the adoption fair was a possibility, but Josh hesitated. Despite her congenial manner and good references, he hadn't quite taken to her. Neither had Nathan and Kimberly.

Raquel was his first choice, yet asking her was out of the question. She attended church on Sunday mornings with friends, declaring it her favorite time of the week. More so since his dad had died. She might be willing to babysit once she returned, but that wouldn't be for hours.

"I'll watch them," Cara offered.

"I can't impose."

"You can. I don't mind. That was our deal. You help me with the sanctuary, and I help you with Nathan and Kimberly." She smiled. "Besides, you know how much I like them."

"Only them?"

She'd told him last night, but he wanted to hear her say it again.

"I did spend the night with you."

There was the tiniest hint of flirtation in her answer. It was enough to send his heart into overdrive.

"Thank you. For everything," he added before giving her the kind of good morning kiss he'd planned all along. "When I get back, we'll talk more about the equine therapy program and...other stuff."

"Other stuff?"

"Are you free for dinner tonight?"

Uncertainty flashed in her eyes. He didn't let that deter him. In fourteen years of professional rodeoing, he'd learned to rely on his gut. Right now, it was telling him one thing. Cara Alverez was special. She'd be worth the wait and worth the effort.

"Think about it," he said.

A moment later, after another quick kiss, he left the bedroom. While Cole watched from the open doorway, Josh sat in a dining chair and pulled on his boots, having kicked them off sometime last night after lying down with Cara. He ignored Cara's boots tossed on the floor at the end of the couch and hoped Cole didn't notice them.

Last, he grabbed his canvas duster from where it hung on the back of the door and plucked his hat from the table. His remaining rain gear was in his saddlebags, which were stowed in the tack room along with the rest of his equipment.

Cole continued staring at Josh as they walked briskly down the stairs and through the horse stable, stopping at Wanderer's stall. He didn't ask about the kids or who was with them.

"What are you looking at?" Josh finally demanded, his hand on the latch, his impatience ready to boil over.

"You never changed your shirt."

Josh sent his brother a warning look. "Don't ask me why, because I won't answer."

Cole broke into raucous laughter, startling several of the nearby horses, who huffed and snorted in annoyance.

"It's about damn time, brother. About damn time."

Chapter Twelve

"I wanted to let you know where I was." Cara balanced her cell phone in the crook of her neck while spoon-feeding Kimberly rice cereal and supervising Nathan's breakfast of toaster waffles and fruit.

"I figured it out," Raquel said. "Your Jeep was in the driveway all night."

"It's not what you think."

"I don't think anything." Raquel's voice truly held no censure. "Your business is your business. You aren't a teenager with a curfew, and you certainly don't have to report in to me."

"Nothing happened. I fell asleep on the couch. Josh didn't wake me."

He hadn't woken her, not intentionally. Though every time he moved, her eyes had snapped open and she'd lain there, listening to his breathing and feeling the pressure of his arm circling her middle. Once or twice, she could have sworn he was also awake, but they didn't talk.

Instead, they'd communicated through tender touches and quiet sighs. It was amazing how beautifully their bodies fit together. If that hadn't been the case, they'd have never managed a full night on that uncomfortable couch. Josh was on the tall side, his physique athletic without being gym addict muscled out. It was, she decided, the perfect body to spoon with.

How might it be to spend an entire night with him in a real bed? Did she dare find out?

"Again, you have nothing to explain," Raquel said. "To me or anyone."

"Thank you." Cara heard people talking in the background. Raquel must be walking into the church.

"All I want is for you to be happy. And if Josh is the one who makes you that way, then you have my full support."

"Let's not get ahead of ourselves. We haven't even gone on our first date yet." They would soon. Perhaps as early as tonight.

She used the baby spoon to scrape away cereal dribbling down Kimberly's chin. Like her brother, the little girl wore her pajamas. Unlike her brother, hers were rainbow-striped. Nathan's had cartoon cowboys riding ponies and waving their hats in the air.

"I knew from the moment I met August he was the one I'd been waiting for my whole life."

Raquel was a romantic. The first time Cara had met Josh, she'd been convinced he and his brother cared nothing about Dos Estrellas or their late father, other than what money they could get from the estate. It had taken months for Cara to change her mind about Josh. Hardly the actions of a romantic.

She'd started seeing him in a different light on the day he'd lassoed Wind Walker and returned the escaped mustangs to the sanctuary. The changes continued each time she watched him with his children, showing his—not to sound clichéd—sensitive side. He'd won her over entirely during the exhibition with Teddy and Wind Walker.

Was she wrong? Making a mistake? Doubts crept in, the result of her painful past with Manuel. Maybe, when Josh returned from rescuing the stranded cattle, she'd tell him she needed more time.

Then again, maybe, for once, she should follow her heart and jump in with both feet.

"He's such a fine man." Raquel's remark regarding Josh broke into Cara's thoughts. "A lot like August. He'd have been so proud of Josh."

He *was* a fine man. And a wonderful father. Whatever he lacked in experience, he made up for in heart and effort. And he was so very considerate of her feelings.

Was that enough? Only a man with incredible patience and a huge capacity to love would be right for her. From what she'd seen of Josh, he had those qualities. He was also the father of two young children who required his patience and love. They were his priority, as they should be.

"I finished." Nathan pushed his breakfast plate away and tried to climb down from his booster seat.

The instant Cara lowered him to the floor, Kimberly wanted down from her high chair. Squealing, she slapped the tray, spilling her bottle of apple juice. That triggered a crying fit.

Cara righted the bottle. "Tia Raquel, I have to go."

"Me, too. Service starts in ten minutes." She'd want to find her friends and sit with them.

After clearing the table and washing the dishes, including the mugs from last night's hot chocolate, Cara figured the children could use a bath. Portions of their breakfast had dried to a hard crust on their faces and hands.

She kept them with her, not daring to let them wander. They went to the bedroom, where she selected clean outfits for the day. In the apartment's small bathroom, she turned on the tub's spigots and adjusted the temperature of the water.

To Nathan's delight, she found some bubble bath in the cabinet beneath the sink, a remnant from when she'd lived here, and added it to the running water. He immediately hung over the side of the tub and thrust his hands into the bubbles.

"Careful." Cara reached for him. "Get back."

He did, for two seconds. Long enough for Kimberly to crawl off.

"Come back."

Caring for two children was hard. Cara had her hands full every moment. Literally, had her hands full.

It was overwhelming and challenging, yes, but also exhilarating. She was ready for more. At least, she wanted to be ready for more.

Deciding rambunctious Nathan was probably too much for delicate little Kimberly, Cara chose to bathe them separately. With the water at the right level, not too deep, she sat Kimberly in the safety seat, sticking the suction cups to the tub floor. The baby laughed and kicked her feet, splashing water and launching bubbles into flight.

"Aren't you silly?" Feeling as if she was bathing an octopus rather than a girl, Cara wet a washcloth, added a dab of liquid soap and cleaned Kimberly's crust-covered face.

Nathan wasn't happy about being excluded. He threw

a plastic dinosaur into the water. It landed on Kimberly's foot, and she squealed.

"No, no. Be good."

Nathan tried. His version of being good. Cara no sooner finished washing Kimberly than he was back to shoving his hands in the water. By now, his pajamas were soaked.

Cara released a long breath. Shampooing Kimberly's hair would have to wait. How did Josh manage? He had less experience than she did with children.

Perhaps she'd underestimated him. Recalling their night together and his willingness to respect her wishes, she realized she might have underestimated a lot of things about him.

Lifting Kimberly out of the safety seat, she toweled her dry, put her in a clean diaper and pink T-shirt, then deposited her on the rug for a moment. Freshening the water and adding more bubble bath, she undressed Nathan. He was old enough and big enough that he didn't need a safety seat. The rubber mat would suffice just fine.

He insisted on more toys. Along with the dinosaur, a plastic yellow duck and colorful floating blocks provided handy obstacles around which he could navigate a boat and submarine.

"Let me wash your face, *mijo*."

Kimberly busied herself crawling from one end of the bathroom floor to the other, investigating the vanity cabinet door and the space behind the toilet. Nathan didn't mind the tear-free soap and giggled when Cara tweaked his shiny clean nose.

"This isn't so hard." She'd no sooner spoken the words than Kimberly let loose with a loud cry. Cara twisted sideways. The little girl was trapped behind the laundry hamper. Okay, *trapped* was an exaggeration, but to her very young way of thinking, the hamper held her prisoner.

"I'll get you," Cara said. "Hang on."

Making sure Nathan was fine, Cara moved the hamper aside, freeing Kimberly. The experience had apparently scared the baby, for she wouldn't move and continued crying.

"Now, now," Cara said in a soothing voice and picked her up. "Nothing happened. You're fine."

Kimberly's wails increased. Was she hurt? A quick inspection revealed no obvious injuries. Maybe she was hungry. No, she'd eaten a good breakfast. A wet diaper? Not that, either. Tired? Possibly, but she'd been awake only about an hour after sleeping through the night.

This was perplexing. But weren't babies like that, often crying over nothing? Because they couldn't talk, adults were left with the task of trying to deduce what was wrong.

"Come on, little one." Cara reached for a tissue from the box on the back of the toilet and dabbed at Kimberly's tears.

The tissue fascinated Kimberly and, like that, her crying stopped. She grabbed the tissue with a chubby hand. Cara let her have it.

"Oops. No!"

Big mistake. Kimberly had shoved the tissue in her mouth.

"Give it here." Cara removed the tissue, which resulted in renewed cries. "It's not food."

Thump!

She turned her head, not seeing Nathan. Where was he? A jolt blazed through her. "Oh, God!"

Her realization was followed instantly by his shriek of terror. Nathan had slipped and fallen onto his side in the tub. Impossible! The rubber mat was supposed to prevent accidents.

Cara lunged for the tub. Hitting her knees, she put Kimberly on the floor and hauled Nathan from the tub. His shrieks escalated, and Cara saw the reason at once. He sported a large, angry red welt on his forehead that was already swelling.

"No, no, no!"

This couldn't be happening. Not again. She'd been right there the entire time. Nathan wasn't out of her sight for a moment.

Except, that wasn't true. She'd looked away to help Kimberly.

It had taken Javier a minute to climb the shelving unit in the laundry room and fall, hitting his head and fatally injuring himself.

"Please, not again." Cara squeezed Nathan to her, then released him in order to examine the welt more closely.

He squirmed in protest. "Want down!"

"Let me see, *mijo*." She didn't like the looks of the welt. What to do, what to do?

Wait, where was Kimberly? Cara twisted around, going weak with relief when she spotted the baby once again behind the toilet.

"Think," she told herself. Nathan's wails in her ear didn't help her concentration.

Standing, she retrieved Kimberly with her free arm. Somehow, she managed to wrap Nathan in a towel and carry both children to the kitchen. There, she put Kimberly in her high chair. The baby girl wasn't happy about being confined, but Cara decided the chair was the safest place for her. She needed to focus her attention on Nathan.

Should she call his pediatrician? Did he have one? She inspected the welt again. Had it swollen more? Hard to tell.

She studied his pupils, remembering how often the doctors had done that with Javier. Nathan's appeared normal, but what did she know? She had no medical training.

"Nathan, are you okay? Please, tell me."

He didn't answer, merely stared at her with tears running down his cheeks.

Ice. She should put ice on the welt. Wait, that wasn't enough. She should take him to the medical clinic in town, just to be on the safe side. Were they open Sundays? She didn't know or couldn't remember. Her thoughts were too jumbled.

Raquel would know. She'd taken August to the clinic on several occasions. Locating her cell phone, Cara started to dial, only to disconnect. Raquel was in church, and she'd have her phone shut off.

Another glance at Nathan's welt made Cara's concern shoot through the roof. It was definitely swelling. What if he had a concussion or, worse, a fracture?

"Want down," Nathan insisted.

He was active and alert. That was a good sign.

Josh. Should she call him? Let him know what happened and that she was taking Nathan to the clinic? If it was closed, she'd drive into Rio Verde. All the way to the nearest hospital in Scottsdale if necessary.

"Damn," she muttered when the call went straight to voice mail. He was probably out of range. Reception was iffy on many parts of the ranch. She left a message, but didn't hold much hope he'd get it before she left.

Cara hurriedly finished dressing Nathan, then put him in the crib to keep him contained while she attended Kimberly. He objected fiercely and tried to climb out.

"Stay," she admonished, for all the good it did.

Luckily, the diaper bag was packed and ready to take. Cara grabbed it, the children, their coats, and Josh's truck key and was off.

Barely holding herself together, she loaded the children into the truck. Thankfully, the clinic was just opening when they arrived. Nathan was their first patient for the day, and the nurse practitioner on duty saw him immediately.

"I think he'll be fine," she assured Cara after examining him.

"Does he need a CAT scan?"

The matronly woman in scrubs shook her head. "Let's see how he does. Watch for any symptoms of concussion." She listed them. "If you're the least bit worried, take him to the emergency room. But in my opinion, it's no more than a bump." She touched Cara's arm. "Kids are resilient."

They weren't. They were fragile as fine china. But Cara didn't argue.

In the truck, with everyone loaded and the paperwork in her purse, Cara sat behind the steering wheel. She couldn't bring herself to turn the key in the ignition. Her hands were shaking too badly.

"I hungry," Nathan said from the backseat.

If he wanted to eat, he must be feeling better.

Every ounce of strength Cara possessed instantly

drained from her body, leaving her light-headed and boneless. Resting her forehead on the steering wheel, she cried great racking sobs. She didn't stop until someone knocked on the window. Through the glass, she heard a man's muffled voice asking if she was all right.

She hadn't been all right for over two years. She was a fool to think one night in Josh's arms could heal her.

JOSH PUSHED OPEN the back door and stormed into the kitchen. "Cara! Where are you?" He'd gone to the apartment first and discovered it empty. Fear propelling him, he'd raced to the ranch house. "Cara!"

"In here."

The response came from the family room. Only it wasn't Cara's voice, but Raquel's.

Josh covered the distance in three seconds flat. Raquel sat on the couch with his children, Nathan in her lap, drinking from a sippy cup, and Kimberly beside her, curled in a ball and fast asleep.

"How is he?" Josh headed straight for Nathan, who stopped drinking and raised his arms in a bid for attention.

"Fine," Raquel said, stroking his hair.

"Daddy! I fell."

"I heard, buddy." He lifted Nathan up and held him close, relief coursing through him.

When he'd finally gotten a signal on his phone, the display showed two messages, both from Cara. The first one frantically summarized what had happened and informed that she was taking Nathan to the clinic. The second one let him know Nathan was pronounced okay by the nurse practitioner, and they were headed home.

While all appeared good, the odd quality in Cara's

voice had alarmed Josh. Was she holding back? Waiting to deliver the bad news until he got home?

"Look." Nathan showed Josh his bump and told the story of what happened, much of his baby talk hard to understand.

"That's some goose egg you have." He patted the boy's back.

The bump didn't look too bad to Josh. A little worse, he supposed, than others his son had sustained. Likely there would be a lot more in his future, along with scraped knees, bruised elbows and maybe a broken bone or two.

Nathan hooked an arm around Josh's neck and resumed drinking his juice. Josh relaxed. His kids were safe, and the crisis had passed. Now he could concentrate on Cara.

Come to think of it, where was she? Raquel spoke before he could ask.

"I've been keeping an eye on him. Cara told me what to look for. I haven't noticed any signs of concussion but, to be safe, we have to watch him for the next twenty-four hours."

"Thank you, Raquel."

"You know I'm happy to help." Her expression softened as she gazed fondly at each child. "Cara mentioned the sitter you hired didn't work out."

"She was nice enough, but the kids didn't warm to her. Me, either, for that matter."

"I'd be happy to keep watching them. For as long as you need me."

Josh shook his head. "I can't impose."

"It's my pleasure. They're your father's grandchildren. Taking care of them makes me feel closer to him.

It also gives me something to fill my time. I spend too much of it with only myself for company since August passed."

Josh studied the woman who had shared his father's life and owned his heart, wondering if he'd be able to make the same kind of sacrifices for love his father had. Though, to be fair, his father had been put in a difficult, almost impossible, situation.

The actions of Josh's mother and Raquel's father had affected so many. Did they know or even care?

"Where's Cara?" he asked.

"At the sanctuary."

Josh should have guessed. "Is she all right? Her voice mail message sounded strange."

"Nathan falling, hurting his head…it was hard on her."

"But he's fine."

"She was reminded of Javier."

His birthday! Of course. Josh should have remembered. "She must be a wreck."

Raquel smiled. "Why don't you go see her? I'll take Nathan." She held out her arms as if Josh had already agreed.

"I won't be long." He kissed Nathan's head and passed the boy to Raquel.

"Abuela," Nathan happily said as he plopped onto the couch. "Read Rabbit and Fox."

Grandmother. Josh's brows rose.

Raquel blushed guiltily. "I hope you don't mind."

He discovered he didn't. Not in the least. His kids already had two grandmothers, but, considering the unusual blending of their families, Nathan calling Raquel by *Abuela* seemed to fit right in.

"I promise I won't be long."

"Take your time," she called after him as he headed through the house and out the kitchen door and leaped over the puddles left by the rain.

Cara was in the feeding station, unloading hay. She didn't appear to have heard his approach. No surprise. Rain pelted the metal roof like a thousand hammers. There was less need to supplement the mustangs' feed these days. Forty fewer head made a difference. Besides those adopted out and the one raffled off at the fair, Rusty had taken three in exchange for farrier services and Josh had his two, Wind Walker and Hurry Up.

Soon enough, Cara would have more to take their places. She never turned away a mustang in need. It wasn't in her nature.

He walked through the gate. His movements must have alerted her, for she stopped in the middle of tossing hay into the feeder and turned to stare at him.

Not the welcome he was expecting and far different from their parting this morning. Still, he flashed her a warm smile.

"Hey, honey."

"Hi." She resumed loading hay.

He came up behind her and, slipping an arm around her waist, pulled her against him. He wanted her to know he understood and was there for her. "I'm sorry you had to go through that with Nathan."

She didn't move, every muscle tensing. "Don't."

Don't what? Hold her?

He let his arm drop. "What's wrong?"

"Not now." She walked away, in the direction of the flatbed trailer, which was hooked behind the ranch pickup.

Okay. She was obviously more distraught than he'd first realized. He probably should have started out talking rather than touching. But he'd missed her and been worried.

Following her to the trailer, he grabbed a bale of hay by the twine binding it together and carried the bale to the next feeder. He let go, and the bale dropped heavily to the ground. Three cuts to the twine with his brand-new pocketknife freed the flakes.

He loaded the feeder. Several minutes passed in silence with neither him nor Cara talking.

Finally she paused, hands on her hips. "What are you doing?"

"Helping you."

"Not that."

He also paused. "I'm waiting for you to tell me what's wrong."

"Nothing." She loaded more hay.

"Cara, Nathan's fine. The bump is no big deal."

She froze and gaped at him. "No big deal? I was scared out of my mind. He could have died."

"Don't take this wrong—I'm not minimizing your feelings—but he slipped in the tub and hurt his head. That's all."

"That's all! Javier died from a fall."

"Six feet. He fell six feet onto bare concrete. Nathan slipped in the tub."

"You *are* minimizing my feelings."

Josh advanced. At her frown, he halted. Three feet separated them. "I'm simply trying to put things into perspective."

"Now I'm insulted."

"Then help me understand."

Cara's chin trembled making it hard for her to speak. "I lost control."

He was confused. "Are you kidding? You were the epitome of control and took Nathan to the clinic. Handled the situation like a pro."

"I stayed calm when Javier fell. I told Manuel to call 9-1-1 and administered first aid. It didn't make a difference. He died anyway." Tears welled in her eyes. "Afterward, in the hospital, I broke down. I did today, too, and before, when Nathan fell off the gate. I can't help myself."

He hesitated, then tried a different approach. "I know today is Javier's birthday—"

"You think that's what this is about? I'm upset because I'm having a bad day?"

"No. Not exactly."

She drew back. "Your son fell and hit his head. It might have been life-threatening."

"The nurse said he was fine. Raquel is with him now, watching him like a hawk."

"Admit it. You think I'm overreacting."

Josh wanted to be patient and understanding. It was starting to get difficult, especially since she seemed intent on lashing out at him. "What I think is that Nathan's fall was a painful reminder of Javier's, made worse by it happening on Javier's birthday. You're distraught, and you have every reason to be."

In a flash, her eyes turned from sad to angry. "You're missing the whole point."

"Enlighten me. Please."

Some of her bluster diminished, and her shoulders sagged. Josh was tempted to go to her. He didn't, figuring she wouldn't be any more receptive to his touch than she'd been when he'd first arrived.

She began haltingly. "We made a mistake. I made a mistake. This is wrong. Us. I'm not ready for a relationship."

"You came to this conclusion because of Nathan's fall?"

"Yes."

For the first time since he'd arrived at the feeding station, Josh was worried. "I'm not sure what one has to do with the other."

"I told you before. You have children. You're a package deal. There is no dating you without your children becoming a part of my life."

"Don't you like them?"

"If I let myself, I could love them."

"How is that bad?" He was hoping she felt the same about him.

"They're babies. They need constant, reliable supervision. I'm not that person."

"Javier's death wasn't your fault, and neither was Nathan's fall."

She shook her head. "I should have checked on him. I wanted to. Instead, I listened to Manuel."

"Which sounds to me like Javier's fall was his fault, not yours. He put arguing with you ahead of his son's welfare."

"Letting him take the blame is the coward's way out. I was Javier's mother," she insisted. "It was my job to protect him. Something kept telling me to check on him, and I didn't. That's why he fell."

"It was a freak accident."

"And what if it happens again? It almost did today.

I took my eyes off Nathan for a minute. A minute! The next time could be much worse."

"Kids constantly have mishaps."

"I'm not strong enough." She looked away.

"So, you're content to remain alone the rest of your life, and miss out on being in a happy relationship and being a mother, because you're afraid something *might* happen?"

"Don't belittle me."

"I'm hardly doing that." He paused. "But if everyone had that same attitude, we'd be living in a world full of miserable people."

"You haven't lost one of your children."

"No, you're right." He didn't like the tone creeping into his voice, but was unable to stop it. "I lost a dad. Twice. When I was seven and again four months ago. I lost my wife to addiction. Spent a lot of time beating myself up over that. I lost my kids twice when she ran off with them." Josh attempted to lower his rising voice. "I don't want to sound mean, but we've all experienced our share of heartache. It's part of life. It's also not a reason to give up on finding that someone special and falling in love."

"You're stronger than me. Or, you're further along in the healing process."

"It's not that. I had to pull myself together for Nathan's and Kimberly's sakes."

"I don't have anyone needing me."

Wow, that hurt. "I guess I know where I stand."

"Josh." She rubbed her forehead. "I'm sorry."

He stepped forward. "You have someone who cares about you. Who wants you. Who'd like to see how deep his feelings for you go. Who's standing right here."

She began to cry, crumpling in front of his eyes. "I can't."

Can't? Won't? Was there any difference? She was scared. All right. But if his willingness to be her partner in their journey together wasn't enough, he didn't know what else he could do or what more he could offer her.

"I won't beg, Cara, or pressure you. I want to be with you like you can't imagine, but only if you want that, too."

"I do, I think. But I'm not ready."

"How long until you are?"

"It doesn't work that way."

Her words struck a familiar chord with Josh. "The counselor at Trista's rehab center told me the person has to want to get better."

"I'm not an addict." She wiped at her cheeks with the back of her hand.

"No. But the recovery process for grief isn't much different. And until you're ready to embrace it, we don't stand a chance."

She stiffened. "I'm not sure we ever had one."

He chuckled mirthlessly. "My mistake."

She'd given up without ever trying. The realization left Josh numb—for a moment—until anger rushed in to take its place.

"Is that what you want?" he demanded. "For this to be done with before it began?"

She swallowed. "I don't see another way."

Well, there was no reason to stay. Josh had opened himself to Cara and she'd kicked him to the curb.

Probably better now than later, when the hurt would be worse and the wounds deeper. This way, he'd get over her in a few days or a few weeks.

Right. Who was he kidding? Cara had become a part of him. He wouldn't get over her anytime soon, if at all.

The short walk back to his truck was the hardest one he'd ever made. Even so, he didn't turn around and go back to her.

Chapter Thirteen

Six people from Teddy's learning center were at Dos Estrellas, including Summer and Teddy. Dr. Franklin Armstrong, the head of the center, had brought one of his colleagues plus another patient, a little girl—or, did they call them students?—and the girl's mother.

Cara walked among the group, trying to make sense of everything they said. There was so much to learn. Terms, designations, phrases, acronyms, slang. Some of it sounded like a foreign language to her. The reading material Dr. Armstrong had given her remained on her bedside table, barely touched.

It wasn't just a lack of time, though she had been busy these past ten days since the adoption fair. Rather, she'd found it impossible to concentrate.

The argument with Josh had taken a toll on Cara, draining her emotionally and physically. She felt flushed much of the time, yet she wasn't running a fever. Food tasted bland, and she'd taken to pushing her plate away, half of her meal eaten.

After Javier died, the mustang sanctuary had become her refuge. Now it was a constant reminder of Josh, the time they'd spent together and the wonderful moments they'd shared. He'd taught her—allowed her—to put her regrets in the past and look forward to the future.

No more. Sadly, she had new regrets to replace the old ones.

Raquel had noticed Cara's funk and constantly fussed over her. She refused to answer the other woman's questions, well intended though they were. Cara went out of her way to avoid Josh, but it wasn't necessary. Lately he'd kept to himself, taking extra effort not to cross her path.

At his request, Raquel babysat the children in the apartment rather than the house, at least while Cara was there. The excuse given was the new puppy, which Josh and the kids had picked up on Wednesday from Rusty Collins. Cara didn't question the new arrangement. Seeing the children, missing them, was almost as painful as seeing and missing Josh.

She'd hoped throwing herself into the equine therapy program would lift her spirits. It hadn't happened yet. Maybe soon. This meeting and demonstration was their first step forward. The goal was to open early enrollment by the first of May and begin classes in May.

She sighed, not realizing how loudly until all the adults looked at her. The two children weren't interested. They paid attention only to each other, though they didn't interact.

"Sorry," Cara said.

Dr. Armstrong smiled. "As I was saying, you'll have plenty of professional help. One trained teacher for every child."

That was right. She'd asked about assistance, picturing a group of children with special needs riding around the arena with no one except herself in charge.

"And an administrator will also be here for every session," Dr. Armstrong's colleague added.

Cara was giving the group a tour of the facilities, including the round pen and horse stable. She'd also introduced them to three rehabilitated mustangs hand-picked for the program. Last on the tour was the make-shift riding arena constructed with Violet and Cole's help. Josh had stayed away.

She didn't care. When more funds rolled in, if they did, Cara would expand the sanctuary and build a permanent riding arena as planned.

If. The biggest two-letter word in the English language.

She sneaked another peek at the children. They were the future of the program, the key to its success.

"Ride, ride." The girl tugged on her mother's coat sleeve.

"Soon, Lexie."

She was a bit older than Teddy and not as severely autistic. Cara should know the term, something about a spectrum. Would have known the term if she'd done her reading.

Summer smiled fondly at Lexie and patted her head. Apparently, the girl didn't mind being touched. Another difference between her and Teddy. "Don't worry. Cara has a special horse for you to ride."

Teddy walked beside Summer and appeared to be sulking. Cara couldn't be sure, though. He probably wanted to ride Wind Walker. That wouldn't be happening. The stallion had made great progress, but was hardly a child's mount. And, besides, Wind Walker and Hurry Up belonged to Josh, who was under no obligation to lend either of them to the therapy program.

It was for the best. The last thing Cara wanted was to be beholden to him, even for a good reason.

Earlier today, she'd readied an old gelding for Lexie, grooming him for a full hour. The saddle somewhat hid his deep swaybacked and bony frame. Not that it mattered. For the needs of the equine therapy program, a docile and trustworthy personality far outweighed good looks, and this horse was a bundle of love.

Cara had tied him to the railing inside the makeshift arena. "Here's Astro," she said by way of introduction.

After putting a helmet on the little girl, Cara lifted her onto the saddle and buckled the harness, then led Astro in circles and figure eights. The horse performed beautifully—slow, steady and calm.

Like Teddy had with Wind Walker, Lexie responded well to Astro. Wearing a huge grin, she patted his neck and repeated his name over and over. Dr. Armstrong and his colleague were delighted with both the horse and Lexie's interaction. Her mother was thrilled.

"Very promising," Dr. Armstrong announced when Cara met everyone at the gate. "I'm impressed."

Summer beamed. Cara should have been over the moon. This was what she'd wanted, what she'd prayed for. The sanctuary would become self-sufficient. She'd be able to continue her work and provide a home for more mustangs.

Instead, she felt hollow. Had things gone differently, Josh would have been here with her, joining in the celebration.

"I'm still a little concerned about the potential for injury." Cara had brought the subject up before. She'd yet to get Nathan's fall out of her head; though, as Josh had predicted, the boy had made a full recovery.

Dr. Franklin nodded. "We, of course, will carry a liability insurance policy."

"It's not that."

"What, then?" Dr. Franklin asked.

"I wouldn't want any of the children to get hurt."

"Rest assured, we'll take every precaution. Have a safety protocol in place."

"Accidents happen."

Lexie's mother's cleared her throat, contributing for the first time to the conversation. "We have to weigh the benefits against the potential risks. I can see there's little chance of anything going wrong. And look how happy my daughter is."

It was true. The girl radiated joy.

The meeting finished up a short time later. Summer asked if it was all right for Teddy to visit Wind Walker in his stall. Cara couldn't refuse her friend or the look of longing on Teddy's face. The moment they arrived, the stallion hung his big head over the stall door and reveled in the attention.

There really was something to be said about the positive impact animals had on all people.

"What the heck is wrong with you?" Summer demanded.

"I beg your pardon?"

"I've been talking for the last three minutes, and you haven't heard a single word."

Cara's cheeks warmed. "I've got a lot on my mind. The meeting was—"

"Nonsense."

"It isn't."

"When are you going to tell me what happened between you and Josh? I've been waiting all week."

"Nothing happened."

"Right. Up until the adoption fair, he was all you talked about. You haven't mentioned him once since then."

Cara resisted at first, but Summer was relentless. Finally, Cara broke down. Starting with the night she spent in the apartment with Josh, she relayed the entire story.

"You're nuts," Summer said when Cara was done.

"Thanks for the support."

"Come on. Nathan had a tumble. If I freaked out every time Teddy fell, I'd be a basket case. He has no coordination."

Cara didn't answer.

"Do you think you might have overreacted a tiny smidge?"

"Fine. I did. But my son died from a fall."

"I get that, sweetie. I do. I'm not being critical, truly. Getting upset, flashing back to Javier, is completely normal. But to end things with Josh? You said yourself, he was very understanding."

"Yes. Very." He hadn't done anything wrong. Cara had come to that conclusion several restless nights ago.

"Come on," Summer coaxed. "We've been through plenty of counseling and support group sessions."

Cara's defenses started to rise. "Meaning what?"

Summer planted her hands on her hips in a not-so-subtle gesture. She was growing irritated. "Is there another reason you don't want to get involved with Josh besides the fact that he has children who might get into a scrape or two now and again?"

"You're reaching."

"And you're being intentionally obtuse."

Cara knew what her friend was talking about, though she hated admitting it. "Manuel cheated on me, and I'm afraid it will happen again."

Was it possible? Could she be using Javier's death and Nathan's falls as excuses not to get involved with Josh when the real reason was Manuel and how much he'd hurt her?

Dammit. She was an even bigger mess than she'd thought.

"I was genuinely frightened the day Nathan got hurt."

"I'm sure you were," Summer said. "That day. But once you knew he was fine, weren't you relieved?"

"I was. For a while. Then I started thinking."

"About?"

As she spoke, her voice grew hoarse. "If Josh and I were to become involved, I'd be vulnerable again."

"I find your choice of words interesting. Just what do you think you're vulnerable to?"

"Panicking if Nathan or Kimberly gets hurt."

Summer studied Cara with interest. "You didn't panic when Lexie rode Astro earlier. She might have fallen."

"Because it was important that everything went well today."

"Exactly. You were motivated. Aren't you motivated to be with Josh?"

Cara swallowed. It was surprisingly difficult. Her throat had gone completely dry. "It's scary."

"Josh isn't Manuel. He didn't cheat on his ex-wife despite all the terrible things she did to him."

"I know."

"You can't have one without the other," Summer said

gently. "Falling in love is opening yourself to the other person."

"I'm not in love," Cara insisted.

"Are you sure? Because if you're not, I might go after Josh myself."

"You'd do that?"

"Why not? He's a great guy. Good-looking. Employed. A family man with two of the cutest kids on the planet. Exactly the kind of husband material I've been looking for."

"Are you serious?"

Summer laughed. "You should see the look on your face. It's priceless."

Cara glanced away. "Manuel betrayed me. That's not easy to deal with."

"And Hal walked out on me because our son is autistic. You don't have the market cornered on feeling betrayed."

Cara was immediately chagrined. "I'm sorry. That was thoughtless of me."

"You have no idea what I'd give for a chance with a guy like Josh." The laughter left Summer's eyes, and she became teary eyed. "You're a fool to let him go."

Cara put an arm around her friend.

Summer sniffed. "I'm the one who should be comforting you."

"Even if I wanted a second chance with Josh, I don't think he'd give me one." She might not deserve one after the horrible way she'd treated him.

"You don't know if you don't try." Summer smiled through her tears. "And I'll hate you if you don't."

Cara didn't answer. She couldn't.

"Cara!" Summer exclaimed. "Do you want to be lonely your whole life?"

"No. But I'm not like that. Impulsive."

"Oh, sweetie. What if, just this once, you were?"

Cara went over to Wind Walker and patted his head. The horse nuzzled her arm. Feeling a soft sensation on her other arm, she turned.

Teddy's hand rested slightly above her wrist.

Summer stared in astonishment. "He's touching you."

Teddy spoke. "Jah, Jah."

Josh. Of course. It seemed everyone, including Teddy, was championing him.

Summer laughed. "Who are you to argue with an eight-year-old?"

CARA SPENT FOUR full days diligently not thinking about her conversation with Summer. Her friend was wrong. Josh didn't want to get back together and had clearly moved on. Otherwise he'd approach her, right? Make an effort. Break the ice.

Except why would he? She was the one who'd insisted on ending their fledgling romance. The one who'd gotten cold feet.

"Stupid, stupid, stupid," she said, unsure if she was summing up her actions or calling herself a name. Both, perhaps.

At least she'd stopped ducking around corners every time Josh came within glimpsing distance. And her appetite had returned. Somewhat. Enough that Raquel no longer pestered her. Cara almost missed the constant reminder.

"Time heals all wounds," she said, searching her jacket pocket for keys and making her way to her Jeep.

Did it? Then why wasn't she healed? For a while, she'd thought it possible. When she'd spent the night wrapped in Josh's arms and they'd shared their feelings as comfortably as any established couple.

Then she'd gone and messed it all up.

If she believed that, it stood to reason she must also believe she and Josh had something worthwhile. Something too precious to lose.

"Stupid!"

Which was worse? Ending things with Josh, or not going after him as Summer had suggested?

Cara was tired of the endless questions and the endless circles her mind kept running in. Either she spoke to Josh and tested the waters or she forgot about him entirely.

Starting the engine, she shoved the Jeep into first gear and accelerated. Rather than ride by horseback to the far east corner of the mustang sanctuary, she'd driven. Yesterday, she'd returned the mare and foal to this section, where she pastured pregnant mares and those with foals. It was Cara's belief horses thrived better when kept with others, similar to how they once existed in the wild.

The drive back to the ranch passed quickly, the Jeep bouncing and bumping over deep ruts carved in the dirt road after the recent rains. Weeds and other low-growing vegetation had sprouted seemingly overnight and lined both sides of the road. Soon they'd be knee-high.

Entering the ranch by the back way, she headed straight to the horse stable and parked in her usual spot next to the supply shed.

Another Sunday afternoon. Two weeks since Nathan's fall and Cara's emotional crash and burn. And like most Sundays at the ranch, a lazy atmosphere prevailed. Family and workers were resting, pursuing recreational pastimes, off visiting friends or relatives or running errands. Cara alone worked.

She no sooner stepped out of the Jeep than her gaze traveled to the round pen as if pulled by a strong magnet. Josh was there. She spotted his tall frame and familiar cowboy hat through the railings. Hurry Up was in the pen with him and so were the children. She knew that because she could hear Nathan's gleeful chatter.

Go. That was her first inclination, and it was a powerful one. Cara didn't, however. She stayed, resisting the pull for as long as possible. Eventually she strolled toward the pen, her feet deciding for her.

"Come on, buddy," Josh said. "Cooperate, will you?"

He'd put Nathan in the saddle atop Hurry Up. As always, the small horse stood quiet. Nathan was the one moving. He wiggled and fidgeted and complained.

"I wanna ride."

"You will. As soon as you let me take a picture of you and your sister." Josh stood beside the small horse, Kimberly in one arm and his phone in the other hand. At his feet, the puppy dug in the dirt, then yipped and shot sideways, stumbling over its own front feet. "Come on, Nathan. I promised your mother I'd send her some pictures of you and your sister."

With everything his ex-wife had done, and done to him, Josh continued to send her pictures of the children. There were plenty who wouldn't be so kind and considerate. Plenty who wouldn't recognize how a simple picture could provide enough inspiration and hope to get a person through the day.

Finally, Nathan sat still long enough for Josh to place Kimberly in front of him in the saddle. Retrieving the puppy, he deposited it in Kimberly's arms. At once, it licked her face. She burst into baby laughter.

"One, two, three, smile." Josh took a step back and held up the phone, snapping several more shots.

By now, Cara was close enough to see the big grins the children wore. The pictures would be adorable. What Cara wouldn't give for a copy.

Josh, or perhaps Raquel, had dressed the children for the pictures. Kimberly wore overalls, and Nathan jeans, boots and a child-size cowboy hat. A string under his chin held the hat in place. He looked like a miniature version of his father.

Cara had done that with Javier, dressed him in cowboy clothes.

She stopped in front of the railing, waiting for the grief and the guilt to assail her as it always did. The emotions came...then went. Not in a rush, but rather like a soft breeze disappearing over the next rise.

They'd return, she was sure of it. But something told her each time would be less harsh until the memories of Javier became something she cherished. Not painful reminders. Wouldn't that be wonderful?

"Ride, Daddy, please." Nathan swung his feet in an entirely ineffectual attempt to get the horse moving.

"One second." Josh removed the puppy from Kimberly's grasp and set it on the ground. Her cry of protest dissolved into a whimper of complaint.

Nap time was Cara's first thought. Kimberly always whimpered like that when she was tired.

"Hold on to your sister," Josh said. Only when Nathan had a firm grip on Kimberly did he cluck to the horse. They started slow and went no faster, the puppy rollicking behind them.

With a less dependable horse and someone less attentive in charge, there might have been cause for concern. Not with Hurry Up and Josh.

He didn't see her until the end of their first circuit. Their gazes locked, and he drew up short. Hurry Up automatically stopped. The puppy did, too. Finding something interesting, he began digging in the dirt.

"Hi." It was Cara who spoke first.

Nathan, not Josh, answered her. "Cara!" He raised his arms above his head, fingers splayed. "We riding Hurry Up."

"I see. But you'd better hold on to your sister so she doesn't fall."

The boy obediently hugged Kimberly and squeezed. She squealed in protest, making an unhappy face.

Josh had yet to say a single word. She supposed her unexpected appearance had taken him by surprise.

"I got a puppy," Nathan gushed.

"I see." Her knees weakened, and she grabbed the top railing with both hands to steady herself. "What's his name?"

"Trouble."

"Cute. Did your dad name him after you?"

Nathan giggled.

Wait. Was that a twinkle in Josh's eyes?

Finally he spoke. "What's up?"

She considered his tone, deciding it was cautiously friendly. Better than cool and distant.

"Want me to take a picture of the three of you?"

"That's all right. I'm sending these to Trista. She probably wouldn't appreciate me being included."

His tone contained the barest trace of humor.

"For you," Cara clarified. "Don't you want a copy for yourself?"

His brows rose. After a pause, he activated his phone's camera and passed it to her through the railing.

A minute later, six new pictures were saved to his phone. Josh's features relaxed as he viewed the images, swiping his finger across the display screen.

"Thanks." He pocketed the phone, not offering to take one of her and the children.

What did she expect?

"Daddy, wanna ride."

"Don't let me keep you," Josh said. He made three more circuits before Cara turned and walked away. *Stupid, stupid, stupid.* He must think she was an idiot.

"Wait."

She stopped but didn't turn around.

This was no game. She needed to be 100 percent certain he wanted to give them another shot and to say as much out loud.

A lot was at stake. She'd realized that seeing the pictures on his phone. The longing to be included in those shots was a physical ache, almost as intense as the pain she'd endured when Javier died.

Why not? Both were terrible losses.

"If you're free later…" Josh let the sentence drop.

Cara swallowed. She needed more from him, not just an inquiry about whether she happened to be free.

"What, Josh?"

"We could talk."

"About?"

"I made a mistake. I should have been more patient with you." He cleared his throat. "You made a mistake, too. You should have admitted your fears, talked to me like a grown-up. Instead, you lashed out at me."

That made her turn around. At the sight of his smiling face, her annoyance vanished.

"Come with me," he said. "Up to the apartment. It's past time for the kids' naps. I'll put them to bed."

"And then?"

"We have that talk."

She still wasn't sure.

"Cara!" Nathan started kicking his feet again. "Read Rabbit and Fox."

"Okay." She walked to the gate and unlocked it.

Josh didn't take his eyes off her. "You accept his offer, but not mine?"

"He made a better one."

"Bested by a two-year-old." Josh chuckled and led Hurry Up through the gate. "Come on. Help me unsaddle."

"No, let me take Kimberly to the apartment." Cara lifted the little girl by the waist. "She's tired."

Nathan protested. "Me, too. Take me."

"Sorry, buddy." Josh patted his son's leg. "She can only manage one of you at a time."

"Nooooo!"

"It's all right," Cara insisted.

"Are you sure?" Josh seemed to be asking her something other than whether she was willing to take Nathan.

"Yes." She was. Very sure. "Come on, *mijo*." To Josh, she said, "See you shortly."

Kimberly was asleep by the time Cara opened the

door. After changing both children, she laid Kimberly down in her crib and covered her with a blanket. In the living room, she sat on the couch, Nathan cuddled by her side, his favorite book open on her lap.

They weren't halfway through the book when he nodded off. Cara had just put him to bed and Josh returned. A thrill wound through her at the sound of his steps crossing to the kitchen. Closing the bedroom door behind her, she made her way to him. He was fixing hot chocolate. Without a word, she sat at the dining table.

He placed the mug in front of her. "Kids asleep?"

"Out like lights."

"Good." He lowered himself into the chair beside her. "You first."

"Me?" She stared at him over the rim of her mug.

"You have more to say."

Perhaps she did. "You'd think with all the counseling I've had, I'd be better at understanding myself and communicating my feelings."

"It's not always easy."

"No. But you're an easy guy to talk to. That's something I've always liked about you and found…attractive."

"And here I thought it was my good looks."

"There is that." His smile encouraged her to continue. "I told you once before, I'm broken, and it's going to take time before I'm fixed, if ever." She held up a hand when he would have replied, afraid she might lose her nerve. "The difference between now and before is that I want to be fixed. I want to feel happiness bubbling up inside me every time we kiss and not think it's a betrayal of Javier."

"You deserve to be happy again, Cara."

"I don't know if *deserve* is the right word, but I'd

like to be happy again. I'll always have regrets, and I'll always have bad days. They don't need to run one into the other anymore."

"You also don't have to face them alone."

"I do have my family."

"I was referring to me."

Her heart beat faster. "I was wrong, thinking I needed to push people away. Being with you, with Nathan and Kimberly, has made me stronger. Not weaker."

"I'm glad to hear you say that, because my intentions are to be with you a lot."

"Are you sure?"

"Very." He reached for her hand.

She brought it to her face and pressed his knuckles to her cheek, a gentle sensation washing over her. "You didn't see Raquel and your father together. Trust me when I tell you, what they had was special."

"What we have is special, too."

She happened to agree.

Returning their linked hands to the table, she said, "We're exclusive."

"Goes without saying."

"This isn't casual, either. We date for the long haul, with the intention of seeing where this can lead."

He grinned at her. "Ground rules."

She liked the way his eyes softened. "Too much?"

"I wouldn't have it any other way." He tugged on her hand, pulling her toward him. "Are there more, or can I kiss you now?"

"Much as I adore the children, we have a date night once a week—"

"Shut up." He wrapped a strong hand around her neck and drew her to him.

Their lips met. The kiss was incredible, but then, weren't they always? She'd thought at first it was him and his skill. She knew now it was the two of them together and the wonderful combination of their hearts meeting and joining.

It was too soon to tell for sure, but Cara thought the wild emotion sailing through her just might be love. Of the variety that lasted a lifetime. The idea no longer scared her. Instead, she couldn't wait to see what tomorrow brought. Heck, she couldn't wait for the next few minutes.

As the kiss continued, she felt the shattered pieces of her life mending, and her difficult past give way to a bright new future.

Epilogue

One month later

"Congratulations." Josh shook Gabe's hand. "Best of luck to you, man. You got yourself a good one."

His brother startled him by pulling him into a back-slapping hug. In the five months since he'd returned to Mustang Valley and Dos Estrellas, this was their first. Things had obviously changed.

He needed only to look at Cara to realize that. She sat on the couch with Kimberly between her legs, helping the little girl "walk" as she held on to the edge of the coffee table. Nathan, on the move as usual, ran in circles around the room, tapping the legs of guests in his own version of tag. Cara watched him with a smile on her face.

Josh hated leaving the task of minding the kids to her, but they adored her and chose her company over his whenever they were all together. He didn't blame them. He enjoyed her company, too, especially when they were alone.

"We set a date." Reese appeared beside Gabe and took his arm. "November fifteenth."

Gabe had made their engagement official with a proposal two weeks ago. Raquel was beyond excited and had immediately insisted on throwing a fiesta to celebrate. Between the two families and all their friends, the house was packed. She'd spent three full days preparing the food.

Reese's father had insisted on supplying the beverages. He sat in a leather chair by the side table, enjoying the attention and looking better than he had in weeks.

The one person not appearing to enjoy himself was Cole. He stood in a corner, nursing a glass of champagne and talking hardly at all. Josh didn't know what was bothering his brother. Maybe he was missing the rodeo circuit and wanted to go home. Josh made a mental note to spend some time with Cole and get to the bottom of his recent discontent.

"Interesting day for a wedding. The fifteenth," Josh said and exchanged glances with Gabe. It was the day they'd had the reading of his late father's will, when Reese showed up at the ranch and announced she was the trustee for the estate.

Gabe shrugged. "The calves should be born by then."

Reese laughed brightly and gave him a playful swat. "Leave it to him to pick a day that coincides with ranch business."

Nathan squealed. Typical for him, he'd tripped and face-planted on the living room floor.

"Be right back." Josh reached his son one second ahead of Cara. He lifted Nathan and set him on his feet. "Be careful, buddy."

"Sorry." Cara held Kimberly, who wore a frilly dress that she and Raquel had bought specifically for the party. "I lost track of him for a second."

The noticeable lack of panic in her face was accompanied by no trace of it in her voice. Josh relaxed. She'd come a long way this past month. *They'd* come a long way.

Her request, and Josh's promise, to go slow had quickly fallen by the wayside. Whenever they weren't working, they were together. As of last week, Cara had started spending nights with him. Josh hadn't known it could be so incredible with a woman or so satisfying. The passion he'd seen in Cara and hoped to unlock was more exciting than he'd imagined.

He had no intentions of ever letting this woman go and had told her so their first night in his bed. She'd answered the same, making him feel like the luckiest guy in the world.

"Maybe we should take the kids outside for a bit," he said. "Let Nathan blow off some steam."

"Good idea."

Josh had ulterior motives. He'd been wanting to get Cara alone from the start of the party, when he'd first spotted her in that snug-fitting dress and high heels. Quite a change from her usual jeans and boots.

Instead of the backyard, they ambled out front to the courtyard. The weather was perfect, a glorious Arizona spring day. Josh was surprised more people weren't sitting on the twin benches, enjoying the sunshine. Then again, he had Cara to himself. Well, almost.

While Nathan darted from one end of the courtyard to the other, Cara held Kimberly's hand. The girl stood at her side, babbling and pointing at her brother.

"This is nice," Cara said.

Josh put an arm around her waist. It was too soon to talk about their own engagement party, but he thought it might be possible one day in the not-too-distant future. There were still decisions to be made and issues to resolve.

The spring calf sale hadn't brought in as much money as they'd hoped, but the ranch finances were in okay shape for the next couple of months. Trista was doing well at the halfway home, and Josh would soon be taking the kids to see her as promised. He wondered how that would go. Nathan hadn't asked about his mother for weeks.

Whatever problems they faced, he was confident he and Cara had what it took to see them through. They'd both weathered marital blows and were committed to putting everything necessary into their relationship.

"Josh!" Cara jerked. "Look."

For a moment, he shot back to the day Nathan had fallen in the round pen and cut his forehead. The tension coursing through Cara transmitted to him like an electrical current.

"What?" He glanced around. Nathan played happily by the rock garden. "He's fine."

"No, silly. Kimberly."

Josh looked down…and watched his daughter take her first solo steps, tottering unsteadily toward her brother.

"She's walking," Cara exclaimed.

With each step, Kimberly gained confidence. She'd be running soon. In a matter of days.

"Well, I'll be." He held Cara tighter and kissed the top of her head.

He felt a lot like his little daughter. He and Cara might have started off wobbly, but they were strong now, and growing stronger by the day. It gave Josh a sense of contentment to think his father would approve of them.

"I love you, Cara."

She peered at him, emotion glinting in her eyes. "I love you, too."

They stood for some time, gazing at each other and the distant pasturelands and hills rising in the distance. Josh didn't see just the ranch and the hard work that lay ahead. He saw the future, with the woman who meant the world to him and the children they would raise.

The next generation of Dempseys. It wasn't only his late father's wish. Somewhere along the way, it had become Josh's, too.

* * * * *

Watch for the next book in Cathy McDavid's
MUSTANG VALLEY *miniseries,*
HAVING THE RANCHER'S BABY,
coming June 2016,
only from
Harlequin American Romance!

MY FUNNY VALENTINE

Debbie Macomber

One

Dianne Williams had the scenario all worked out. She'd be pushing her grocery cart down the aisle of the local grocery store and gazing over the frozen-food section when a tall, dark, handsome man would casually stroll up to her and with a brilliant smile say, "Those low-cal dinners couldn't possibly be for you."

She'd turn to him and suddenly the air would fill with the sounds of a Rimsky-Korsakov symphony, or bells would chime gently in the distance—Dianne didn't have that part completely figured out yet—and in that instant she would know deep in her heart that this was the man she was meant to spend the rest of her life with.

All right, Dianne was willing to admit, the scenario was childish and silly, the kind of fantasy only a teenage girl should dream up. But reentering the dating scene after umpteen years of married life created problems Dianne didn't even want to consider.

Three years earlier, Dianne's husband had left her and the children to find himself. Instead he found a SYT (sweet young thing), promptly divorced Dianne and moved across the country. It hurt; in fact, it hurt more than anything Dianne had ever known, but she was a survivor, and always had been. Perhaps that was the reason Jack didn't seem to suffer a single pang of guilt about abandoning her to raise Jason and Jill on her own.

Her children, Dianne had discovered, were incredibly resilient. Within a year of their father's departure, they were urging her to date. Their father did, they reminded Dianne with annoying frequency. And if it wasn't her children pushing her toward establishing a new relationship, it was her own dear mother.

When it came to locating Mr. Right for her divorced daughter, Martha Janes knew no equal. For several months, Dianne had been subjected to a long parade of single men. Their unmarried status, however, seemed their sole attribute.

After dinner with the man who lost his toupee on a low-hanging chandelier, Dianne had insisted enough was enough and she would find her own dates.

This proved to be easier said than done. Dianne hadn't gone out once in six months. Now, within the next week, she needed a man. Not just any man, either. One who was tall, dark and handsome. It would be a nice bonus if he was exceptionally wealthy, too, but she didn't have time to be choosy. The Valentine's dinner at the Port Blossom Community Center was Saturday night. *This* Saturday night.

From the moment the notice was posted six weeks earlier, Jason and Jill had insisted she attend. Surely their mother could find a date given that much time! And someone handsome to boot. It seemed a matter of family honor.

Only now the dinner was only days away and Dianne was no closer to achieving her goal.

"I'm home," Jason yelled as he walked into the house. The front door slammed in his wake, hard enough to shake the kitchen windows. He threw his books on the counter, moved directly to the refrigerator, opened the door and stuck the upper half of his fourteen-year-old body inside.

"Help yourself to a snack," Dianne said, smiling and shaking her head.

Jason reappeared with a chicken leg clenched between his teeth like a pirate's cutlass. One hand was filled with a piece of leftover cherry pie while the other held a platter of cold fried chicken.

"How was school?"

He shrugged, set down the pie and removed the chicken leg from his mouth. "Okay, I guess."

Dianne knew what was coming next. It was the same question he'd asked her every afternoon since the notice about the dinner had been posted.

"Do you have a date yet?" He leaned against the counter as his steady gaze pierced her. Her son's eyes could break through the firmest resolve, and cut through layers of deception.

"No date," she answered cheerfully. At least as cheerfully as she could under the circumstances.

"The dinner's this Saturday night."

As if she needed reminding. "I know. Stop worrying, I'll find someone."

"Not just anyone," Jason said emphatically, as though he were speaking to someone with impaired hearing. "He's got to make an impression. Someone decent."

"I know, I know."

"Grandma said she could line you up with—"

"No," Dianne interrupted. "I categorically refuse to go on any more of Grandma's blind dates."

"But you don't have the time to find your own now. It's—"

"I'm working on it," she insisted, although she knew she wasn't working very hard. She *was* trying to find someone to accompany her to the dinner, only she'd never dreamed it would be this difficult.

Until the necessity of attending this affair had been forced upon her, Dianne hadn't been aware of how limited her choices were. In the past couple of years, she'd met few single men, apart from the ones her mother had thrown at her. There were a couple of unmarried men at the office where she was employed part-time as a bookkeeper. Neither, however, was anyone she'd seriously consider dating. They were both too suave, too urbane—too much like Jack. Besides, problems might arise if she were to mingle her social life with her business one.

The front door opened and closed again, a little less noisily this time.

"I'm home!" ten-year-old Jill announced from the entryway. She dropped her books on the floor and marched toward the kitchen. Then she paused on the threshold and planted both hands on her hips as her eyes sought out her brother. "You better not have eaten all the leftover pie. I want some, too, you know."

"Don't grow warts worrying about it," Jason said sarcastically. "There's plenty."

Jill's gaze swiveled from her brother to her mother. The level of severity didn't diminish one bit. Dianne met her daughter's eye and mouthed the words along with her.

"Do you have a date yet?"

Jason answered for Dianne. "No, she doesn't. And she's got five days to come up with a decent guy and all she says is that she's working on it."

"Mom..." Jill's brown eyes filled with concern.

"Children, please."

"Everyone in town's going," Jill claimed, as if Dianne wasn't already aware of that. "You've *got* to be there, you've just got to. I told all my friends you're going."

More pressure! That was the last thing Dianne needed. Nevertheless, she smiled serenely at her two children and assured them they didn't have a thing to worry about.

An hour or so later, while she was making dinner, she could hear Jason and Jill's voices in the living room. They were huddled together in front of the television, their heads close together. Plotting, it looked like, charting her barren love life. Doubtless deciding who their mother should take to the dinner. Probably the guy with the toupee.

"Is something wrong?" Dianne asked, standing in the doorway. It was unusual for them to watch television this time of day, but more unusual for them to be so chummy. The fact that they'd turned on the TV to drown out their conversation hadn't escaped her.

They broke guiltily apart.

"Wrong?" Jason asked, recovering first. "I was just talking to Jill, is all. Do you need me to do something?"

That offer alone was enough evidence to convict them both. "Jill, would you set the table for me?" she asked, her gaze lingering on her two children for another moment before she returned to the kitchen.

Jason and Jill were up to something. Dianne could only guess what. No doubt the plot they were concocting included their grandmother.

Sure enough, while Jill was setting the silverware on the kitchen table, Jason used the phone, stretching the cord as far as it would go and mumbling into the mouthpiece so there was no chance Dianne could overhear his conversation.

Dianne's suspicions were confirmed when her mother arrived shortly after dinner. And within minutes, Jason and Jill had deserted the kitchen, saying they had to get to their homework. Also highly suspicious behavior.

"Do you want some tea, Mom?" Dianne felt obliged to ask, dreading the coming conversation. It didn't take Sherlock Holmes to deduce that her children had called their grandmother hoping she'd find a last-minute date for Dianne.

"Don't go to any trouble."

This was her mother's standard reply. "It's no trouble," Dianne said.

"Then make the tea."

Because of her evening aerobics class—W.A.R. it was called, for Women After Results—Dianne had changed and was prepared to make a hasty exit.

While the water was heating, she took a white ceramic teapot from the cupboard. "Before you ask, and I know you will," she said with strained patience, "I haven't got a date for the Valentine's dinner yet."

Her mother nodded slowly as if Dianne had just announced something of profound importance. Martha was from the old school, and she took her time getting around to whatever was on her mind, usually preceding it with a long list of questions that hinted at the subject. Dianne loved her mother, but there wasn't anyone on this earth who could drive her crazier.

"You've still got your figure," Martha said, her expression serious. "That helps." She stroked her chin a couple of times and nodded. "You've got your father's brown eyes, may he rest in peace, and your hair is nice and thick. You can thank your grandfather for that. He had hair so thick—"

"Ma, did I mention I have an aerobics class tonight?"

Her mother's posture stiffened. "I don't want to bother you."

"It's just that I might have to leave before you say what you're obviously planning to say, and I didn't want to miss the reason for your unexpected visit."

Her mother relaxed, but just a little. "Don't worry. I'll say what must be said and then you can leave. Your mother's words are not as important as your exercise class."

An argument bubbled up like fizz from a can of soda, but Dianne successfully managed to swallow it. Showing any sign of weakness in front of her mother was a major tactical error. Dianne made the tea, then carried the pot over to the table and sat across from Martha.

"Your skin's still as creamy as—"

"Mom," Dianne said, "there's no need to tell me all this. I know my coloring is good. I also know I've still got my figure and that my hair is thick and that you approve of my keeping it long. You don't need to sell me on myself."

"Ah," Martha told her softly, "that's where you're wrong."

Dianne couldn't help it—she rolled her eyes. When

Dianne was fifteen her mother would have slapped her hand, but now that she was thirty-three, Martha used more subtle tactics.

Guilt.

"I don't have many years left."

"Mom—"

"No, listen. I'm an old woman now and I have the right to say what I want, especially since the good Lord may choose to call me home at any minute."

Stirring a teaspoon of sugar into her tea offered Dianne a moment to compose herself. Bracing her elbows on the table, she raised the cup to her lips. "Just say it."

Her mother nodded, apparently appeased. "You've lost confidence in yourself."

"That's not true."

Martha's smile was meager at best. "Jack left you, and now you think there must be something wrong with you. But, Dianne, what you don't understand is that he would've gone if you were as beautiful as Marilyn Monroe. Jack's leaving had nothing to do with you and everything to do with Jack."

This conversation was taking a turn Dianne wanted to avoid. Jack was a subject she preferred not to discuss. As far as she could see, there wasn't any reason to peel back the scars and examine the wound at this late date. Jack was gone. She'd accepted it, dealt with it, and gone on with her life. The fact that her mother was even mentioning her ex-husband had taken Dianne by surprise.

"My goodness," Dianne said, checking her watch. "Look at the time—"

"Before you go," her mother said quickly, grabbing her wrist, "I met a nice young man this afternoon in the butcher's shop. Marie Zimmerman told me about him and I went to talk to him myself."

"Mom—"

"Hush and listen. He's divorced, but from what he said it was all his wife's fault. He makes blood sausage and insisted I try some. It was so good it practically melted in my mouth. I never tasted sausage so good. A man who makes sausage like that would be an asset to any family."

Oh, sweet heaven. Her mother already had her married to the guy!

"I told him all about you and he generously offered to take you out."

"Mother, *please.* I've already said I won't go out on any more blind dates."

"Jerome's a nice man. He's—"

"I don't mean to be rude, but I really have to leave now, or I'll be late." Hurriedly, Dianne stood, collected her coat, and called out to her children that she'd be back in an hour.

The kids didn't say a word.

It wasn't until she was in her car that Dianne realized they'd been expecting her to announce that she finally had a date.

Two

"Damn," Dianne muttered, scrambling through her purse for the tenth time. She knew it wasn't going to do the least bit of good, but she felt compelled to continue the search.

"Double damn," she said as she set the bulky leather handbag on the hood of her car. Raindrops spattered all around her.

Expelling her breath, she stalked back into the Port Blossom Community Center and stood in front of the desk. "I seem to have locked my keys in my car," she told the receptionist. "Along with my cell."

"Oh, dear. Is there someone you can get in touch with?"

"I'm a member of the auto club so I can call them for help. I also want to call home and say I'll be late. So if you'll let me use the phone?"

"Oh, sure." The young woman smiled pleasantly, and lifted the phone onto the counter. "We close in fifteen minutes, you know."

A half hour later, Dianne was leaning impatiently against her car in the community center parking lot when a red tow truck pulled in. It circled the area, then eased into the space next to hers.

The driver, whom Dianne couldn't see in the dark, rolled down his window and stuck out his elbow. "Are you the lady who phoned about locking her keys in the car?"

"No. I'm standing out in the rain wearing a leotard for the fun of it," she muttered.

He chuckled, turned off the engine and hopped out of the driver's seat. "Sounds like this has been one of those days."

She nodded, suddenly feeling a stab of guilt at her churlishness. He seemed so friendly.

"Why don't you climb in my truck where it's nice and warm while I take care of this?" He opened the passenger-side door and gestured for her to enter.

She smiled weakly, and as she climbed in, said, "I didn't mean to snap at you just now."

He flashed her a grin. "No problem." She found herself taking a second look at him. He was wearing gray-striped coveralls and the front was covered with grease stains. His name, Steve, was embroidered in red across the top of his vest pocket. His hair, which was neatly styled, appeared to have been recently cut. His eyes were a warm shade of brown and—she searched for the right word—gentle, she decided.

After ensuring that she was comfortable in his truck, Steve walked around to the driver's side of her compact car and used his flashlight to determine the type of lock.

Dianne lowered the window. "I don't usually do things like this. I've never locked the keys in my car before—I don't know why I did tonight. Stupid."

He returned to the tow truck and opened the passen-

ger door. "No one can be smart all the time," he said
cheerfully. "Don't be so hard on yourself." He moved
the seat forward a little and reached for a toolbox in the
space behind her.

"I've had a lot on my mind lately," she said.

Straightening, he looked at her and nodded sympa-
thetically. He had a nice face too, she noted, easy on the
eyes. In fact, he was downright attractive. The coveralls
didn't detract from his appeal, but actually suggested
a certain ruggedness. He was thoughtful and friendly
just when Dianne was beginning to think there wasn't
anyone in the world who was. But then, standing in the
dark and the rain might make anyone feel friendless,
even though Port Blossom was a rural community with
a warm, small-town atmosphere.

Steve went back to her car and began to fiddle with
the lock. Unable to sit still, Dianne opened the truck
door and climbed out. "It's the dinner that's got me so
upset."

"The dinner?" Steve glanced up from his work.

"The Valentine's dinner the community center's
sponsoring this Saturday night. My children are forc-
ing me to go. I don't know for sure, but I think they've
got money riding on it, because they're making it sound
like a matter of national importance."

"I see. Why doesn't your husband take you?"

"I'm divorced," she said bluntly. "I suppose no one
expects it to happen to them. I assumed after twelve
years my marriage was solid, but it wasn't. Jack's re-
married now, living in Boston." Dianne had no idea why
she was rambling on like this, but once she'd opened her
mouth, she couldn't seem to stop. She didn't usually re-
late the intimate details of her life to a perfect stranger.

"Aren't you cold?"

"I'm fine, thanks." That wasn't entirely true—she was a little chilled—but she was more worried about not having a date for the stupid Valentine's dinner than freezing to death. Briefly she wondered if Jason, Jill and her mother would accept pneumonia as a reasonable excuse for not attending.

"You're sure? You look like you're shivering."

She rubbed her palms together and ignored his question. "That's when my mother suggested Jerome."

"Jerome?"

"She seems to think I need help getting my feet wet."

Steve glanced up at her again, clearly puzzled.

"In the dating world," Dianne explained. "But I've had it with the dates she's arranged."

"Disasters?"

"Encounters of the worst kind. On one of them, the guy set his napkin on fire."

Steve laughed outright at that.

"Hey, it wasn't funny, trust me. I was mortified. He panicked and started waving it around in the air until the maitre d' arrived with a fire extinguisher and chaos broke loose."

Dianne found herself smiling at the memory of the unhappy episode. "Now that I look back on it, it was rather amusing."

Steve's gaze held hers. "I take it there were other disasters?"

"None I'd care to repeat."

"So your mother's up to her tricks again?"

Dianne nodded. "Only this time my kids are involved. Mom stumbled across this butcher who specializes in...well, never mind, that's not important. What is important is if I don't come up with a date in the next day or two, I'm going to be stuck going to this stupid dinner with Jerome."

"It shouldn't be so bad," he said. Dianne could hear the grin in his voice.

"How generous of you to say so." She crossed her arms over her chest. She'd orbited her vehicle twice before she spoke again.

"My kids are even instructing me on the kind of man they want me to date."

"Oh?"

Dianne wasn't sure he'd heard her. Her lock snapped free and he opened the door and retrieved her keys, which were in the ignition. He handed them to her, and with a thank-you, Dianne made a move to climb into her car.

"Jason and Jill—they're my kids—want me to go out with a tall, dark, handsome—" She stopped abruptly, thrusting out her arm as if to keep her balance.

Steve looked at her oddly. "Are you all right?"

Dianne brought her fingertips to her temple and nodded. "I think so…" She inhaled sharply and motioned toward the streetlight. "Would you mind stepping over there for a minute?"

"Me?" He pointed to himself as though he wasn't sure she meant him.

"Please."

He shrugged and did as she requested.

The idea was fast gaining momentum in her mind. He was certainly tall—at least six foot three, which was a nice complement to her own slender five ten. And he was dark—his hair appeared to be a rich shade of mahogany. As for the handsome part, she'd noticed that right off.

"Is something wrong?" he probed.

"No," Dianne said, grinning shyly—although what she was about to propose was anything but shy. "By the way, how old are you? Thirty? Thirty-one?"

"Thirty-five."

"That's good. Perfect." A couple of years older than she was. Yes, the kids would approve of that.

"Good? Perfect?" He seemed to be questioning her sanity.

"Married?" she asked.

"Nope. I never got around to it, but I came close once." His eyes narrowed suspiciously.

"That's even better. I don't suppose you've got a jealous girlfriend—or a mad lover hanging around looking for an excuse to murder someone?"

"Not lately."

Dianne sighed with relief. "Great."

"Your car door's open," he said, gesturing toward it. He seemed eager to be on his way. "All I need to do is write down your auto club number."

"Yes, I know." She stood there, arms folded, studying him in the light. He was even better-looking than she'd first thought. "Do you own a decent suit?"

He chuckled as if the question amused him. "Yes."

"I mean something really nice, not the one you wore to your high-school graduation."

"It's a really nice suit."

Dianne didn't mean to be insulting, but she had to have all her bases covered. "That's good," she said. "How would you like to earn an extra hundred bucks Saturday night?"

"I beg your pardon?"

"I'm offering you a hundred dollars to escort me to the Valentine's dinner here at the center."

Steve stared at her as though he suspected she'd escaped from a mental institution.

"Listen, I know this is a bit unusual," Dianne rushed on, "but you're perfect. Well, not perfect, but you're exactly the kind of man the kids expect me to date, and frankly I haven't got time to do a whole lot of recruiting. Mr. Right hasn't showed up, if you know what I mean."

"I think I do."

"I need a date for one night. You fit the bill and you could probably use the extra cash. I realize it's not much, but a hundred dollars sounds fair to me. The dinner starts at seven and should be over by nine. I suspect fifty dollars an hour is more than you're earning now."

"Ah..."

"I know what you're thinking, but I promise you I'm not crazy. I've got a gold credit card, and they don't issue those to just anyone."

"What about a library card?"

"That, too, but I do have a book overdue. I was planning to take it back tomorrow." She started searching through her purse to prove she had both cards before she saw that he was teasing her.

"Ms...."

"Dianne Williams," she said stepping forward to offer him her hand. His long, strong fingers wrapped around hers and he smiled, studying her for perhaps the first time. His eyes softened as he shook her hand. The gesture, though small, reassured Dianne that he was the man she wanted to take her to this silly dinner. Once more she found herself rushing to explain.

"I'm sure this all sounds crazy. I don't blame you for thinking I'm a nutcase. But I'm not, really I'm not. I attend church every Sunday, do volunteer work at the grade school, and help coach a girls' soccer team in the fall."

"Why'd you pick me?"

"Well, that's a bit complicated, but you have nice eyes, and when you suggested I sit in your truck and get out of the rain—actually it was only drizzling—" she paused and inhaled a deep breath "—I realized you were a generous person, and you just might consider something this..."

"...weird," he finished for her.

Dianne nodded, then looked him directly in the eye. Her defenses were down, and there was nothing left to do but admit the truth.

"I'm desperate. No one but a desperate woman would make this kind of offer."

"Saturday night, you say?"

The way her luck was running, he'd suddenly remember he had urgent plans for the evening. Something important like dusting his bowling trophies.

"From seven to nine. No later, I promise. If you don't think a hundred is enough..."

"A hundred's more than generous."

She sagged with relief. "Does this mean you'll do it?"

Steve shook his head slowly, as though to suggest he ought to have it examined for even contemplating her proposal.

"All right," he said after a moment. "I never could resist a damsel in distress."

Three

"Hello, everyone!" Dianne sang out as she breezed in the front door. She paused just inside the living room and watched as her mother and her two children stared openly. A sense of quiet astonishment pervaded the room. "Is something wrong?"

"What happened to you?" Jason cried. "You look awful!"

"You look like Little Orphan Annie, dear," her mother said, her hand working a crochet hook so fast the yarn zipped through her fingers.

"I phoned to tell you I'd be late," Dianne reminded them.

"But you didn't say anything about nearly drowning. What happened?"

"I locked my keys in the car—I already explained that."

Jill walked over to her mother, took her hand and led her to the hallway mirror. The image that greeted Dianne was only a little short of shocking. Her long thick hair hung in limp sodden curls over her shoulders. Her mascara, supposedly no-run, had dissolved into black tracks down her cheeks. She was drenched to the skin and looked like a prize the cat had dragged onto the porch.

"Oh, dear," she whispered. Her stomach muscles tightened as she recalled the odd glances Steve had given her, and his comment that it must be "one of those days." No wonder!

"Why don't you go upstairs and take a nice hot shower?" her mother said. "You'll feel worlds better."

Humbled, for more reasons than she cared to admit, Dianne agreed.

As was generally the rule, her mother was right. By the time Dianne reappeared a half hour later, dressed in her terry-cloth robe and fuzzy pink slippers, she felt considerably better.

Making herself a cup of tea, she reviewed the events of the evening. Even if Steve had agreed to attend the Valentine's dinner out of pity, it didn't matter. What did matter was the fact that she had a date. As soon as she told her family, they'd stop hounding her.

"By the way," she said as she carried her tea into the living room, "I have a date for Saturday night."

The room went still. Even the television sound seemed to fade into nothingness. Her two children and her mother did a slow turn, their faces revealing their surprise.

"Don't look so shocked," Dianne said with a light, casual laugh. "I told you before that I was working on it. No one seemed to believe I was capable of finding a date on my own. Well, that isn't the case."

"Who?" Martha demanded, her eyes disbelieving.

"Oh, ye of little faith," Dianne said, feeling only a small twinge of guilt. "His name is Steve Creighton."

"When did you meet him?"

"Ah…" Dianne realized she wasn't prepared for an inquisition. "A few weeks ago. We happened to bump into each other tonight, and he asked if I had a date for the dinner. Naturally I told him I didn't and he suggested we go together."

"Steve Creighton." Her mother repeated the name slowly, rolling the syllables over her tongue, as if trying to remember where she'd last heard it. Then she shook her head and resumed crocheting.

"You never said anything about this guy before." Jason's gaze was slightly accusing. He sat on the carpet, knees tucked under his chin.

"Of course I didn't. If I had, all three of you would be bugging me about him, just the way you are now."

Martha gave her ball of yarn a hard jerk. "How'd you two meet?"

Dianne wasn't ready for this line of questioning. She'd assumed letting her family know she had the necessary escort would've been enough to appease them. Silly of her.

They wanted details. Lots of details, and the only thing Dianne could do was make them up as she went along. She couldn't very well admit she'd only met Steve that night and was so desperate for a date that she'd offered to pay him to escort her to the dinner.

"We met, ah, a few weeks ago in the grocery store," she explained haltingly, averting her gaze. She prayed that would satisfy their curiosity. But when she paused to sip her tea, the three faces were riveted on her.

"Go on," her mother urged.

"I… I was standing in the frozen-food section and…

Steve was there, too, and…he smiled at me and introduced himself."

"What did he say after that?" Jill wanted to know, eager for the particulars. Martha shared her granddaughter's interest. She set her yarn and crochet hook aside, focusing all her attention on Dianne.

"After he introduced himself, he said surely those low-cal dinners couldn't be for me—that I looked perfect just the way I was." The words fell stiffly from her lips. She had to be desperate to divulge her own fantasy to her family like this.

All right, she *was* desperate.

Jill's shoulders rose with an expressive sigh. "How romantic!"

Jason, however, was frowning. "The guy sounds like a flake to me. A real man doesn't walk up to a woman and say something stupid like that."

"Steve's very nice."

"Maybe, but he doesn't sound like he's got all his oars in the water."

"I think he sounds sweet," Jill countered, immediately defending her mother by championing Steve. "If Mom likes him, then he's good enough for me."

"There are a lot of fruitcakes out there." Apparently her mother felt obliged to tell her that.

It was all Dianne could do not to remind her dear, sweet mother that she'd arranged several dates for her with men who fell easily into that category.

"I think we should meet him," Jason said, his eyes darkening with concern. "He might turn out to be a serial murderer or something."

"Jason—" Dianne forced another light laugh

"—you're being silly. Besides, you're going to meet him Saturday night."

"By then it'll be too late."

"Jason's got a point, dear," Martha said. "I don't think it would do any harm to introduce your young man to the family before Saturday night."

"I… He's probably busy… He's working all sorts of weird hours and…"

"What does he do?"

"Ah…" She couldn't think fast enough to come up with a lie and had to admit the truth. "He drives a truck."

Her words were followed by a tense silence as her children and mother exchanged meaningful looks. "I've heard stories about truck drivers," Martha said, pinching her lips tightly together. "None I'd care to repeat in front of the children, mind you, but…stories."

"Mother, you're being—"

"Jason's absolutely right. I insist we meet this Steve. Truck drivers and cowboys simply aren't to be trusted."

Dianne rolled her eyes.

Her mother forgave her by saying, "I don't expect you to know this, Dianne, since you married so young."

"You married Dad when you were eighteen—younger than I was when I got married," Dianne said, not really wanting to argue, but finding herself trapped.

"Yes, but I've lived longer." She waved her crochet hook at Dianne. "A mother knows these things."

"Grandma's right," Jason said, sounding very adult. "We need to meet this Steve before you go out with him."

Dianne threw her hands in the air in frustration.

"Hey, I thought you kids were the ones so eager for me to be at this dinner!"

"Yes, but we still have standards," Jill said, now siding with the others.

"I'll see what I can do," Dianne mumbled.

"Invite him over for dinner on Thursday night," her mother said. "I'll make my beef Stroganoff and bring over a fresh apple pie."

"Ah...he might be busy."

"Then tell him Wednesday night," Jason advised in a voice that was hauntingly familiar. It was the same tone Dianne used when she meant business.

With nothing left to do but agree, Dianne said, "Okay. I'll try for Thursday." Oh, Lord, she thought, what had she got herself into?

She waited until the following afternoon to contact Steve. He'd given her his business card, which she'd tucked into the edging at the bottom of the bulletin board in her kitchen. She wasn't pleased about having to call him. She'd need to offer him more money if he agreed to this dinner. She couldn't very well expect him to come out of the generosity of his heart.

"Port Blossom Towing," a crisp female voice answered.

"Ah...this is Dianne Williams. I'd like to leave a message for Steve Creighton."

"Steve's here." Her words were followed by a click and a ringing sound.

"Steve," he answered distractedly.

"Hello." Dianne found herself at a loss for words. She'd hoped to just leave a message and ask him to return the call at his convenience. Having him there, on the other end of the line, when she wasn't expecting it left her at a disadvantage.

"Is this Dianne?"

"Yes. How'd you know?"

He chuckled softly, and the sound was pleasant and warm. "It's probably best if I don't answer that. Are you checking up to make sure I don't back out of Saturday night? Don't worry, I won't. In fact, I stopped off at the community center this morning and picked up tickets for the dinner."

"Oh, you didn't have to do that, but thanks. I'll reimburse you later."

"Just add it to my tab," he said lightly.

Dianne cringed, then took a breath and said, "Actually, I called to talk to you about my children."

"Your children?"

"Yes," she said. "Jason and Jill, and my mother, too, seem to think it would be a good idea if they met you. I assured them they would on Saturday night, but apparently that isn't good enough."

"I see."

"According to Jason, by then it'll be too late, and you might turn out to be a serial murderer or something. And my mother found the fact that you drive a truck worrisome."

"Do you want me to change jobs, too? I might have a bit of a problem managing all that before Saturday night."

"Of course not. Now, about Thursday—that's when they want you to come for dinner. My mother's offered to fix her Stroganoff and bake a pie. She uses Granny Smith apples," Dianne added, as though that bit of information would convince him to accept.

"Thursday night?"

"I'll give you an additional twenty dollars."

"Twenty dollars?" He sounded insulted, so Dianne raised her offer.

"All right, twenty-five, but that's as high as I can go. I'm living on a budget, you know." This fiasco was quickly running into a big chunk of cash. The dinner tickets were thirty each, and she'd need to reimburse Steve for those. Plus, she owed him a hundred for escorting her to the silly affair, and now an additional twenty-five if he came to dinner with her family.

"For twenty-five you've got yourself a deal," he said at last. "Anything else?"

Dianne closed her eyes. This was the worst part. "Yes," she said, swallowing tightly. The lump in her throat had grown to painful proportions. "There's one other thing. I… I want you to know I don't normally look that bad."

"Hey, I told you before—don't be so hard on yourself. You'd had a rough day."

"It's just that I don't want you to think I'm going to embarrass you at this Valentine's dinner. There may be people there you know, and after I made such a big deal over whether you had a suit and everything, well, I thought you might be more comfortable knowing…" She paused, closed her eyes and then blurted, "I've decided to switch brands of mascara."

His hesitation was only slight. "Thank you for sharing that. I'm sure I'll sleep better now."

Dianne decided to ignore his comment since she'd practically invited it. She didn't understand why she should find herself so tongue-tied with this man, but then again, perhaps she did. She'd made a complete idiot of herself. Paying a man to escort her to a dinner wasn't exactly the type of thing she wanted to list on a résumé.

"Oh, and before I forget," Dianne said, determined to put this unpleasantness behind her, "my mother and the kids asked me several questions about...us. How we met and the like. It might be a good idea if we went over my answers so our stories match."

"You want to meet for coffee later?"

"Ah...when?"

"Say seven, at the Pancake Haven. Don't worry, I'll buy."

Dianne had to bite back her sarcastic response. Instead she murmured, "Okay, but I won't have a lot of time."

"I promise not to keep you any longer than necessary."

Four

"All right," Steve said dubiously, once the waitress had poured them each a cup of coffee. "How'd we meet?"

Dianne told him, lowering her voice when she came to the part about the low-cal frozen dinners. She found it rather humiliating to have to repeat her private fantasy a second time, especially to Steve.

He looked incredulous when she'd finished. "You've got to be kidding."

Dianne took offense at his tone. This was *her* romantic invention he was ridiculing, and she hadn't even mentioned the part about the Rimsky-Korsakov symphony or the chiming bells.

"I didn't have time to think of anything better," Dianne explained irritably. "Jason hit me with the question first thing and I wasn't prepared."

"What did Jason say when you told him that story?"

"He said you sounded like a flake."

"I don't blame him."

Dianne's shoulders sagged with defeat.

"Don't worry about it," Steve assured her, still frowning. "I'll clear everything up when I meet him

Thursday night." He said it in a way that suggested the task would be difficult.

"Good—only don't make me look like any more of a fool than I already do."

"I'll try my best," he said with the same dubious inflection he'd used when they'd first sat down.

Dianne sympathized. This entire affair was quickly going from bad to worse, and there was no one to fault but her. Who would've dreamed finding a date for the Valentine's dinner would cause so many problems?

As they sipped their coffee, Dianne studied the man sitting across from her. She was somewhat surprised to discover that Steve Creighton looked even better the second time around. He was dressed in slacks and an Irish cable-knit sweater the color of winter wheat. His smile was a ready one and his eyes, now that she had a chance to see them in the light, were a deep, rich shade of brown like his hair. The impression he'd given her of a considerate, generous man persisted. He must be. No one else would have agreed to this scheme, at least not without a more substantial inducement.

"I'm afraid I might've painted my kids a picture of you that's not quite accurate," Dianne admitted. Both her children had been filled with questions about Steve when they'd returned from school that afternoon. Jason had remained skeptical, but Jill, always a romantic—Dianne couldn't imagine where she'd inherited that!—had bombarded her for details.

"I'll do my best to live up to my image," Steve was quick to assure her.

Placing her elbows on the table, Dianne brushed a thick swatch of hair away from her face and tucked it behind her ear. "Listen, I'm sorry I ever got you involved in this."

"No backing out now—I've laid out cold hard cash for the dinner tickets."

Which was a not-so-subtle reminder that she owed him for those. She dug through her bag and brought out her checkbook. "I'll write you a check for the tickets right now."

"I'm not worried." He dismissed her offer with a wave of his hand.

Nevertheless, Dianne insisted. If she paid him in increments, she wouldn't have to think about how much this fiasco would end up costing her. She had the distinct feeling that by the time the Valentine's dinner was over, she would've spent as much as if she'd taken a Hawaiian vacation. Or gone to Seattle for the weekend, anyway.

After adding her signature, with a flair, to the bottom of the check, she kept her eyes lowered and said, "If I upped the ante ten dollars do you think you could manage to look...besotted?"

"Besotted?" Steve repeated the word as though he'd never heard it before.

"You know, smitten."

"Smitten?"

Again he made it sound as though she were speaking a foreign language. "Attracted," she tried for the third time, loud enough to catch the waitress's attention. The woman appeared and splashed more coffee into their nearly full cups.

"I'm not purposely being dense," he said. "I'm just not sure what you mean."

"Try to look as though you find me attractive," she

said, leaning halfway across the table and speaking in a heated whisper.

"I see. So that's what 'besotted' means." He took another sip of his coffee, and Dianne had the feeling he did so in an effort to hide a smile.

"You aren't supposed to find that amusing." She took a gulp of her own drink and nearly scalded her mouth. Under different circumstances she would've grimaced with pain, or at least reached for the water glass. She did none of those things. A woman has her pride.

"Let me see if I understand you correctly," Steve said matter-of-factly. "For an extra ten bucks you want me to look 'smitten.'"

"Yes," Dianne answered with as much dignity as she could muster, which at the moment wasn't a lot.

"I'll do it, of course," Steve said, grinning and making her feel all the more foolish, "only I'm not sure I know how." He straightened, squared his shoulders and momentarily closed his eyes.

"Steve?" Dianne whispered, glancing around, hoping no one was watching them. He seemed to be attempting some form of Eastern meditation. She half expected him to start chanting. "What are you doing?"

"Thinking about how to look smitten."

"Are you making fun of me?"

"Not at all. If you're willing to offer me an extra ten bucks, it must be important to you. I want to do it right."

Dianne thought she'd better tell him. "This isn't for me," she said. "It's for my ten-year-old daughter, who happens to have a romantic nature. Jill was so impressed with the story of how we supposedly met, that I… I was kind of hoping you'd be willing to…you know." Now that she was forced to spell it out, Dianne wasn't certain of anything. But she knew one thing—suggesting he look smitten with her had been a mistake.

"I'll try."

"I'd appreciate it," she said.

"How's this?" Steve cocked his head at a slight angle, then slowly lowered his eyelids until they were half closed. His mouth curved upward in an off-center smile while his shoulders heaved in what Dianne suspected was meant to be a deep sigh of longing. As though in afterthought, he pressed his open hands over his heart while making soft panting sounds.

"Are you doing an imitation of a Saint Bernard?" Dianne snapped, still not sure whether he was laughing at her. "You look like a…a dog. Maybe Jason's right and you really are a flake."

"I was trying to look besotted," Steve said. "I thought that was what you wanted." As if it would improve the image, he cocked his head the other way and repeated the performance.

"You're making fun of me, and I don't appreciate it one bit." Dianne tossed her napkin on the table and stood. "Thursday night, six o'clock, and please don't be late." With that she slipped her purse strap over her shoulder and stalked out of the restaurant.

Steve followed her to her car. "All right, I apologize. I got carried away in there."

Dianne nodded. She'd gone a little overboard herself, but not nearly as much as Steve. Although she claimed she wanted him to give the impression of being attracted to her for Jill's sake, that wasn't entirely true. Steve was handsome and kind, and to have him looking at her with his heart in his eyes was a fantasy that was strictly her own.

Admitting that, even to herself, was a shock. The walls around her battered heart had been reinforced by three years of loneliness. For reasons she couldn't really explain, this tow-truck driver made her feel vulnerable.

"I'm willing to try again if you want," he said. "Only..."

"Yes?" Her car was parked in the rear lot where the lighting wasn't nearly as good. Steve's face was hidden in the shadows, and she couldn't tell if he was being sincere or not.

"The problem," he replied slowly, "comes from the fact that we haven't kissed. I don't mean to be forward, you understand. You want me to wear a certain look, but it's a little difficult to manufacture without having had any, er, physical closeness."

"I see." Dianne's heart was pounding hard enough to damage her rib cage.

"Are you willing to let me kiss you?"

It was a last resort and she didn't have much choice. But she didn't have anything to lose, either. "If you insist."

With a deep breath, she tilted her head to the right, shut her eyes and puckered up. After waiting what seemed an inordinate amount of time, she opened her eyes. "Is something wrong?"

"I can't do it."

Embarrassed in the extreme, Dianne set her hands on her hips. "What do you mean?"

"You look like you're about to be sacrificed to appease the gods."

"I beg your pardon!" Dianne couldn't believe she was hearing him correctly. Talk about humiliation— she was only doing what he'd suggested.

"I can't kiss a woman who acts like she's about to undergo the most revolting experience of her life."

"You're saying I'm…oh…oh!" Too furious to speak, Dianne gripped Steve by the elbow and jerked him over to where his tow truck was parked, a couple of spaces down from her own car. Hopping onto the running board, she glared down at him. Her higher vantage point made her feel less vulnerable. Her eyes flashed with anger; his were filled with mild curiosity.

"Dianne, what are you doing now?"

"I'll have you know I was quite a kisser in my time."

"I don't doubt it."

"You just did. Now listen and listen well, because I'm only going to say this once." Waving her index finger under his nose, she paused and lowered her hand abruptly. He was right, she hadn't been all that thrilled to fall into this little experiment. A kiss was an innocent-enough exchange, she supposed, but kissing Steve put her on the defensive. And that troubled her.

"Say it."

Self-conscious now, she shifted her gaze and stepped off the running board, feeling ridiculous.

"What was so important that you were waving your finger under my nose?" Steve pressed.

Since she'd made such a fuss, she didn't have any alternative but to finish what she'd begun. "When I was in high school…the boys used to like to kiss me."

"They still would," Steve said softly, "if you'd give them a little encouragement."

She looked up at him and had to blink back unexpected tears. A woman doesn't have her husband walk out on her and not find herself awash in pain and self-doubt. Once she'd been confident; now she was dubious and insecure.

"Here," Steve said, holding her by the shoulders. "Let's try this." Then he gently, sweetly slanted his mouth over hers. Dianne was about to protest when their lips met and the option to refuse was taken from her.

Mindlessly she responded. Her arms slid around his middle and her hands splayed across the hard muscles of his back. And suddenly, emotions that had been simmering just below the surface rose like a tempest within her, and her heart went on a rampage.

Steve buried his hands in her hair, his fingers twisting and tangling in its thickness, bunching it at the back of her head. His mouth was soft, yet possessive. She gave a small, shocked moan when his tongue breached the barrier of her lips, but she adjusted quickly to the deepening quality of his kiss.

Reluctantly, Steve eased his mouth from hers. For a long moment, Dianne didn't open her eyes. When she finally did, she found Steve staring down at her.

He blinked.

She blinked.

Then, in the space of a heartbeat, he lowered his mouth back to hers.

Unable to stop, Dianne sighed deeply and leaned into his strength. Her legs felt like mush and her head was spinning with confusion. Her hands crept up and closed around the folds of his collar.

This kiss was long and thorough. It was the sweetest kiss Dianne had ever known—and the most passionate.

When he lifted his mouth from hers, he smiled tenderly. "I don't believe I'll have any problem looking besotted," he whispered.

Five

"Steve's here!" Jason called, releasing the living-room curtain. "He just pulled into the driveway."

Jill's high-pitched voice echoed her brother's. "He brought his truck. It's red and—"

"—wicked," Jason said, paying Steve's choice of vehicles the highest form of teenage compliment.

"What did I tell you," Dianne's mother said, as she briskly stirred the Stroganoff sauce. "He's driving a truck that's red and wicked." Her voice rose hysterically. "The man's probably a spawn of the devil!"

"Mother, 'wicked' means 'wonderful' to Jason."

"I've never heard anything so absurd in my life."

The doorbell chimed just then. Unfastening the apron from around her waist and tossing it aside, Dianne straightened and walked into the wide entryway. Jason, Jill and her mother followed closely, crowding her.

"Mom, please," Dianne pleaded, "give me some room here. Jason. Jill. Back up a little, would you?"

All three moved several paces back, allowing Dianne some space. But the moment her hand went for the doorknob, they crowded forward again.

"Children, Ma, please!" she whispered frantically. The three were so close to her she could barely breathe.

Reluctantly Jason and Jill shuffled into the living room and slumped onto the sofa near the television set. Martha, however, refused to budge.

The bell chimed a second time, and after glaring at her mother and receiving no response, Dianne opened the door. On the other side of the screen door stood Steve, a huge bouquet of red roses in one hand and a large stuffed bear tucked under his other arm.

Dianne stared as she calculated the cost of long-stemmed roses, and a stuffed animal. She couldn't even afford carnations. And if he felt it necessary to bring along a stuffed bear, why hadn't he chosen a smaller, less costly one?

"May I come in?" he asked after a lengthy pause.

Her mother elbowed Dianne in the ribs and smiled serenely as she unlatched the lock on the screen door.

"You must be Steve. How lovely to meet you," Martha said as graciously as if she'd always thought the world of truck drivers.

Holding the outer door for him, Dianne managed to produce a weak smile as Steve entered her home. Jason and Jill had come back into the hallway to stand next to their grandmother, eyeing Dianne's newfound date with open curiosity. For all her son's concern that Steve might turn out to be an ax-murderer, one look at the bright-red tow truck and he'd been won over.

"Steve, I'd like you to meet my family," Dianne said, gesturing toward the three.

"So, you're Jason," Steve said, holding out his hand.

The two exchanged a hearty handshake. "I'm pleased to meet you. Your mother speaks highly of you."

Jason beamed.

Turning his attention to Jill, Steve held out the over-size teddy bear. "This is for you," he said, giving her the stuffed animal. "I wanted something extra-special for Dianne's daughter, but this was all I could think of. I hope you aren't disappointed."

"I *love* teddy bears!" Jill cried, hugging it tight. "Did Mom tell you that?"

"Nope," Steve said, centering his high-voltage smile on the ten-year-old. "I just guessed."

"Oh, thank you, thank you." Cuddling the bear, Jill raced up the stairs, giddy with delight. "I'm going to put him on my bed right now."

Steve's gaze followed her daughter, and then his eyes briefly linked with Dianne's. In that split second, she let him know she wasn't entirely pleased. He frowned slightly, but recovered before presenting the roses to Dianne's mother.

"For me?" Martha brought her fingertips to her mouth as though shocked by the gesture. "Oh, you shouldn't have! Oh, my heavens, I can't remember the last time a man gave me roses." Reaching for the corner of her apron, she discreetly dabbed her eyes. "This is such a treat."

"Mother, don't you want to put those in water?" Dianne said pointedly.

"Oh, dear, I suppose I should. It was a thoughtful gesture, Steve. Very thoughtful."

"Jason, go help your grandmother."

Her son looked as though he intended to object, but

changed his mind and obediently followed Martha into the kitchen.

As soon as they were alone, Dianne turned on Steve. "Don't you think you're laying it on a little thick?" she whispered. She was so furious she was having trouble speaking clearly. "I can't afford all this!"

"Don't worry about it."

"I am worried. In fact I'm experiencing a good deal of distress. At the rate you're spending my money, I'm going to have to go on an installment plan."

"Hush, now, before you attract everyone's attention."

Dianne scowled at him. "I—"

Steve placed his fingers over her lips. "I've learned a very effective way of keeping you quiet—don't force me to use it. Kissing you so soon after my arrival might create the wrong impression."

"You wouldn't dare!"

The way his mouth slanted upward in a slow smile made her afraid he would. "I was only doing my best to act besotted," he said.

"You didn't have to spend this much money doing it. Opening my door, holding out my chair—that's all I wanted. First you roll your eyes like you're going into a coma and pant like a Saint Bernard, then you spend a fortune."

"Dinner's ready," Martha shouted from the kitchen.

With one last angry glare, Dianne led him into the big kitchen. Steve moved behind Dianne's chair and pulled it out for her. "Are you happy now?" he whispered close to her ear as she sat down.

She nodded, thinking it was too little, too late, but she didn't have much of an argument since she'd specifically asked for this.

Soon the five were seated around the wooden table. Dianne's mother said the blessing, and while she did, Dianne offered up a fervent prayer of her own. She wanted Steve to make a good impression—but not too good.

After the buttered noodles and the Stroganoff had been passed around, along with a lettuce-and-cucumber salad and homemade rolls, Jason embarked on the topic that had apparently been troubling him from the first.

"Mom said you met at the grocery store."

Steve nodded. "She was blocking the aisle and I had to ask her to move her cart so I could get to the Hearty Eater Pot Pies."

Jason straightened in his chair, looking more than a little satisfied. "I thought it might be something like that."

"I beg your pardon?" Steve asked, playing innocent.

Her son cleared his throat, glanced carefully around before answering, then lowered his voice. "You should hear Mom's version of how you two met."

"More noodles?" Dianne said, shoving the bowl toward her son.

Jill looked confused. "But didn't you smile at Mom and say she's perfect just the way she is?"

Steve took a moment to compose his thoughts while he buttered his third dinner roll. Dianne recognized that he was doing a balancing act between her two children. If he said he'd commented on the low-cal frozen dinners and her figure, then he risked offending Jason, who seemed to think no man in his right mind would say something like that. On the other hand, if he claimed otherwise, he might wound Jill's romantic little heart.

"I'd be interested in knowing that myself," Martha

added, looking pleased that Steve had taken a second helping of her Stroganoff. "Dianne's terribly close-mouthed about these things. She didn't even mention you until the other night."

"To be honest," Steve said, sitting back in his chair, "I don't exactly recall what I said to Dianne. I remember being irritated with her for hogging the aisle, but when I asked her to move, she apologized and immediately pushed her cart out of the way."

Jason nodded, appeased.

"But when I got a good look at her, I couldn't help thinking she was the most beautiful woman I'd seen in a long while."

Jill sighed, mollified.

"I don't recall any of that," Dianne said, reaching for another roll. She tore it apart with a vengeance and smeared butter on both halves before she realized she had an untouched roll balanced on the edge of her plate.

"I was thinking that after dinner I'd take Jason out for a ride in the truck," Steve said when a few minutes had passed.

"You'd do that?" Jason nearly leapt from his chair in his eagerness.

"I was planning to all along," Steve explained. "I thought you'd be more interested in seeing how all the gears worked than in any gift I could bring you."

"I am." Jason was so excited he could barely sit still.

"When Jason and I come back, I'll take you out for a spin, Dianne."

She shook her head. "I'm not interested, thanks."

Three pairs of accusing eyes flashed in her direction. It was as if she'd committed an act of treason.

"I'm sure my daughter didn't mean that," Martha

said, smiling sweetly at Steve. "She's been very tired lately and not quite herself."

Bewildered, Dianne stared at her mother.

"Can we go now?" Jason asked, already standing.

"If your mother says it's okay," Steve said, with a glance at Dianne. She nodded, and Steve finished the last of his roll and stood.

"I'll have apple pie ready for you when you get back," Martha promised, quickly ushering the two out the front door.

As soon as her mother returned to the kitchen, Dianne asked, "What was all that about?"

"What?" her mother demanded, feigning ignorance.

"That I've been very tired and not myself lately?"

"Oh, that," Martha said, clearing the table. "Steve wants to spend a few minutes alone with you. It's only natural. So I had to make some excuse for you."

"Yes, but—"

"Your behavior, my dear, was just short of rude. When a gentleman makes it clear he wants to spend some uninterrupted time in your company, you should welcome the opportunity."

"Mother, I seem to recall your saying Steve was a spawn of the devil, remember?"

"Now that I've met him, I've had a change of heart."

"What about Jerome, the butcher? I thought you were convinced he was the one for me."

"I like Steve better. I can tell he's a good man, and you'd be a fool to let him slip through your fingers by pretending to be indifferent."

"I am indifferent."

With a look of patent disbelief, Martha Janes shook her head. "I saw the way your eyes lit up when Steve walked into the house. You can fool some folks, but you can't pull the wool over your own mother's eyes. You're falling in love with this young man, and frankly, I'm pleased. I like him."

Dianne frowned. If her eyes had lit up when Steve arrived, it was because she was busy trying to figure out a way to repay him for the roses and the teddy bear. What she felt for him wasn't anything romantic. Or was it?

Dear Lord, she couldn't actually be falling for this guy, could she?

The question haunted Dianne as she loaded the dishwasher.

"Steve's real cute," Jill announced. Her daughter would find Attila the Hun cute, too, if he brought her a teddy bear, but Dianne resisted the impulse to say so.

"He looks a little bit like Hugh Jackman, don't you think?" Jill continued.

"I can't say I've noticed." A small lie. Dianne had noticed a lot more about Steve than she was willing to admit. Although she'd issued a fair number of complaints, he really was being a good sport about this. Of course, she was paying him, but he'd gone above and beyond the call of duty. Taking Jason out for a spin in the tow truck was one example, although why anyone would be thrilled to drive around in that contraption was something Dianne didn't understand.

"I do believe Steve Creighton will make you a decent husband," her mother stated thoughtfully as she removed the warm apple pie from the oven. "In fact, I was just thinking how nice it would be to have a summer wedding. It's so much easier to ask relatives to travel when the weather's good. June or July would be perfect."

"Mother, please! Steve and I barely know each other."

"On the contrary," Steve said, sauntering into the kitchen. He stepped behind Dianne's mother and sniffed appreciatively at the aroma wafting from her apple pie. "I happen to be partial to summer weddings myself."

Six

"Don't you think you're overdoing it a bit?" Dianne demanded as Steve eased the big tow truck out of her driveway. She was belted into the seat next to him, feeling trapped—not to mention betrayed by her own family. They had insisted Steve take her out for a spin so the two of them could have some time alone. Steve didn't want to be alone with her, but her family didn't know that.

"Maybe I did come on a little strong," Steve agreed, dazzling her with his smile.

It was better for her equilibrium if she didn't glance his way, Dianne decided. Her eyes would innocently meet his and he'd give her one of those heart-stopping, lopsided smiles, and something inside her would melt. If this continued much longer, she'd be nothing more than a puddle by the end of the evening.

"The flowers and the stuffed animal I can under-stand," she said stiffly, willing to grant him that much. "You wanted to make a good impression, and that's fine, but the comment about being partial to summer weddings was going too far. It's just the kind of thing my mother was hoping to hear from you."

"You're right."

The fact that he was being so agreeable should have forewarned Dianne that something was amiss. She'd sensed it from the first moment she'd climbed into the truck. He'd closed the door and almost immediately something pulled wire-taut within her. The sensation was peculiar, even wistful—a melancholy pining she'd never felt before.

She squared her shoulders and stared straight ahead, determined not to fall under his spell the way her children and her mother so obviously had.

"As it is, I suspect Mom's been faithfully lighting votive candles every afternoon, asking God to send me a husband. She thinks God needs her help—that's why she goes around arranging dates for me."

"You're right, of course. I should never have made that comment about summer weddings," Steve said, "but I assumed that's just the sort of thing a *besotted* man would say."

Dianne sighed, realizing once again that she didn't have much of an argument. But he was doing everything in his power to make her regret that silly request.

"Hey, where are you taking me?" she asked when he turned off her street onto a main thoroughfare.

Steve turned his smile on her full force and twitched his thick eyebrows a couple of times for effect. "For a short drive. It wouldn't look good if we were to return five minutes after we left the house. Your family—"

"—will be waiting at the front door. They expect me back any minute."

"No, they don't."

"And why don't they?" she asked, growing uneasy. This wasn't supposed to be anything more than a ride around the block, and she'd had to be coerced into even that.

"Because I told your mother we'd be gone for an hour."

"An hour?" Dianne cried, as though he'd just announced he was kidnapping her. "But you can't do that! I mean, what about your time? Surely it's valuable."

"I assumed you'd want to pay me a few extra dollars— after all, I'm doing this to create the right impression. It's what—"

"I know, I know," she interrupted. "You're just acting smitten." The truth of the matter was that Dianne was making a fuss over something that was actually causing her heart to pound hard and fast. The whole idea of being alone with Steve appealed to her too much. *That* was the reason she fought it so hard. Without even trying, he'd managed to cast a spell on her family, and although she hated to admit it, he'd cast one on her, too. Steve Creighton was laughter and magic. Instinctively she knew he wasn't another Jack. Not the type of man who would walk away from his family.

Dianne frowned as the thought crossed her mind. It would be much easier to deal with the hand life had dealt her if she wasn't forced to associate with men as seemingly wonderful as Steve. It was easier to view all men as insensitive and inconsiderate.

Dianne didn't like that Steve was proving to be otherwise. He was apparently determined to crack the hard shell around her heart, no matter how hard she tried to reinforce it.

"Another thing," she said stiffly, crossing her arms

with resolve, but refusing to glance in his direction. "You've got to stop being so free with my money."

"I never expected you to reimburse me for those gifts," he explained quietly.

"I insist on it."

"My, my, aren't we prickly. I bought the flowers and the toy for Jill of my own accord. I don't expect you to pick up the tab," he said again.

Dianne didn't know if she should argue with him or not. Although his tone was soft, a thread of steel ran through his words, just enough to let her know nothing she said was going to change his mind.

"That's not all," she said, deciding to drop that argument for a more urgent one. She probably did sound a bit shrewish, but if he wasn't going to be practical about this, *she'd* have to be.

"You mean there's more?" he cried, pretending to be distressed.

"Steve, please," she said, shocked at how feeble she sounded. She scarcely recognized the voice as her own. "You've got to stop being so…so wonderful," she finally said.

He came to a stop at a red light and turned to her, draping his arm over the back of the seat. "I don't think I heard you right. Would you mind repeating that?"

"You can't continue to be so—" she paused, searching for another word "—charming."

"Charming," he echoed. "Charming?"

"To my children and my mother," she elaborated. "The gifts were one thing. Giving Jason a ride in the tow truck was fine, too, but agreeing with my mother about summer weddings and then playing basketball with Jason—none of that was necessary."

"Personally, I would've thought your mother measuring my chest and arm length so she could knit me a sweater would bother you the most."

"That, too!"

"Could you explain why this is such a problem?"

"Isn't it obvious? If you keep doing that sort of thing, they'll expect me to continue dating you after the Valentine's dinner, and, frankly, I can't afford it."

He chuckled at that as if she was making some kind of joke. Only it wasn't funny. "I happen to live on a budget—"

"I don't think we should concern ourselves with that," he broke in.

"Well, I *am* concerned." She expelled her breath sharply. "One date! That's all I can afford and that's all I'm interested in. If you continue to be so…so…"

"Wonderful?" he supplied.

"Charming," she corrected, "then I'll have a whole lot to answer for when I don't see you again after Saturday."

"So you want me to limit the charm?"

"Please."

"I'll do my best," he said, and his eyes sparked with laughter, which they seemed to do a good deal of the time. If she hadn't been so flustered, she might have been pleased that he found her so amusing.

"Thank you." She glanced pointedly at her watch. "Shouldn't we head back to the house?"

"No."

"No? I realize you told my mother we'd be gone an hour, but that really is too long and—"

"I'm taking you to Jackson Point."

Dianne's heart reacted instantly, zooming into her

throat and then righting itself. Jackson Point overlooked
a narrow water passage between the Kitsap Peninsula
and Vashon Island. The view, either at night or during
the day, was spectacular, but those who came to appreciate it at night were generally more interested in each
other than the glittering lights of the island and Seattle
farther beyond.

"I'll take the fact that you're not arguing with me as
a positive sign," he said.

"I think we should go back to the house," she stated
with as much resolve as she could muster. Unfortunately it didn't come out sounding very firm. The last
time she'd been to Jackson Point had been a lifetime
ago. She'd been a high-school junior and madly in love
for the first time. The last time.

"We'll go back in a little while."

"Steve," she cried, fighting the urge to cry, "why are
you doing this?"

"Isn't it obvious? I want to kiss you again."

Dianne pushed her hair away from her face with both
hands. "I don't think that's such a good idea." Her voice
wavered, just like her teenage son's.

Before she could come up with an argument, Steve
pulled off the highway and down the narrow road that
led to the popular lookout. She hadn't wanted to think
about that kiss they'd shared. It had been a mistake. Dianne knew she'd disappointed Steve—not because of
the kiss itself, but her reaction to it. He seemed to be
waiting for her to admit how deeply it had affected her,
but she hadn't given him the satisfaction.

Now, she told herself, he wanted revenge.

Her heart was still hammering when Steve stopped
the truck and turned off the engine. The lights across

the water sparkled in welcome. The closest lights were from Vashon Island, a sparsely populated place accessible only by ferry. The more distant ones came from West Seattle.

"It's really beautiful," she whispered. Some of the tension eased from her shoulders and she felt herself begin to relax.

"Yes," Steve agreed. He moved closer and placed his arm around her shoulder.

Dianne closed her eyes, knowing she didn't have the power to resist him. He'd been so wonderful with her children and her mother—more than wonderful. Now it seemed to be her turn, and try as she might to avoid it, she found herself a willing victim to his special brand of magic.

"You *are* going to let me kiss you, aren't you?" he whispered close to her ear.

She nodded.

His hands were in her hair as he directed his mouth to hers. The kiss was slow, as though he was afraid of frightening her. His mouth was warm and moist over her own, gentle and persuasive. Dianne could feel her bones start to dissolve and knew that if she was going to walk away from this experience unscathed, she needed to think fast. Unfortunately, her mind was already overloaded.

When at last they drew apart, he dragged in a deep breath. Dianne sank back against the seat and noted that his eyes were still closed. Taking this moment to gather her composure, she scooted as far away from him as she could, pressing the small of her back against the door handle.

"You're very good at this," she said, striving to sound unaffected, and knowing she hadn't succeeded.

He opened his eyes and frowned. "I'll assume that's a compliment."

"Yes. I think you should." Steve was the kind of man who'd attract attention from women no matter where he went. He wouldn't be interested in a divorcée and a ready-made family, and there was no use trying to convince herself otherwise. The only reason he'd agreed to take her to the Valentine's dinner was because she'd offered to pay him. This was strictly a business arrangement.

His finger lightly grazed the side of her face. His eyes were tender as he studied her, but he said nothing.

"It would probably be a good idea if we talked about Saturday night," she said, doing her best to keep her gaze trained away from him. "There's a lot to discuss and...there isn't much time left."

"All right." His wayward grin told her she hadn't fooled him. He knew exactly what she was up to.

"Since the dinner starts at seven, I suggest you arrive at my house at quarter to."

"Fine."

"We don't need to go to the trouble or the expense of a corsage."

"What are you wearing?"

Dianne hadn't given the matter a second's thought. "Since it's a Valentine's dinner, something red, I suppose. I have a red-and-white striped dress that will do." It was a couple of years old, but this dinner wasn't exactly the fashion event of the year, and she didn't have the money for a new outfit, anyway.

She looked at her watch, although she couldn't possibly read it in the darkness.

"Is that a hint you want to get back to the house?"

"Yes," she said.

Her honesty seemed to amuse him. "That's what I thought." Without argument, he started the engine and put the truck in Reverse.

The minute they turned onto her street, Jason and Jill came vaulting out the front door. Dianne guessed they'd both been staring out the upstairs window, eagerly awaiting her return.

She was wrong. It was Steve they were eager to see.

"Hey, what took you so long?" Jason demanded as Steve climbed out of the truck.

"Grandma's got the apple pie all dished up. Are you ready?" Jill hugged Steve's arm, gazing anxiously up at him.

Dianne watched the unfolding scene with dismay. Steve walked into her house with one arm around Jason and Jill clinging to the other.

It was as if she were invisible. Neither of her children had said a single word to her!

To his credit, Jason paused at the front door. "Mom, you coming?"

"Just bringing up the rear," she muttered.

Jill shook her head, her shoulders lifting, then falling, in a deep sigh. "You'll have to forgive my mother," she told Steve confidingly. "She can be a real slowpoke sometimes."

Seven

"Oh, Mom," Jill said softly. "You look so beautiful."

Dianne examined her reflection in the full-length mirror. At the last moment, she'd been gripped by another bout of insanity. She'd gone out and purchased a new dress.

She couldn't afford it. She couldn't rationalize that expense on top of everything else, but the instant she'd seen the flowered pink creation in the shop window, she'd decided to try it on. That was her first mistake. Correction: that was just one mistake in a long list of recent mistakes where Steve Creighton was concerned.

The dress was probably the most flattering thing she'd ever owned. The price tag had practically caused her to clutch her chest and stagger backward. She hadn't purchased it impulsively. No, she was too smart for that. The fact that she was nearly penniless and it was only the middle of the month didn't help matters. She'd sat down in the coffee shop next door and juggled figures for ten or fifteen minutes before crumpling up the paper and deciding to buy the dress, anyway. It was her birthday, Mother's Day and Christmas gifts to herself all rolled into one.

"I brought my pearls," Martha announced as she bolted breathlessly into Dianne's bedroom. She was late, which wasn't like Martha, but Dianne hadn't been worried. She knew her mother would be there before she had to leave for the dinner.

Martha stopped abruptly, folding her hands prayerfully and nodding with approval. "Oh, Dianne. You look…"

"Beautiful," Jill finished for her grandmother.

"Beautiful," Martha echoed. "I thought you were going to wear the red dress."

"I just happened to be at the mall and stumbled across this." She didn't mention that she'd made the trip into Tacoma for the express purpose of looking for something new to wear.

"Steve's here," Jason yelled from the bottom of the stairs.

"Here are my pearls," Martha said, reverently handing them to her daughter. The pearls were a family heirloom and worn only on the most special occasions.

"Mom, I don't know…"

"Your first official date with Steve," she said as though that event was on a level with God giving Moses the Ten Commandments. Without further ado, Martha draped the necklace around her daughter's neck. "I insist. Your father insists."

"Mom?" Dianne asked, turning around to search her mother's face. "Have you been talking to Dad again?" Dianne's father had been gone for more than ten years. However, for several years following his death, Martha claimed they carried on regular conversations.

"Not exactly, but I know your father would have insisted, had he been here. Now off with you. It's rude to keep a date waiting."

Preparing to leave her bedroom, Dianne closed her eyes. She was nervous. Which was silly, she told herself. This wasn't a *real* date, since she was paying Steve for the honor of escorting her. She'd reminded herself of that the entire time she was dressing. The only reason they were even attending this Valentine's dinner was because she'd asked him. Not only asked, but offered to pay for everything.

Jill rushed out of the bedroom door and down the stairs. "She's coming and she looks beautiful."

"Your mother always looks beautiful," Dianne heard Steve say matter-of-factly as she descended the steps. Her eyes were on him, standing in the entryway dressed in a dark gray suit, looking tall and debonair.

He glanced up and his gaze found hers. She was gratified to see that his eyes widened briefly.

"I was wrong, she's extra-beautiful tonight," he whispered, but if he was speaking to her children, he wasn't looking at them. In fact, his eyes were riveted on her, which only served to make Dianne more uneasy.

They stood staring at each other like star-crossed lovers until Jill tugged at Steve's arm. "Aren't you going to give my mom the corsage?"

"Oh, yes, here," he said. Apparently he'd forgotten he was holding an octagon-shaped plastic box.

Dianne frowned. They'd agreed earlier that he wasn't going to do this. She was already over her budget, and flowers were a low-priority item, as far as Dianne was concerned.

"It's for the wrist," he explained, opening the box

for her. "I thought you said the dress was red, so I'm afraid this might not go with it very well." The corsage was fashioned of three white rosebuds between a froth of red-and-white silk ribbons. Although her dress was several shades of pink, there was a smattering of red in the center of the flowers that matched the color in the ribbon perfectly. It was as if Steve had seen the dress and chosen the flowers to complement it. "It's…"

"Beautiful," Jill supplied once more, smugly pleased with herself.

"Are you ready?" Steve asked.

Jason stepped forward with her wool coat as though he couldn't wait to be rid of her. Steve took the coat from her son's hands and helped Dianne into it, while her son and daughter stood back looking as proud as if they'd arranged the entire affair themselves.

Before she left the house, Dianne gave her children their instructions and kissed them each on the cheek. Jason wasn't much in favor of letting his mother kiss him, but he tolerated it.

Martha continued to stand at the top of the stairs, dabbing her eyes with a tissue and looking down as if the four of them together were the most romantic sight she'd ever witnessed. Dianne sincerely prayed that Steve wouldn't notice.

"I won't be late," Dianne said as Steve opened the front door.

"Don't worry about it," Jason said pointedly. "There's no need to rush home."

"Have a wonderful time," Jill called after them.

The first thing Dianne realized once they were out the door was that Steve's tow truck was missing from her driveway. She looked around, half expecting to find the red monstrosity parked on the street.

With his hand cupping her elbow, he led her instead to a luxury car. "What's this?" she asked, thinking he might have rented it. If he had, she wanted it understood this minute that she had no intention of paying the fee.

"My car."

"Your car?" she asked. He opened the door for her and Dianne slid onto the supple white leather. Tow-truck operators obviously made better money than she'd assumed. If she'd known that, she would've offered him seventy-five dollars for this evening instead of a hundred.

Steve walked around the front of the sedan and got into the driver's seat. They chatted on the short ride to the community center, with Dianne making small talk in an effort to cover her nervousness.

The parking lot was nearly full, but Steve found a spot on the side lot next to the sprawling brick building.

"You want to go in?" he asked.

She nodded. Over the years, Dianne had attended a dozen of these affairs. There was no reason to feel nervous. Her friends and neighbors would be there. Naturally there'd be questions about her and Steve, but this time she was prepared.

Steve came around the car, opened her door and helped her out. She saw that he was frowning.

"Is something wrong?" she asked anxiously.

"You look pale."

She was about to reply that it was probably nerves when he said, "Not to worry, I have a cure for that." Before she'd guessed his intention, he leaned forward and brushed his mouth over hers.

He was right. The instant his lips touched hers, hot color exploded in her cheeks. She felt herself swaying toward him, and Steve caught her gently by the shoulders.

"That was a mistake," he whispered once they'd moved apart. "Now the only thing I'm hungry for is you. Forget the dinner."

"I...think we should go inside now," she said, glancing around the parking lot, praying no one had witnessed the kiss.

Light and laughter spilled out from the wide double doors of the Port Blossom Community Center. The soft strains of a romantic ballad beckoned them in.

Steve took her coat and hung it on the rack in the entry. She waited for him, feeling more jittery than ever. When he'd finished, Steve slipped his arm about her waist and led her into the main room.

"Steve Creighton!" They had scarcely stepped into the room when Steve was greeted by a robust man with a salt-and-pepper beard. Glancing curiously at Dianne, the stranger slapped Steve on the back and said, "It's about time you attended one of our functions."

Steve introduced Dianne to the man, whose name was Sam Horton. The name was vaguely familiar to her, but she couldn't quite place it.

Apparently reading her mind, Steve said, "Sam's the president of the Chamber of Commerce."

"Ah, yes," Dianne said, impressed to meet one of the community's more distinguished members.

"My wife, Renée," Sam said, absently glancing around, "is somewhere in this mass of humanity." Then he turned back to Steve. "Have you two found a table yet? We'd consider it a pleasure to have you join us."

"Dianne?" Steve looked at her.

"That would be very nice, thank you." Wait until her mother heard this. She and Steve dining with the Chamber of Commerce president! Dianne couldn't help smiling. No doubt her mother would attribute this piece of good luck to the pearls. Sam left to find his wife, in order to introduce her to Dianne.

"Dianne Williams! It's so good to see you." The voice belonged to Beth Martin, who had crossed the room, dragging her husband, Ralph, along with her. Dianne knew Beth from the PTA. They'd worked together on the spring carnival the year before. Actually, Dianne had done most of the work while Beth had done the delegating. The experience had been enough to convince Dianne not to volunteer for this year's event.

Dianne introduced Steve to Beth and Ralph. Dianne felt a small sense of triumph as she noted the way Beth eyed Steve. This man was worth every single penny of the money he was costing her!

The two couples chatted for a few moments, then Steve excused himself. Dianne watched him as he walked through the room, observing how the eyes of several women followed him. He did make a compelling sight, especially in his well-cut suit.

"How long have you known Steve Creighton?" Beth asked the instant Steve was out of earshot. She moved closer to Dianne, as though she was about to hear some well-seasoned gossip.

"A few weeks now." It was clear that Beth was hoping Dianne would elaborate, but Dianne had no intention of doing so.

"Dianne." Shirley Simpson, another PTA friend,

moved to her side. "Is that Steve Creighton you're with?"

"Yes." She'd had no idea Steve was so well known.

"I swear he's the cutest man in town. One look at him and my toes start to curl."

When she'd approached Steve with this proposal, Dianne hadn't a clue she would become the envy of her friends. She really *had* got a bargain.

"Are you sitting with anyone yet?" Shirley asked. Beth bristled as though offended she hadn't thought to ask first.

"Ah, yes. Sam Horton's already invited us, but thanks."

"Sam Horton," Beth repeated and she and Shirley shared a significant look. "My, my, you are traveling in elevated circles these days. Well, more power to you. And good luck with Steve Creighton. I've been saying for ages that it's time someone bagged him. I hope it's you."

"Thanks," Dianne said, feeling more than a little confused by this unexpected turn of events. Everyone knew Steve, right down to her PTA friends. It didn't make a lot of sense.

Steve returned a moment later, carrying two slender flutes of champagne. "I'd like you to meet some friends of mine," he said, leading her across the room to where several couples were standing. The circle immediately opened to include them. Dianne recognized the mayor and a couple of others.

Dianne threw Steve a puzzled look. He certainly was a social animal, but the people he knew... Still, why should she be surprised? A tow-truck operator would have plenty of opportunity to meet community leaders. And Steve was such a likable man, who obviously made friends easily.

A four-piece band began playing forties' swing, and after the introductions, Dianne found her toe tapping to the music.

"Next year we should make this a dinner-dance," Steve suggested, smiling down on Dianne. He casually put his hand on her shoulder as if he'd been doing that for months.

"Great idea," Port Blossom's mayor said, nodding. "You might bring it up at the March committee meeting."

Dianne frowned, not certain she understood. It was several minutes before she had a chance to ask Steve about the comment.

"I'm on the board of directors for the community center," he explained briefly.

"You are?" Dianne took another sip of her champagne. Some of the details were beginning to get muddled in her mind, and she wasn't sure if it had anything to do with the champagne.

"Does that surprise you?"

"Yes. I thought you had to be, you know, a business owner to be on the board of directors."

Now it was Steve's turn to frown. "I am."

"You are?" Dianne asked. Her hand tightened around the long stem of her glass. "What business?"

"Port Blossom Towing."

That did it. Dianne drank what remained of her champagne in a single gulp. "You mean to say you *own* the company?"

"Yes. Don't tell me you didn't know."

She glared up at him, her eyes narrowed and distrusting. "I didn't."

Eight

Steve Creighton had made a fool of her.

Dianne was so infuriated she couldn't wait to be alone with him so she could give him a piece of her mind. Loudly.

"What's that got to do with anything?" Steve asked.

Dianne continued to glare at him, unable to form any words yet. It wasn't just that he owned the towing company or even that he was a member of the board of directors for the community center. It was the fact that he'd deceived her.

"You should've told me you owned the company!" she hissed.

"I gave you my business card," he said, shrugging.

"You gave me your business card," she mimicked in a furious whisper. "The least you could've done was mention it. I feel like an idiot."

Steve was wearing a perplexed frown, as if he found her response completely unreasonable. "To be honest, I assumed you knew. I wasn't purposely keeping it from you."

That wasn't the only thing disturbing her, but the

second concern was even more troubling than the first. "While I'm on the subject, what are you? Some sort of...love god?"

"What?"

"From the moment we arrived all the women I know, and even some I don't, have been crowding around me asking all sorts of leading questions. One friend claims you make her toes curl and another...never mind."

Steve looked exceptionally pleased. "I make her toes curl?"

How like a man to fall for flattery! "That's not the point."

"Then what is?"

"Everyone thinks you and I are an item."

"So? I thought that's what you wanted."

Dianne felt like screaming. "Kindly look at this from my point of view. I'm in one hell of a mess because of you!" He frowned as she went on. "What am I supposed to tell everyone, including my mother and children, once tonight is over?" Why, oh why hadn't she thought of this sooner?

"About what?"

"About you and me," she said slowly, using short words so he'd understand. "I didn't even *want* to attend this dinner. I've lied to my own family and, worse, I'm actually paying a man to escort me. This is probably the lowest point of my life, and all you can do is stand there with a silly grin."

Steve chuckled and his mouth twitched. "This silly grin you find so offensive is my besotted look. I've been practicing it in front of a mirror all week."

Dianne covered her face with her hands. "Now... now I discover that I'm even more of a fool than I realized. You're this upstanding businessman and, worse, a...a playboy."

"I'm not a playboy," he corrected. "And that's a pretty dated term, anyway."

"Maybe—but that's the reputation you seem to have. There isn't a woman at this dinner who doesn't envy me."

All she'd wanted was someone presentable to escort her to this dinner so she could satisfy her children. She lived a quiet, uncomplicated life, and suddenly she was the most gossip-worthy member of tonight's affair.

Sam Horton stepped to the microphone in front of the hall and announced that dinner was about to be served, so would everyone please go to their tables.

"Don't look so discontented," Steve whispered in her ear. He was standing behind her, and his hands rested gently on her shoulders. "The woman who's supposed to be the envy of every other one here shouldn't be frowning. Try smiling."

"I don't think I can," she muttered, fearing she might break down and cry. Being casually held by Steve wasn't helping. She found his touch reassuring and comforting when she didn't want either, at least not from him. She was confused enough. Her head was telling her one thing and her heart another.

"Trust me, Dianne, you're blowing this out of proportion. I didn't mean to deceive you. Let's just enjoy the evening."

"I feel like such a fool," she muttered again. Several people walked past them on their way to the tables, pausing to smile and nod. Dianne did her best to respond appropriately.

"You're not a fool." He slipped his arm around her

waist and led her toward the table where Sam and his wife, as well as two other couples Dianne didn't know, were waiting.

Dianne smiled at the others while Steve held out her chair. A gentleman to the very end, she observed wryly. He opened doors and held out chairs for her, and the whole time she was making an idiot of herself in front of the entire community.

As soon as everyone was seated, he introduced Dianne to the two remaining couples—Larry and Louise Lester, who owned a local restaurant, and Dale and Maryanne Atwater. Dale was head of the town's most prominent accounting firm.

The salads were delivered by young men in crisp white jackets. The Lesters and the Atwaters were discussing the weather and other bland subjects. Caught in her own churning thoughts, Dianne ate her salad and tuned them out. When she was least expecting it, she heard her name. She glanced up to find six pairs of eyes studying her. She had no idea why.

She lowered the fork to her salad plate and glanced at Steve, praying he'd know what was going on.

"The two of you make such a handsome couple," Renée Horton said. Her words were casual, but her expression wasn't. Everything about her said she was intensely curious about Steve and Dianne.

"Thank you," Steve answered, then turned to Dianne and gave her what she'd referred to earlier as a silly grin and what he'd said was his besotted look.

"How did you two meet?" Maryanne Atwater asked nonchalantly.

"Ah…" Dianne's mind spun, lost in a haze of half-truths and misconceptions. She didn't know if she dared repeat the story about meeting in the local grocery, but she couldn't think fast enough to come up with anything else. She thought she was prepared, but the moment she was in the spotlight, all her self-confidence deserted her.

"We both happened to be in the grocery store at the same time," Steve explained smoothly. The story had been repeated so often it was beginning to sound like the truth.

"I was blocking Steve's way in the frozen-food section," she said, picking up his version of the story. She felt embarrassed seeing the three other couples listening so intently to their fabrication.

"I asked Dianne to kindly move her cart, and she stopped to apologize for being so thoughtless. Before I knew it, we'd struck up a conversation."

"I was there!" Louise Lester threw her hands wildly in the air, her blue eyes shining. "That was the two of you? I saw the whole thing!" She dabbed the corners of her mouth with her napkin and checked to be sure she had everyone's attention before continuing. "I swear it was the most romantic thing I've ever seen."

"It certainly was," Steve added, smiling over at Dianne, who restrained herself from kicking him in the shin, although it was exactly what he deserved.

"Steve's cart inadvertently bumped into Dianne's," Louise went on, grinning broadly at Steve.

"Inadvertently, Steve?" Sam Horton teased, chuckling loudly enough to attract attention. Crazy though it was, it seemed that everyone in the entire community center had stopped eating in order to hear Louise tell her story.

"At any rate," Louise said, "the two of them stopped

to chat, and I swear it was like watching a romantic comedy. Naturally Dianne apologized—she hadn't realized she was blocking the aisle. Then Steve started sorting through the stuff in her cart, teasing her. We all know how Steve enjoys kidding around."

The others shook their heads, their affection for their friend obvious.

"She was buying all these diet dinners," Steve said, ignoring Dianne's glare. "I told her she couldn't possibly be buying them for herself."

The three women at the table sighed audibly. It was all Dianne could do not to slide off her chair and disappear under the table.

"That's not the best part," Louise said, beaming with pride at the attention she was garnering. A dreamy look stole over her features. "They must've stood and talked for ages. I'd finished my shopping and just happened to stroll past them several minutes later, and they were still there. It was when I was standing in the checkout line that I noticed them coming down the aisle side by side, each pushing a grocery cart. It was so cute, I half expected someone to start playing a violin."

"How sweet," Renée Horton whispered.

"I thought so myself and I mentioned it to Larry once I got home. Remember, honey?"

Larry nodded obligingly. "Louise must've told me that story two or three times that night," her husband reported.

"I just didn't know it was you, Steve. Imagine, out of all the people to run into at the grocery store, I happened to stumble upon you and Dianne the first time you met. Life is so ironic, isn't it?"

"Oh, yes, life is very ironic," Dianne said. Steve sent

her a subtle smile, and she couldn't hold back an answering grin.

"It was one of the most beautiful things I've ever seen," Louise finished.

"Can you believe that Louise Lester?" Steve said later. They were sitting in his luxury sedan waiting for their turn to pull out of the crowded parking lot.

"No," Dianne said simply. She'd managed to make it through the rest of the dinner, but it had demanded every ounce of poise and self-control she possessed. From the moment they'd walked in the front door until the time Steve helped her put on her coat at the end of the evening, they'd been the center of attention. And the main topic of conversation.

Like a bumblebee visiting a flower garden, Louise Lester had breezed from one dinner table to the next, spreading the story of how Dianne and Steve had met and how she'd been there to witness every detail.

"I've never been so…" Dianne couldn't think of a word that quite described how she'd felt. "This may have been the worst evening of my life." She slumped against the back of the seat and covered her eyes.

"I thought you had a good time."

"How could I?" she cried, dropping her hand long enough to glare at him. "The first thing I get hit with is that you're some rich playboy."

"Come on, Dianne. Just because I happen to own a business doesn't mean I'm rolling in money."

"Port Blossom Towing is one of the fastest-growing enterprises in Kitsap County," she said, repeating what Sam Horton had been happy to tell her. "What I don't understand is why my mother hasn't heard of you. She's been on the lookout for eligible men for months. It's a miracle she didn't—" Dianne stopped abruptly.

"What?"

"My mother was looking all right, but she was realistic enough to stay in my own social realm. You're a major-league player. The only men my mother knows are in the minors—butchers, teachers, everyday sort of guys."

Now that she thought about it, however, her mother had seemed to recognize Steve's name when Dianne first mentioned it. She probably *had* heard of him, but couldn't remember where.

"Major-league player? That's a ridiculous analogy."

"It isn't. And to think I approached you, offering you money to take me to this dinner." Humiliation washed over her again, then gradually receded. "I have one question—why didn't you already have a date?" The dinner had been only five days away, so surely the most eligible bachelor in town, a man who could have his choice of women, would've had a date!

He shrugged. "I'm not seeing anyone."

"I bet you got a good laugh when I offered to pay you." Not to mention the fact that she'd made such a fuss over his owning a proper suit.

"As a matter of fact, I was flattered."

"No doubt."

"Are you still upset?"

"You could say that, yes." *Upset* was putting it mildly.

Since Dianne's house was only a couple of miles from the community center, she reached for her purse and checkbook. She waited until he pulled into the driveway before writing a check and handing it to him.

"What's this?" Steve asked.

"What I owe you. Since I didn't know the exact cost of Jill's stuffed animal, I made an educated guess. The cost of the roses varies from shop to shop, so I took an average price."

"I don't think you should pay me until the evening's over," he said, opening his car door.

As far as Dianne was concerned, it had been over the minute she'd learned who he was. When he came around to her side of the car and opened her door, she said, "Just what are you planning now?" He led her by the hand to the front of the garage, which was illuminated by a floodlight. They stood facing each other, his hands on her shoulders.

She frowned, gazing up at him. "I fully intend to give you your money's worth," he replied.

"I beg your pardon?"

"Jason, Jill and your mother."

"What about them?"

"They're peering out the front window waiting for me to kiss you, and I'm not going to disappoint them."

"Oh, no, you don't," she objected. But the moment his eyes held hers, all her anger drained away. Then, slowly, as though he recognized the change in her, he lowered his head. Dianne knew he was going to kiss her, and in the same instant she knew she wouldn't do anything to stop him…

Nine

"You have the check?" Dianne asked once her head was clear enough for her to think again. It was a struggle to pull herself free from the magic Steve wove so easily around her.

Steve pulled the check she'd written from his suit pocket. Then, without ceremony, he tore it in two. "I never intended to accept a penny."

"You have to! We agreed—"

"I want to see you again," he said, clasping her shoulders firmly and looking intently at her.

Dianne was struck dumb. If he'd announced he was an alien, visiting from the planet Mars, he couldn't have surprised her more. Not knowing what to say, she eyed him speculatively. "You're kidding, aren't you?"

A smile flitted across his lips as though he'd anticipated her reaction. The left side of his mouth rose slightly higher in that lazy, off-center grin of his. "I've never been more serious in my life."

Now that the shock had worn off, it took Dianne all of one second to decide. "Naturally, I'm flattered— but no."

"No?" Steve was clearly taken aback, and he needed a second or two to compose himself. "Why not?"

"After tonight you need to ask?"

"Apparently so," he said, stepping away from her a little. He paused and shoved his fingers through his hair with enough force to make Dianne flinch. "I can't believe you," he muttered. "The first time we kissed I realized we had something special. I thought you felt it, too."

Dianne couldn't deny it, but she wasn't about to admit it, either. She lowered her gaze, refusing to meet the hungry intensity of his eyes.

When she didn't respond, Steve continued, "I have no intention of letting you out of my life. In case you haven't figured it out yet—and obviously you haven't— I'm crazy about you, Dianne."

Unexpected tears clouded her vision as she gazed up at him. She rubbed her hands against her eyes and sniffled. This wasn't supposed to be happening. She wanted the break to be clean and final. No discussion. No tears.

Steve was handsome and ambitious, intelligent and charming. If anyone deserved an SYT, it was this oh-so-eligible bachelor. She'd been married, and her life was complicated by two children and a manipulative mother.

"Say something," he demanded. "Don't just stand there looking at me with tears in your eyes."

"Th-these aren't tears. They're…" Dianne couldn't finish as fresh tears scalded her eyes.

"Tomorrow afternoon," he said, his voice gentle. "I'll stop by the house, and you and the kids and I can all go to a movie. You can bring your mother, too, if you want."

Dianne managed to swallow a sob. "That's the lowest, meanest thing you've ever suggested."

He frowned. "Taking you and the kids to a movie?"

"Y-yes. You're using my own children against me and that's—"

"Low and mean," he finished, scowling more fiercely. "All right, if you don't want to involve Jason and Jill, then just the two of us will go."

"I already said no."

"Why?"

Her shoulders trembled slightly as she smeared the moisture across her cheek. "I'm divorced." She said it as if it had been a well-kept secret and no one but her mother and children were aware of it.

"So?" He was still scowling.

"I have children."

"I know that, too. You're not making a lot of sense, Dianne."

"It's not that—exactly. You can date any woman you want."

"I want to date *you*."

"No!" She was trembling from the inside out. She tried to compose herself, but it was hopeless with Steve standing so close, looking as though he was going to reach for her and kiss her again.

When she was reasonably sure she wouldn't crumble under the force of her fascination with him, she looked him in the eye. "I'm flattered, really I am, but it wouldn't work."

"You don't know that."

"But I do, I do. We're not even in the same league, you and I, and this whole thing has got completely out of hand." She stood a little straighter, as though the extra inch in height would help. "The deal was I pay you to escort me to the Valentine's dinner—but then I had to go and complicate matters by suggesting you look smitten with me and you did such a good job of it that you've convinced yourself you're attracted to me and you aren't. You couldn't be."

"Because you're divorced and have two children," he repeated incredulously.

"You're forgetting my manipulative mother."

Steve clenched his fists at his sides. "I haven't forgotten her. In fact, I'm grateful to her."

Dianne narrowed her eyes. "Now I *know* you can't be serious."

"Your mother's a real kick, and your kids are great, and in case you're completely blind, I think you're pretty wonderful yourself."

Dianne fumbled with the pearls at her neck, twisting the strand between her fingers. The man who stood before her was every woman's dream, but she didn't know what was right anymore. She knew only one thing. After the way he'd humiliated her this evening, after the way he'd let her actually pay him to take her to the Valentine's dinner, make a total fool of herself, there was no chance she could see him again.

"I don't think so," she said stiffly. "Goodbye, Steve."

"You really mean it, don't you?"

She was already halfway to the front door. "Yes."

"All right. Fine," he said, slicing the air with his hands. "If this is the way you want it, then fine, just fine." With that he stormed off to his car.

Dianne knew her family would give her all kinds of flack. The minute she walked in the door, Jason and

Jill barraged her with questions about the dinner. Dianne was as vague as possible and walked upstairs to her room, pleading exhaustion. There must have been something in her eyes that convinced her mother and children to leave her alone, because no one disturbed her again that night.

She awoke early the next morning, feeling more than a little out of sorts. Jason was already up, eating a huge bowl of cornflakes at the kitchen table.

"Well," he said, when Dianne walked into the kitchen, "when are you going to see Steve again?"

"Uh, I don't know." She put on a pot of coffee, doing her best to shove every thought of her dinner companion from her mind. And not succeeding.

"He wants to go out on another date with you, doesn't he?"

"Uh, I'm not sure."

"You're not sure?" Jason asked. "How come? I saw you two get mushy last night. I like Steve. He's fun."

"Yes, I know," she said, standing in front of the machine while the coffee dripped into the glass pot. Her back was to her son. "Let's give it some time. See how things work out," she mumbled.

To Dianne's relief, he seemed to accept that and didn't question her further. That, however, wasn't the case with her mother.

"So talk to me," Martha insisted later that day, working her crochet hook as she sat in the living room with Dianne. "You've been very quiet."

"No, I haven't." Dianne didn't know why she denied it. Her mother was right, she had been introspective.

"The phone isn't ringing. The phone should be ringing."

"Why's that?"

"Steve. He met your mother, he met your children, he took you out to dinner…"

"You make it sound like we should be discussing wedding plans." Dianne had intended to be flippant, but the look her mother gave her said she shouldn't joke about something so sacred.

"When are you seeing him again?" Her mother tugged on her ball of yarn when Dianne didn't immediately answer, as if that might bring forth a response.

"We're both going to be busy for the next few days."

"Busy? You're going to let busy interfere with love?"

Dianne ignored the question. It was easier that way. Her mother plied her with questions on and off for the rest of the day, but after repeated attempts to get something more out of her daughter and not succeeding, Martha reluctantly let the matter drop.

Three days after the Valentine's dinner, Dianne was shopping after work at a grocery store on the other side of town—she avoided going anywhere near the one around which she and Steve had fabricated their story—when she ran into Beth Martin.

"Dianne," Beth called, racing down the aisle after her. Darn, Dianne thought. The last person she wanted to chitchat with was Beth, who would, no doubt, be filled with questions about her and Steve.

She was.

"I've been meaning to phone you all week," Beth said, her smile so sweet Dianne felt as if she'd fallen into a vat of honey.

"Hello, Beth." She made a pretense of scanning the grocery shelf until she realized she was standing in front of the disposable-diaper section. She jerked away as though she'd been burned.

Beth's gaze followed Dianne's. "You know, you're not too old to have more children," she said. "What are you? Thirty-three, thirty-four?"

"Around that."

"If Steve wanted children, you could—"

"I have no intention of marrying Steve Creighton," Dianne answered testily. "We're nothing more than friends."

Beth arched her eyebrows. "My dear girl, that's not what I've heard. All of Port Blossom is buzzing with talk about the two of you. Steve's been such an elusive bachelor. He dates a lot of women, or so I've heard, but from what everyone's saying, and I do mean *everyone*, you've got him hooked. Why, the way he was looking at you on Saturday night was enough to bring tears to my eyes. I don't know what you did to that man, but he's yours for the asking."

"I'm sure you're mistaken." Dianne couldn't very well announce that she'd paid Steve to look besotted. He'd done such a good job of it, he'd convinced himself and everyone else that he was head over heels in love with her.

Beth grinned. "I don't think so."

As quickly as she could, Dianne made her excuses, paid for her groceries and hurried home. Home, she soon discovered, wasn't exactly a haven. Jason and Jill were waiting for her, and it wasn't because they were eager to carry in the grocery sacks.

"It's been three days," Jill said. "Shouldn't you have heard from Steve by now?"

"If he doesn't phone you, then you should call him,"

Jason insisted. "Girls do that sort of thing all the time now, no matter what Grandma says."

"I..." Dianne looked for an escape. Of course there wasn't one.

"Here's his card," Jason said, taking it from the corner of the bulletin board. "Call him."

Dianne stared at the raised red lettering. Port Blossom Towing, it said, with the phone number in large numbers below. In the corner, in smaller, less-pronounced lettering, was Steve's name, followed by one simple word: *owner.*

Dianne's heart plummeted and she closed her eyes. He'd really meant it when he said he had never intentionally misled her. He assumed she knew, and with good reason. The business card he'd given her spelled it out. Only she hadn't noticed...

"Mom." Jason's voice fragmented her introspection.

She opened her eyes to see her son and daughter staring up at her, their eyes, so like her own, intent and worried.

"What are you going to do?" Jill wanted to know.

"W.A.R."

"Aerobics?" Jason said. "What for?"

"I need it," Dianne answered. And she did. She'd learned long ago that when something was weighing on her, heavy-duty exercise helped considerably. It cleared her mind. She didn't enjoy it, exactly; pain rarely thrilled her. But the aerobics classes at the community center had seen her through more than one emotional trauma. If she hurried, she could be there for the last session of the afternoon.

"Kids, put those groceries away for me, will you?" she said, heading for the stairs, yanking the sweater over her head as she raced. The buttons on her blouse were too time-consuming, so she peeled that over her head the moment she entered the bedroom, closing the door with her foot.

In five minutes flat, she'd changed into her leotard, kissed the kids and was out the door. She had a small attack of guilt when she pulled out of the driveway and glanced back to see both her children standing on the porch looking dejected.

The warm-up exercises had already begun when Dianne joined the class. For the next hour she leapt, kicked, bent and stretched, doing her best to keep up with everyone else. By the end of the session, she was exhausted—and no closer to deciding whether or not to phone Steve.

With a towel draped around her neck, she walked out to her car. Her cardiovascular system might've been fine, but nothing else about her was. She searched through her purse for her keys and then checked her coat pocket.

Nothing.

Dread filled her. Framing the sides of her face with her hands, she peered inside the car. There, innocently poking out of the ignition, were her keys.

Ten

"Jason," Dianne said, closing her eyes in thanks that it was her son who'd answered the phone and not Jill. Her daughter would have plied her with questions and more advice than "Dear Abby."

"Hi, Mom. I thought you were at aerobics."

"I am, and I may be here a whole lot longer if you can't help me out." Without a pause, she continued, "I need you to go upstairs, look in my underwear drawer and bring me the extra set of car keys."

"They're in your underwear drawer?"

"Yes." It was the desperate plan of a desperate woman. She didn't dare contact the auto club this time for fear they'd send Port Blossom Towing to the rescue in the form of one Steve Creighton.

"You don't expect me to paw through your, uh, stuff, do you?"

"Jason, listen to me, I've locked my keys in the car, and I don't have any other choice."

"You locked your keys in the car? *Again?* What's with you lately, Mom?"

"Do we need to go through this now?" she demanded. Jason wasn't saying anything she hadn't already said to herself a hundred times over the past few minutes. She was so agitated it was a struggle not to break down and weep.

"I'll have Jill get the keys for me," Jason agreed, with a sigh that told her it demanded a good deal of effort, not to mention fortitude, for him to comply with this request.

"Great. Thanks." Dianne breathed out in relief. "Okay. Now, the next thing you need to do is get your bicycle out of the garage and ride it down to the community center."

"You mean you want me to *bring* you the keys?"

"Yes."

"But it's raining!"

"It's only drizzling." True, but as a general rule Dianne didn't like her son riding his bike in the winter.

"But it's getting dark," Jason protested next.

That did concern Dianne. "Okay, you're right. Call Grandma and ask her to come over and get the keys from you and then have her bring them to me."

"You want me to call Grandma?"

"Jason, are you hard of hearing? Yes, I want you to call Grandma, and if you can't reach her, call me back here at the community center." Needless to say, her cell phone was locked in the car. *Again.* "I'll be waiting." She read off the number for him. "And listen, if my car keys aren't in my underwear drawer, have Grandma bring me a wire clothes hanger, okay?"

He hesitated. "All right," he said after another burdened sigh. "Are you sure you're all right, Mom?"

"Of course I'm sure." But she was going to remember his attitude the next time he needed her to go on a Boy Scout campout with him.

Jason seemed to take hours to do as she'd asked. Since the front desk was now busy with the after-work crowd, Dianne didn't want to trouble the staff for the phone a second time to find out what was keeping her son.

Forty minutes after Dianne's aerobic class was over, she was still pacing the foyer of the community center, stopping every now and then to glance outside. Suddenly she saw a big red tow truck turn into the parking lot.

She didn't need to be psychic to know that the man driving the truck was Steve.

Mumbling a curse under her breath, Dianne walked out into the parking lot to confront him.

Steve was standing alongside her car when she approached. She noticed that he wasn't wearing the gray-striped coveralls he'd worn the first time they'd met. Now he was dressed in slacks and a sweater, as though he'd come from the office.

"What are you doing here?" The best defense was a good offense, or so her high-school basketball coach had advised her about a hundred years ago.

"Jason called me," he said, without looking at her.

"The traitor," Dianne muttered.

"He said something about refusing to search through your underwear and his grandmother couldn't be reached. And that all this has to do with you going off to war."

Although Steve was speaking in an even voice, it was clear he found the situation comical.

"W.A.R. is my aerobics class," Dianne explained stiffly. "It means Women After Results."

"I'm glad to hear it." He walked around to the passenger side of the tow truck and brought out the instrument he'd used to open her door the first time. "So," he said, leaning against the side of her compact, "how have you been?"

"Fine."

"You don't look so good, but then I suppose that's because you're a divorced woman with two children and a manipulative mother."

Naturally he'd taunt her with that. "How kind of you to say so," she returned with an equal dose of sarcasm.

"How's Jerome?"

"Jerome?"

"The butcher your mother wanted to set you up with," he answered gruffly. "I figured by now the two of you would've gone out." His words had a biting edge.

"I'm not seeing Jerome." The thought of having to eat blood sausage was enough to turn her stomach.

"I'm surprised," he said. "I would've figured you'd leap at the opportunity to date someone other than me."

"If I wasn't interested in him before, what makes you think I'd go out with him now? And why aren't you opening my door? That's what you're here for, isn't it?"

He ignored her question. "Frankly, Dianne, we can't go on meeting like this."

"Funny, very funny." She crossed her arms defiantly.

"Actually I came here to talk some sense into you," he said after a moment.

"According to my mother, you won't have any chance of succeeding. I'm hopeless."

"I don't believe that. Otherwise I wouldn't be here."

He walked over to her and gently placed his hands on her shoulders. "Maybe, Dianne, you've been fine these past few days, but frankly I've been a wreck."

"You have?" As Dianne looked at him she thought she'd drown in his eyes. And when he smiled, it was all she could do not to cry.

"I've never met a more stubborn woman in my life."

She blushed. "I'm awful, I know."

His gaze became more intent as he asked, "How about if we go someplace and talk?"

"I...think that would be all right." At the moment there was little she could refuse him. Until he'd arrived, she'd had no idea what to do about the situation between them. Now the answer was becoming clear...

"You might want to call Jason and Jill and tell them."

"Oh, right, I should." How could she have forgotten her own children?

Steve was grinning from ear to ear. "Don't worry, I already took care of that. While I was at it, I phoned your mother, too. She's on her way to your house now. She'll make the kids' dinner." He paused, then said, "I figured if I was fortunate enough, I might be able to talk you into having dinner with me. I understand Walker's has an excellent seafood salad."

If he was fortunate enough, he might be able to talk her into having dinner with him? Dianne felt like weeping. Steve Creighton was the sweetest, kindest, handsomest man she'd ever met, and *he* was looking at *her* as if he was the one who should be counting his blessings.

Steve promptly opened her car door. "I'm going to buy you a magnetic key attachment for keeping a spare key under your bumper so this doesn't happen again."

"You are?"

"Yes, otherwise I'll worry about you."

No one had ever worried about her, except her immediate family. Whatever situation arose, she handled. Broken water pipes, lost checks, a leaky roof—nothing had ever defeated her. Not even Jack had been able to break her spirit, but one kind smile from Steve Creighton and she was a jumble of emotions. She blinked back tears and made a mess of thanking him, rushing her words so that they tumbled over each other.

"Dianne?"

She stopped and bit her lower lip. "Yes?"

"Either we go to the restaurant now and talk, or I'm going to kiss you right here in this parking lot."

Despite everything, she managed to smile. "It wouldn't be the first time."

"No, but I doubt I'd be content with one kiss."

She lowered her lashes, thinking she probably wouldn't be, either. "I'll meet you at Walker's."

He followed her across town, which took less than five minutes, and pulled into the empty parking space next to hers. Once inside the restaurant, they were seated immediately by a window overlooking Sinclair Inlet.

Dianne had just picked up her menu when Steve said, "I'd like to tell you a story."

"Okay," she said, puzzled. She put the menu aside. Deciding what to eat took second place to listening to Steve.

"It's about a woman who first attracted the attention of a particular man at the community center about two months ago."

Dianne took a sip of water, her eyes meeting his

above the glass, her heart thumping loudly in her ears. "Yes…"

"This lady was oblivious to certain facts."

"Such as?" Dianne prompted.

"First of all, she didn't seem to have a clue how attractive she was or how much this guy admired her. He did everything but stand on his head to get her attention, but nothing worked."

"What exactly did he try?"

"Working out at the same hours she did, pumping iron—and looking exceptionally good in his T-shirt and shorts."

"Why didn't this man say something to…this woman?"

Steve chuckled. "Well, you see, he was accustomed to women giving him plenty of attention. So this particular woman dented his pride by ignoring him, then she made him downright angry. Finally it occurred to him that she wasn't *purposely* ignoring him—she simply wasn't aware of him."

"It seems to me this man is rather arrogant."

"I couldn't agree with you more."

"You couldn't?" Dianne was surprised.

"That was when he decided there were plenty of fish in the sea and he didn't need a pretty divorcée with two children—he'd asked around about her, so he knew a few details like that."

Dianne smoothed the pink linen napkin across her lap. "What happened next?"

"He was sitting in his office one evening. The day had been busy and one of his men had phoned in sick, so he'd been out on the road all afternoon. He was ready to go home and take a hot shower, but just about then the phone rang. One of the night crew answered it and it was the auto club. Apparently some lady had locked her keys in her car at the community center and needed someone to come rescue her."

"So you, I mean this man, volunteered?"

"That he did, never dreaming she'd practically throw herself in his arms. And not because he'd unlocked her car, either, but because she was desperate for someone to take her to the Valentine's dinner."

"That part about her falling in your arms is a slight exaggeration," Dianne felt obliged to tell him.

"Maybe so, but it was the first time a woman had ever offered to pay him to take her out. Which was the most ironic part of this entire tale. For weeks he'd been trying to gain this woman's attention, practically killing himself to impress her with the amount of weight he was lifting. It seemed every woman in town was impressed except the one who mattered."

"Did you ever stop to think that was the very reason he found her so attractive? If she ignored him, then he must have considered her a challenge."

"Yes, he thought about that a lot. But after he met her and kissed her, he realized that his instincts had been right from the first. He was going to fall in love with this woman."

"He was?" Dianne's voice was little more than a hoarse whisper.

"That's the second part of the story."

"The second part?" Dianne was growing confused.

"The happily-ever-after part."

Dianne used her napkin to wipe away the tears, which had suddenly welled up in her eyes again. "He can't possibly know that."

Steve smiled then, that wonderful carefree, vagabond smile of his, the smile that never failed to lift her heart. "Wrong. He's known it for a long time. All he needs to do now is convince her."

Sniffing, Dianne said, "I have the strangest sensation that this woman has trouble recognizing a prince when she sees one. For a good part of her life, she was satisfied with keeping a frog happy."

"And now?"

"And now she's…now *I'm* ready to discover what happily-ever-after is all about."

* * * * *

She wasn't sure about that. "Yeah, but look at all the time I'm taking from you. You're stuck babysitting me until the Quinns get home."

He leaned back in the chair, and she couldn't help but stare at his muscular chest and those massive shoulders. Did the military do that for him, or the ranch work?

He caught her stare and she quickly glanced away.

"Hey, I'll take your kind of trouble any day. You rescued me yesterday by helping me pack up all that wedding stuff. You took charge yesterday like a drill sergeant."

She felt a blush cover her cheeks. "What can I say? I have a knack for getting things done."

Those dark eyes captured her attention for far too long. She couldn't let this man get to her. Once he learned the truth about her, he might not like that she'd kept it from him.

He rested his elbows on the table. "Have you ever ridden?"

She swallowed hard. "You mean on a horse?"

He gave her an odd look, but she could tell he was trying not to laugh. "Yes, as far as I'm concerned, it's the best way to see the countryside."

"You want to take me riding?"

"You seem surprised. I'm sure your sister will want to show you around, too."

"To be honest, I've never been on or around a horse until today."

Brooke's first instinct was to say no, but then she realized she'd never taken time just for herself. And why wouldn't she want to go riding with this rugged cowboy? "I'll go, but only if you put me on a gentle horse. You've got one named Poky or Snail?"

"Don't worry, I'll make sure you're safe."

She wanted to believe him, but something deep inside told her if she wasn't careful she could get hurt, and in more ways than one.

Don't miss
COUNT ON A COWBOY by Patricia Thayer,
available March 2016 wherever
Harlequin® American Romance®
books and ebooks are sold.

www.Harlequin.com

WORLD IS BETTER
WITH

Romance

Harlequin has everything from contemporary, passionate and heartwarming to suspenseful and inspirational stories.

Whatever your mood,
we have a romance just for you!

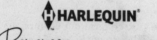